WHERE YOU GO

CLAIRE CAIN

CONTENTS

Book Cover Design by Rainbeau Decker

Formatting by Jeff Senter, Indie Formatting

ISBN-13: 978-1-7327718-0-2

To my husband: I'll always want to go where you go.

CHAPTER ONE

"So... you're back," I said abruptly, flopping down in the plastic chair and huffing out a breath to calm myself.

Simmer, Alex. Simmer.

"It's been a long year," he said. One side of his mouth quirked in a smile, but it was more weary than lighthearted.

"And now what?" I heard myself ask.

It wasn't that I didn't mean to ask him, but that I was amazed I was able to speak in a somewhat normal tone instead of the croak and squeak I felt like making. My whole body was lit with an awareness of him—his closely cropped hair and glacially blue eyes.

Years ago, I visited Alaska with my family. We took a helicopter to a glacier and hiked around on the slab of melting ice with rain jackets on our bodies and crampons on our feet. I remember looking into one of the crevices, which the guide had called a "crevaahsss," and thinking it looked like the most terrifying depth. The white snow intensified as it slipped down into the unknown oblivion of the hole, and the outer edges were bright blue. As the slopes gave way to darkness, the blue deepened into a navy-black that chilled me in a way I'd never forgotten.

So when I said his eyes were glacially blue, I meant it. They chilled me. It was a haunting kind of blue. And maybe it was my imagination, but I was sure they'd gotten more intense since I'd seen him a few years back, maybe because of the slight tan on his face or the gentle silver streaks in the longer hair at the crest of his widow's peak.

There was nothing left of the boy whose mom had shared my mom's nursing bras.

Which was ridiculous. Because what universe was this? Yes, of course it was him. Just older. Wiser. Hotter.

Ok, stop.

This was Luke Waterford, longtime friend, friend from in utero, former co-creator of Mud Pies, Inc., in the sandbox in the backyard at his parents' house. Absolutely no cause for alarm.

"I have some time off now, so I'll stick around another day or so. Then report back and we start training again in a few months." He folded his hands on the table and looked at them now laced together and stretched out between us in a strangely open gesture.

"Wow. Training again? You just got back." I was still working to clear my head, forgetting all sense of the art of conversation. I took a deep breath and inhaled the sultry smell of coffee surrounding us at our corner table in the coffee shop that had sprung up in our town sometime after we both moved away. We hadn't even ordered coffee, but I wished we had so I'd have something purposeful to do with my hands, my mouth.

We'd run into each other at the grocery store that was just a few blocks south of our parents', and formerly our own, neighborhood. Luke's family's house was an easy five minute walk, just a few streets over from mine. The fact that I'd only run into him one other time in the past decade since we said goodbye before I left for New York, also at that same grocery store, was amazing. But this time, instead of an awkward greeting in the canned vegetable aisle and a review of recent life events—including a deployment to Iraq and a girlfriend back in North Carolina for him, and a master's degree and a boyfriend for me—he asked me to meet him at the coffee shop next door.

By the time I checked out with my grapes, triangle of sharp cheddar, and a fresh baguette and tossed them in the car, he was already seated at a two-person table in the corner of the bright, bustling shop. It didn't occur to me to stop and get in line, both because it was after three pm and if I had coffee I'd never sleep, and because once I saw him sitting there, waiting for me, I entered his gravitational pull and there was no escaping it.

"Yeah. Deployments are slowing down so there should be a break. We used to be lucky if we got nine months of dwell time, let alone a year."

"Dwell time?"

"Time between deployments. This time it should be at least a year, I think." He was looking at my face again, and I didn't know why, but the word "dwell" made a twinge of wanting prick my spine. Like maybe, in some version of this story, instead of awkwardly staring at each other and catching up with surface-level factoids, he'd spend that *dwell time* with me. Like we hadn't only exchanged casual emails for the last decade and had that one awkward-but-friendly run in five years ago, but were instead closer.

"Wow." Apparently, all I knew how to say was "wow." My education and all of my grown-up experience was failing me. So long, composure.

I looked down at my lap and traced the hem of my khaki shorts with a nude fingernail I'd painted earlier that morning. My olive skin looked darker in the summer, and with the subtle, skin-toned polish, it looked down right *tan*. My bright white tank top also accentuated my skin and my dark hair now spilled over one shoulder and reached to my ribs. Dark brown hair, dark brown eyes, and olive skin were the trade-offs gifted me by my Italian heritage to balance the very necessary relationship I had with my tweezers and aesthetician.

Luke was looking at me when I finally looked up at him.

His stare—because it was a stare, not a gaze or a passing glance—sent a jolt through me. Something in his look felt heavy and purposeful. No longer was I haunted by that blue —now I was hunted. To what end, I didn't know. I smiled at him and must have furrowed my brow in question.

"It's been so long since I've seen you. Since we've been in the same room together, on purpose, for more than a minute. It's strange." He said it in a gravelly, quiet voice that seeped into my rib cage, and I forgot we weren't alone. He shifted in his seat and squared himself to the table, and to me.

"I know. It's crazy seeing you again but so good. You look..." I stopped before my mind betrayed me.

Hot.

Dangerous.

Dangerously hot.

"Old? Tired?" he offered with a chuckle. His eyes softened.

"No! I mean yes, you do look older, but who doesn't just shy of thirty when the last I saw you was nearly five years ago, and the last time we had a full conversation in person was almost ten?" I couldn't keep eye contact with this person. This man. I looked away a moment and then braved the glance back at him. "It'd be pretty strange if you still looked eighteen.

You look like this life suits you, I guess. Like it fits." I smiled at him, trying to make sure that smile didn't convey any of the wistfulness I felt or just *how* great he looked. I pressed my hands to the table to avoid reaching out and touching him.

"Well, fair enough. I guess it better suit me since I'm practically halfway to retirement. But you." He stopped a minute, waited for me to look at him. I did. "I mean, wow, Alex. You look..." He trailed off too, giving me that focused stare again. I looked away.

"Old? Tired?" I offered with another smile, rigging my courage and meeting his eyes again.

"Damn good. Damn good is what I was going to say." He said it with certainty and an edge that surprised me. He'd been casual and calm and quiet so his vehemence was startling and more than a little thrilling. His eyes skipped across my face and followed my hair over my shoulder, then jumped back to meet mine.

I swallowed hard and chuckled nervously, trying to force my dry lips to form actual word. "... thank you. Thanks? Thank you."

I wasn't sure why I said it three times, ok? It just happened. It was better than letting my jaw hang down to the table and giving him a clear view of the state of my tonsils. His mouth quirked up into a crooked smile like he was both amused by and pleased with my response.

And then, his eyes again. They seemed... something— heated, maybe? But also genuinely happy. The wrinkles around them were visible—proof of the ten years we'd been apart and some of the squinting against the sun and smiling he must have done. He always did have the best laugh, and so many of my earliest memories with him were of us laughing together.

The summers before third grade, we used to lie in the

shade of the Russian olive tree in my parents' front yard, and I'd lie with my head on his stomach. We'd be there for hours, throwing the tiny white olives up in the air, trying to hit each other in the face and then laughing hysterically. When his belly rumbled under my head signaling it was time to eat, I'd laugh even more. I'd turn my head slightly to look up at him and press my ear and listen to his voice bounce around his body. Our hair would be matted and dirty from running around the yard all day and resting in the dirt and giggling when we'd eventually surrender to the call to dinner or time for him to go home. The memory hit me with a surprising force and all the while, I was staring at him.

He looked back at me with a striking intensity, and I had to look away. I forced my gaze down and focused on his hands, still outstretched on the table. They looked strong, and big, and warm. My own hands were my typical cold limbs, and I realized they were still pressing hard into the table, bracing me.

For what? I didn't know. But I felt the need to brace myself.

I was still looking at his hands when I saw them moving— stretching out farther. Well really, just one, the right hand, sliding across the table another three inches before it covered my own.

Impossible.

My mind stuttered with the movement, and I tried to memorize each detail of that moment. His hand was impossibly warm. And big. My hand was covered completely before his continued forward and wrapped lightly around my wrist. I was still gaping at his hand—his warm, perfect, lovely, big hand—encircling my wrist when I heard him speak and my eyes jumped to meet his.

His full lips curved upward at the edges just a bit, and his blue eyes sparkled like he was some kind of movie star. I tried not to leave my mouth agape as I watched his every movement and my brain circled around the sensation of his hand on my arm like he owned me. Like he'd carved the moment out of marble and I couldn't move, and I didn't ever want to move.

"I'm so glad I got to see you. I have to head out, but maybe we could get dinner this week?" He raised his eyebrows and I realized it was my turn to speak.

"Oh! Yeah. Yes. I leave Wednesday, so I'm not sure when you had in mind but—"

"How about Monday?" He interrupted me before my waffling could continue.

"Monday?" I swallowed. "Like, tomorrow?" I felt a tingle of nervousness and a simultaneous overwhelming feeling of annoyance at my hesitancy. This was Luke. My friend.

My extremely handsome, war-hardened, blue-eyed, gloriously warm-handed friend. But still, my friend.

"Yeah. I'll pick you up. How's six? I've got an early flight on Tuesday morning." He let go of my wrist, and I immediately felt an unreasonable urge to grab his other hand or at least force him back to that place and recover the warmth on my now-bereft and apparently needy wrist.

"Yes. Yes. I'll be ready," I said as I busied my hands with grabbing my purse, rising out of my chair at the same time, clearly too eager to get away from him. He stood too and stepped in front of me, spreading his arms. Before I knew what hit me—and it did feel like a hit—he wrapped his arms around me.

To say that my lungs ceased functioning might have been an understatement. To say he smelled like everything a beautiful, grown man should smell like was too obvious. To say that feeling myself crushed against what was the very hard, tall, muscular, grown-up body of my childhood best friend was confusing and thrilling and terrifying and delicious and somehow also embarrassing... well clearly that was an understatement, too.

I wrapped my now gelatinous arms around him and patted him politely on his back twice—a friendly pat—and as I stepped away I found myself still unable to breathe as I stood so close to him. I turned and made for the door like my tail was on fire and heard him laughingly shout, "See you tomorrow!" as I just barely avoided knocking a woman and her child over.

Smooth exit, obviously.

I sat staring out at the Great Salt Lake from my parents' back deck in our small Northern Utah town. They lived on the bench of the mountains and even though I made every effort to escape the place growing up, I missed it from the moment I left. I savored the cool air that filtered around me as I sat in the shade and reveled in the fresh scent of grass and the chirps of birds—so different from my apartment in New York. June in Utah was like heaven compared to the humidity and permanent garbage smell that saturated the New York air when it got hot.

My thoughts swirled around my encounter with Luke.

Luke!

I never managed to tell him everything I wanted to at eighteen or any point before that, and back then I had convinced myself it was right. But I wasn't sure, even still, that it was the right choice. Or at least, I wondered what might have been if I had told him everything.

I'd geared up for it more than once and then stepped back, too scared of what life after high school and my own ambitions would suffer if I admitted it. If I admitted how terrifying and all-encompassing my feelings for him were, even when I'd hardly seen him since we'd entered high school.

At the time, it didn't feel like I had a choice.

We'd been friends since childhood, or really before, as our moms liked to point out by telling stories of how they'd been friends while pregnant and Sal, Luke's mom, had borrowed the nursing bras my mom used for my older sister and brother for Luke's first six months until I was born. This created an incredibly awkward space for us in the moments after Sal shared it so matter-of-factly since we'd been just on the other side of puberty and painfully aware of bodies and breasts and just exactly how one became pregnant. I knew for a fact that the lovely Adriana Moore, my own beloved mother, reveled in making us squirm.

That comment made eye contact with Luke unacceptable for a solid week. Then we forgot it, or pretended we did, and moved on to other woes of middle school.

We moved in different groups in high school—me, fairly studious and involved with clubs, friends, and dances, and he, essentially non-existent. The divide began in ninth grade, and I never knew why, but we eased away from each other. I wondered if what happened with Louis, his older brother, was the wedge between us, but at the time I had no idea why it would be. With distance, I decided it was at least a factor.

Louis was Luke's idol, and late in his senior year, his on-again off-again girlfriend Jen got pregnant. They both graduated, but instead of heading off to Stanford like he'd hoped and like Luke's father, Dr. Louis Waterford, Sr. had done, Louis and his then-fiancée moved to a small apartment in town and got jobs. Jen had planned on college in Hawaii, but living so far from home was impossible with a new baby on the way. Their aspirations of college—and Louis's dream of becoming a doctor—were indefinitely placed on hold.

Luke was quiet when it happened. He didn't seem to want to talk to me about it, and after we overheard the news while my mom talked with Luke's mom one day after school before he walked back to his house, we just sat in my backyard and watched our breath puff out like smoke in the frigid Utah winter. Not long after that, the space between us grew.

From what I could see, Luke did the minimum to get by in school, and while it drove me crazy that he seemed so nonchalant, I couldn't bother with his attitude. I knew my goal was to get out of the town we grew up in, out of the Rocky Mountain and Utahan culture that felt suffocating to me even before I knew it, and out into the world. New York City or Chicago or LA or Paris. Somewhere big and metropolitan and awake all night.

He had other plans. I didn't realize how much I had hoped I'd be a part of them until the end of our senior year. We weren't talking much at that time, but we kept tabs on each other through our mothers (or at least, I did him). He approached me one day in the senior parking lot. To get a real picture of what life was like, let me drop you in the moment, there with eighteen-year-old Alex and perpetually missing Luke:

"So, you're leaving?" he asked with a kind of edge that came out of nowhere since we hadn't talked to or seen each other in weeks. He said it like it was a personal affront.

"Sorry?" I shut the car door and turned to face him directly. I suppressed the nervous excitement that crept up the back of my neck when I heard his voice.

"You're leaving. My mom just told me you got in everywhere you applied and it's just a matter of the financial aid packages. So you're leaving in the fall," he said, a little less gruffly. He stood there looking big and focused and basically like the embodiment of every single one of my teenage dreams. His dark hair was messy and a little long, but his jaw had squared off in the last few years. I hadn't stood and just looked at him in a while, and he seemed a bit more like a grown-up than me in some way.

I felt painfully aware of my body—its size and proximity in comparison to his, and what he might be seeing in me as he looked me over. I felt positively delicate at 5'5" in the face of his 6'2", which continued to be a relief following years of middle school riddled with moments of towering over him and all of the other boys. Then he grew six inches in the span of eighteen months, and I finally felt like I wasn't so far ahead of him. Then, he just kept going.

I squared my shoulders to him and took a breath.

"Yes. I'm leaning toward Columbia but it's the most expensive, so we'll see what they come up with." I gave him a small smile. I wasn't uncomfortable with my achievements—I was proud and ready—but it felt strange telling him about them. Maybe because I wasn't sure he'd even gotten in to college or bothered to apply. It wasn't that he wasn't smart—rather, he was brilliant. It was just that I knew he was never there, never in any of my AP classes or anything else. Come junior year, he'd just kind of checked out.

"You always talked about New York. I guess I never thought you'd do it." He squinted at me, but I couldn't read whatever it was that was in his eyes.

"Why would you think that? I've planned on leaving for school since eighth grade." I felt defensive at his suggestion that he didn't believe in me. Why wouldn't he? What about me would say I didn't mean business? I knew my face betrayed my confusion at his disbelief. Or at least I hoped it showed confusion and not the deep ache with which my heart was now pulsing.

"I don't know. I don't know." He shook his head and his toes busied a rock underfoot. "It just seems crazy. We've been here all our lives, and now we're leaving. Seems unnatural or something." He said this, his blue eyes clouding over and looking into mine, trying to find something in them. I couldn't tell what, but I wished I could give it to him.

"Well, it's pretty normal. Kids do this all the time. That's sort of what the whole point is, isn't it? Launch out on your own and live a little? Try not to come crawling back after graduation and hole up in your parents' house like some jobless failure?"

He snorted a laugh. "Yeah, well. I'm not going to be crawling back, that's for sure." There was the edge again. One hand reached back to grab onto the back of his neck—a familiar gesture I'd seen him do whenever he felt unsure or uncomfortable.

"What school did you decide on?" Was this a safe line of questioning? I had no idea what else to talk about. It'd been long enough since we actually talked, and there hadn't been a time in the last three years when our interactions were less than tense. I knew that on my end there was a bit of unrequited crushing, but what was his issue with me?

"I'm enlisting." He kind of spat this at me, like he knew it would be a shock.

"Huh?" The sound was more a whoosh than a word, and I felt my stomach clench in a weird way. "Enlisting?"

"Yeah, Army. It's been my plan all along, and after 9/11, I knew there was no other option for me. I don't want to be stuck with my head in some stupid textbook when I could be doing something that actually matters." He stepped toward my car, crossed his arms, and leaned against the door. My pulse picked up its pace as I felt the air shift around me, disturbed and buzzing from his nearness.

"But... you don't want to do school first?" I tried not to sound too motherly. He had a mom—a great one, and I didn't want him thinking I thought I knew everything. He'd told me I was a know-it-all once, and I never forgot it.

"No." He seemed almost angry, like he was proving some point I wasn't grasping by saying it.

"Well, good luck, I guess. I mean, that's really great... or I hope it is. I hope it's the right thing for you." I stuttered and fumbled with my response. I didn't know why it shocked me since it wasn't a huge surprise that he'd go Army—he had often mentioned it, or at least I'd heard it was a possibility. But I had assumed he would go to college first. There was nothing wrong with starting now, but it filled me with a sense of dread.

"Thanks. I head to Basic on Tuesday. Good luck to you, too."

I didn't speak immediately since I was still searching for what I could say that would be supportive or... something, but before I could get a word out, he'd pushed away from the car and turned on his heel. I heard him say, "Well, see you later, Alex."

I waved weakly, knowing he couldn't see me with his back to me, but I couldn't find my voice to say goodbye.

CHAPTER TWO

That same summer we said goodbye, while Luke was slogging it out in boot camp, I spent my summer working and interning for a local event planning company. When Luke's mom passed me his basic training mailing address, I shoved it in my desk drawer and tried to forget about it between wedding receptions and the formal art auction that was my pet project. But soon enough, after hearing how lonely he was and how much his family's letters meant to him, I decided to write.

Ok, that wasn't true. One night at a little get-together a few weeks after graduation, I heard another friend of mine, Amber Watkins—someone who certainly hadn't been his childhood best friend—say she wrote Luke a letter. I felt jealous and annoyed and decided I'd write him once a week. So I did.

At the end of the summer, just before taking my flight out to New York, finally off to college, I saw him again. He was back for a few days in the wake of his training. I saw him in the parking lot of the mall, sun glinting off his sunglasses and no doubt burning his scalp through his buzz cut. He seemed taller and somehow bigger all around. He seemed grown.

"What? How are you here?" I dropped the bag I planned to load into the trunk and ran over to him, feeling my stomach flip at the sight of him. He smiled back at me, totally uninhibited, and pulled me into a hug before I knew what was happening. I crushed into his firm frame. It was the first time we'd hugged since we were kids. "I guess letters worked as a form of bribery to stay my friend."

"You look great, Al. About ready to head off to New York, huh?" he said, ignoring my first comment, while his broad, warm smile was still in place. He held me away from him by the wrists, gently, and his eyes skated over me. I felt my cheeks warm at his review and I chuckled nervously. I couldn't figure out what else to do with his close attention or the way I felt like a whole butterfly farm had been released in my stomach.

"Well, yes. But that's not exciting. How was basic training? How do you not look emaciated and ill like so many who've gone before you and been starved? Casey Whitlock came back last year looking like the angel of death!" I tried to look him in the eye, but the sun blared just over his head, blinding me. Casey had gone to Marine Corps boot camp the year before. He was somewhere out there, saving the world, but the week he came home for leave after boot camp, he looked like he'd lost twenty pounds he didn't have to begin with.

Luke grinned and shook his head. "I ate everything in sight every time they gave me a chance. And I was lucky enough not to get too sick, so that helped, though I did lose weight. Now I'm a few months older, and maybe a bit smarter about some stuff, a bit dumber about others. I heard Basic makes you dumb, and I can confirm, the 'Army dumb' syndrome is real." He still held my wrists, but I felt a heat where his hand met my arm and stepped back a bit, using the discarded bag and my open trunk as an excuse. I walked slowly back over to my car, making sure he was following me.

"Well you look good. The haircut suits you. You look hardcore," I said. He beamed at that, and then his eyes seemed to shift from smiling to serious all at once.

"I want you to know that after we talked in the spring, I changed my plan a bit." He always had a knack for sincerity.

I remembered overhearing my mom say something about that to my dad after Luke went home one day. Earlier that day, Luke had dived into a flower bed to save a Frisbee, smashing the daylilies to death. His apology, which was lengthy and amazingly sincere, had brought my mom to tears. And the thing was, he wasn't manipulating her. He was genuinely *that* sweet and knowing he'd done something wrong must have pained him, based on the way he bared his confession. His sense of justice was stunningly strong, even at ten.

I set the bag in the trunk and closed it, turning back to him. "You did?" I couldn't imagine what might have changed in the wake of our clipped, almost unfriendly conversation that past May.

"Yeah, I thought about the college thing. It's not that I didn't want to go, but I felt this urgency to get started with my life and *do* something. I ended up talking with the ROTC guys up at Miller College, and I signed a contract with them. So now I'm back, and I'll be earning my degree first and then commissioning when I graduate. I'll start as an officer." It might have been my imagination, but I was sure he stood a bit taller as he said that.

"Good for you. So four years until you're back at the Army stuff again?" I felt relieved at this news on several fronts.

"Well, not quite. Probably more like two since I have my associate's degree. I'll start as a junior in the fall and be right on track to graduate and commission in two years." He said it casually and leaned against the bumper of my car, waiting for my response.

"What? Wait. How do you already have an associate's degree?" I couldn't make sense of that news.

"I was taking classes at Miller College all through high school. You know the Early College program?" His smile was a little triumphant, like he was glad he could spring this on me and also surprised I didn't know. I knew that smile well.

"Are you kidding me? This whole time I thought you were some underachieving slouch who thought he was too good for high school, and now I find out you were an overachieving genius who *was* actually too good for high school?" I couldn't believe it. This did not line up with the Luke I'd known in high school. Or at least the Luke I imagined I knew but never saw or spent time with.

This version was markedly more dangerous. I had a thing for guys with brains who knew how to use them. My thought that he seemed more mature or experienced months ago was right—he had been. He'd moved on to college before he ever left high school.

"Ah, well not so much too good as just kind of over it. After sophomore year I could feel myself getting restless and talked to the counselors about what I needed to do to graduate early. It wasn't an option, but I did summer school to get all the rest of my high school classes done and by junior year I was taking classes at Miller."

"I'm—I just—I feel like such a jerk for thinking you were a slacker. It's not like you were ever like that before, you just..."

"I just wasn't into school? Or good at it?" he asked with a

brilliant smile. I could hardly look at him. The sun was behind me now and yet he was still too bright.

"Well, yeah. Yes. But I guess you figured it out. You always have been determined when you make a decision." I'd always admired that about him. It was like if he decided to do something, the universe got in line and made it happen. Like he had the power to speak his future into existence.

Ok, maybe that was a tad dramatic. But when he wanted something, he did it, even if it wasn't in his wheelhouse. This happened countless times as we were growing up, whether with a science fair project winning due to his unwavering determination to make his project the best or his maddening ability to charm any of his middle school crushes (I didn't know about the older ones as we'd not been that close). This latest news was a prime example of that tenacity, or whatever it was.

"Thanks. I see how you could think that. But hey, before you have to run, I have to say thank you for your letters. I—it meant a lot. You taking the time to do that—it meant a lot." He reached out and touched my arm lightly and suddenly I felt incoherent.

His blue eyes were twinkling at me, all smiley and friendly and sincere, and his hand was on my wrist, and I felt about as close to hysteria as I'd ever been.

I swallowed down the words bubbling up, the quick confession that wanted to jump out of my mouth. I leashed the impulse to pounce him and finally feel his lips against my own.

I cleared my voice. "I'm so glad your mom passed along your address. It was fun to write you. I'm surprised you didn't get bored with the letters, but I'm glad they helped. Pretty much the least I could do."

I tried to sound casual, but his thanking me was important. I'd shared a lot with him in the letters about my hopes for college and what I'd do after, and several times in the weeks of writing to my silent pen pal, I had to stop myself from asking weighty questions like, "Why didn't we date in high school?" or say things like, "I always thought we'd end up together." Somehow, I kept those feelings under wraps.

"I don't think I could be bored with you, Alex. Not ever," he said lightly, and I had to look away from him. I swallowed and took a deep breath before meeting his eyes again.

"Well listen. Keep in touch, ok? I know we'll both be busy, but I don't want to read about your receipt of the Nobel Peace Prize in the newspaper—that news has to come from your lips, got it?" I joked.

The fatal mistake was saying anything about his perfect, lush lips, because now I was looking at them—the bottom one fuller, the top curved and peaked in just the right way, so right that I swayed toward him a little, and he undoubtedly saw me do it. I shook myself to force my eyes away from his mouth.

Before I finished mentally punishing myself for being so obvious, he was leaning toward me, his previously inspected lips brushing against my cheek and his voice clear and strong in my ear saying, "I promise," before he leaned back away.

"Bye for now," I said softly, still tingly and shaken in the wake of his nearness, the feel of his lips on my cheek, and the brush of his smooth, shaven face against mine.

"Bye for now," he said and then sauntered off in the direction of the mall.

～

A day after our first modern day encounter, Monday, I

worked to convince myself there was nothing to be nervous about. This was Luke. Old friend. Childhood friend. We were meeting to catch up, have a friendly meal, and go our separate ways as friends. Because we were friends. So this was no big deal.

So I wore jeans. I didn't want to look too done up and figured if I wore basically anything other than jeans, I would. But I wore my best fitting jeans, the kind that hugged my curves just right, and depending on my level of carb consumption at dinner, may or may not fit as well by the end of the night. Because also, I planned to be a fully functioning adult woman and eat a real meal rather than let my general gut-bust of nerves prevent me from eating. If I prided myself on anything in life, it was that I wasn't dainty about food.

So I was wearing jeans that may or may not fit in a few more hours, and I was going to eat. I wore a v-neck black t-shirt and my nearly black hair long down my back and tried to wear enough makeup that I felt good but not so much I looked like I was trying. Because again, this was a friend thing.

As I widened my eyes to swipe on a layer of mascara, I knew I didn't stand a chance being near him again and acting normal. I still felt the same crazy urge to yell at him for being gone (even though I had been away too), and then crush myself against him. How would I sit still across from him and act like it was a "fun seeing you again" moment instead of something I'd thought about so often it might as well have been my one and only reoccurring dream?

How would I sit at a table with this man, look into his painfully blue eyes, look at his gorgeous, chiseled, completely appealing face, and still hold a conversation?

I shook my head at myself in the mirror, feeling excitement tinged with a sense of doom that accompanied the knowledge I was more nervous for this date with my old friend than I'd probably ever been for any other night out. I took a deep, grounding breath and made my way to the stairs so I'd be ready when he arrived. The doorbell rang just as I started down, and I clutched the bannister to steady myself.

As I knew he would, Luke arrived promptly at six and I managed to avoid tumbling down the stairs into the hallway of my childhood home where he met me at the door with a relaxed smile. He greeted me through the screen door with a calm "good to see you" and seemed far too relaxed compared to the edginess I couldn't ignore roiling around in my own stomach. And that was before I had a chance to really look at him.

When I saw this man wearing jeans and a plaid blue and white button-down shirt with the sleeves rolled up at the elbows, I did not feel my mouth go dry. My hands did not get clammy as I inspected him through the flimsy screen door still between us and noticed his perfectly styled hair and clean-shaven jaw. I did not wish I could pee again, one last time, and surreptitiously check to make sure I was wearing deodorant. No, I marched out confidently and greeted him with a "good to see you" in return and a wide smile.

He opened the car door for me, and I climbed into his dad's white Honda. It was strange, both of us living adult lives in other places but reuniting here in our hometown without any of our own stuff. In some ways it felt simpler not to be in *his* car, and in other ways it felt like sixteen-year-old me was finally getting to live out her fantasy date in high school, just a decade or so too late. I'd already stopped short of yelling, "I'll be home by eleven!" as I left the house.

He drove downtown and parked, and we wandered in to one of my favorite restaurants. My parents knew the owners and growing up we ate there nearly every Sunday after church. I even did a stint as hostess there during high school before I graduated. The microbrewery and restaurant was home to many of my favorites—illogically good fish tacos, considering it was in the heart of a land-locked state, a salmon sandwich on house-made focaccia bread that would blow minds, and bread pudding worth crying over—and I prayed my stomach would settle and my appetite would return. I was beginning to feel frustrated that so far, I couldn't relax and just enjoy the time with this old friend.

And so there we sat, smiling at each other and looking around. "I haven't been here in so long. I love Pete's. My last few visits have been so short, I haven't made it in." I wiped a hand over the laminated menu, brushing off invisible crumbs and fingerprints.

"It is good. I've been dreaming of their porter for a while. Not much good beer drinking in Afghanistan as it turns out. That whole general order number one really keeps us in check." The waiter returned with our beers then, and Luke smiled down at his tall, cold pint.

He took it in his hand almost reverently, and I couldn't look away as he sipped the still-foamy head of his first drink. He closed his eyes and smiled to himself. When he opened them, he found me watching and smiled ruefully.

"I feel like maybe I should give you two some time alone..." I joked and moved to stand.

"You know, you're right. You can leave. I'll be right here. Waiter?" We laughed as I sat back down and took a sip of my beer.

"Mm, it is good, isn't it? Nothing like a beer from the tap." Beer wasn't my favorite, but there was something homey about having a beer at this place. I'd had my first sip, an illicit one given to me by my father, at just thirteen. I'd begged him, the same way I'd begged to taste his coffee years before, and when he finally gave in, I was completely repulsed.

I knew what I would order the moment we walked in—the same thing I'd eaten every time I'd visited for years, and since the waiter turned to me first, I rattled off my order. The waiter took Luke's order and I looked down at the menu, tracing the black diamond emblem in the brewery's logo on the front. I thought about all the times I'd been there in the past, and amazingly, I'd never been on a date there. Most of my high school dating happened in malls or at movies, and then after that, I was off to college and not in these old familiar places. My time at Pete's spanned decades, but it was almost always with family or dear friends. I guessed that fit.

"What are you thinking?" His voice cut through my laser focus on the menu.

"I was thinking about how I've never actually been on a date here before," I said without thinking. And just as quickly, the twinge of heat crept over my chest, up my neck, and burned my cheeks—I'd implied this was a date. At twenty-seven years old, shouldn't I be over the whole blushing embarrassment thing?

"I mean, not that this is a date. I just mean—"

"Why is this not a date?" he interrupted me. He looked at me expectantly, head tilted to the side, and took another sip of his beer.

"Um—because, you know, it's you! It's us. We've always just been friends. It's great," I stumbled, trying to cover over my fumble and stifle my awkwardness. I looked down into the amber of my ale and hoped he'd change the subject, so I looked back up at him to signal him to move on.

He kept looking at me, but his brow was furrowed. He slowly set his beer down and rested that hand on the table. He leaned back in his seat without breaking eye contact. He seemed impossibly confident and comfortable with himself. Did they teach that in the Army?

"We've always been friends, that's true," he said, almost to himself. He was nodding in slow motion, still looking at me.

"Yes." Because I wasn't sure what else to say, or what to do. I felt like I was getting a gentle letdown from some place high up I wasn't even reaching for.

"But what if it is a date?"

CHAPTER THREE

He was looking at me like he expected me to say something specific. "I have no idea how to respond to that," I said.

"You have no idea how to respond to my asking how you'd feel if this was a date?" he asked, leaning farther forward and resting his hands on the menu.

Still unsure of what to say and feeling incredibly nervous with him watching me so carefully, I picked up my beer and took a long, slow drink to give me another minute before I had to respond. With unnecessary precision, I set down my glass on the little cardboard coaster and touched my napkin to my mouth before I said, "Yeah. I don't know how to respond to that."

So... that was worth waiting for.

My eyes darted around and tried to find an excuse to look anywhere but in his eyes, but my little compass arrow was drawn back to his blue-eyed north. After he didn't speak, I continued, "I mean—sorry. What do you mean?"

He didn't wait to reply but said, "This is a date Alex. We're friends, and we're on a date. A friendly date. Just because it hasn't happened before doesn't mean it shouldn't happen now."

I absorbed his words while taking another sip of my beer. Ok, so a date. But a friend date. A friendly date. So basically *not* a date, then? Oh good grief, I had no idea how to interpret that. "Well sure, you're right. Of course. That's exactly what I meant, too. Friendly date." I could hear the rambling again but couldn't seem to stop myself. Maybe food would help. The waiter arrived then, like mercy and sunlight after a hurricane of idiocy, and I forced myself to relax.

My mouth watered as I pulled in a deep breath filled with the glory of my meal. I bit into one of the highly anticipated tacos I had actively longed for when I was away. Absence indeed made the heart grow fonder where delicious, flakey, spicy fish tacos were concerned. My eyes might have rolled back in my head. I stifled a groan to avoid embarrassing him— I would never be embarrassed by enjoyment of delicious food. I guessed I missed that gene because I couldn't bring myself to give a second thought to someone else's perception of me when I was eating something so good. I piled crisp, fresh julienned cabbage into another soft corn tortilla already containing the perfectly toothsome fish and punishingly spicy fresh salsa, my full focus on the food.

"I'm glad to see nothing has changed," I heard him say and opened my eyes to find him looking at me with full attention, elbows resting on either side of his plate, chin resting on his folded hands.

I feigned ignorance. "How so?" I smiled and took another bite. The flavors peppered my tongue, and I blinked a few times in ecstasy.

"I don't think I've ever met someone who enjoys food like you do. Even at ten, you could savor food like it was your job. I remember reading about food writers in some class I took in high school and thinking that sounded like a perfect job for you." He took a bite of his burger, and said, still chewing, "Oh man, I missed real food." He finished that bite before taking another.

"They don't feed you real food while you're deployed? What do you eat?" I asked. I didn't feel nervous anymore. The food had done it—kicked me off my little spiral into neuroticism and back into reality.

"They do. But it's sort of like school lunch, you know? You can have a burger at school, and it tastes ok. Tastes like a burger. But you go to a restaurant or grill one up at home, and you control the flavor, the toppings, the kind of ketchup—it tastes how you *want* it to taste. It's not coming from the freezer or a vacuum-sealed package. It's fresh. I'm looking forward to getting home and cooking again." His attention returned to his burger, and I watched him devour the thing in just three more bites.

"I guess it makes sense the food isn't fresh. I've never thought that through." It felt like a silly thing to admit—that I hadn't ever thought about what he, or any of the soldiers who were deployed, ate. But then maybe that was obvious. Maybe no one but their wives and mothers thought about that.

"Most people don't." He took a swallow of his beer and leaned back in his chair looking sated and relaxed.

"Wait, go back to what you said before. You cook?" This was a new development, but not a surprising one. He was never interested in cooking—not even with my mother, who made cooking entertaining and sensual and alluring. Not many kids spent hours with their mothers learning to cook like I had, and he was no different. It never occurred to me he might have learned when he got older, but of course he would.

I wondered who had taught him and felt an unwelcomed pang at the thought it might have been a girlfriend, or *per favore Dio dice no*—please God, tell me no, fiancée. But I would have known if he'd been engaged, wouldn't I? His mom would have told my mom who definitely would have told me.

No. There hadn't been a fiancée.

"After living on my own for a few years, I decided I needed to figure it out. I gained weight when I got back from my first Iraq deployment—drank too much beer and ate too many burgers. So I took some classes, read a few cookbooks, and now I can make what I need to make." He sounded so nonchalant, like deciding to learn to cook and taking classes for it was a typical thing.

"You took classes?" I could hear the disbelief in my voice.

"Yes, why?" His eyes narrowed as he looked at me, maybe wondering if I was going to make fun of him.

"I think that's awesome. How many people make time for cooking classes? And maybe especially men, and especially a soldier?" I swallowed the last of my beer and dabbed my lips with my napkin.

"Well, I did. I really liked it. The chef and her daughter who ran the classes were great. And you know my mom cooked nothing but ground hamburger and jars of spaghetti sauce, so I needed help." He shook his head, likely remembering the full gamut of offerings his mom Sal had provided over the years. This was one of many reasons he was usually over at my house for dinner whenever he could swing it.

"I love knowing that, and when I think about it, it's no surprise. That's so you—realizing you need to figure something out, and just... doing it. Do you use recipes online, or...?" I asked, trying not to seem overly excited by what recipes he used. Because I was definitely excited by the subject, it took some effort.

"I've relied on Bittman's *How to Cook Everything* and then I use the *New Best Recipes* a lot. And then, yeah, stuff I find online or whatever." He seemed a little confused, and just before he could speak again I started babbling.

"Those are both great ones! *New Best Recipes* is seriously so good. Do you ever watch the *Test Kitchen* show on *PBS*?" Before he could respond, I kept talking, my love of cooking on full display. "So good. I could watch that for hours. I have in fact. Bittman's is good too. I don't find it as appealing as some because I love good food photography, but his recipes are reliable, and I appreciate that."

"You're a cookbook fanatic, then? This makes total sense." He moved his fork and knife to his plate, signaling he was finished, and sat back in his chair, crossing his arms as he studied me.

"Well yes, if you must know, I am a serious cookbook freak. I have an entire bookshelf dedicated to cookbooks and a separate wish list on Amazon for the ones I want to add to the collection. I can't ever enjoy cooking from a library book, and I feel restless when I print off a recipe from a website if I know I could have it in glossy bound form sitting on my shelf to hoard forever." I piled my silverware on my plate as well and nudged it out of my way so I could lean my elbows on the edge of the table.

"Ok, so we're talking addictive levels of cookbook collection here."

"It's no more an addiction than any other kind of collecting." I raised my eyebrows at him in challenge, wondering whether he still collected Star Wars Legos with as much relish as he had when he was younger. He smiled brightly and shook his head—I took that as a yes. "But yes. I admit that when I open a new cookbook, my heart rate increases with anticipation and it feels a little bit like the night before

Thanksgiving or what I imagine a small hit of cocaine might be like."

He smiled a full, broad smile at that, and my whole nervous system stuttered and skipped over itself. Ready to move on from my attachment to cookbooks, I shifted in my seat and crossed one leg over the other. "What did you major in? It's crazy that I don't even know what you did in college or anything. We've done a terrible job of staying in touch."

"True. We have. And I regret that." His voice was clear and his sincerity warmed me. Or maybe that was the beer.

"Me too."

"I majored in Poli Sci and had a minor in military science —that's automatic when you do ROTC."

"ROTC is the thing you do when you're in college?" I felt like I should know this. Or I felt bad for not knowing, for some reason.

"Yeah. You basically sign a contract with the Army and you get all the training for commissioning as an officer when you graduate. That way you commission right after you graduate and then start active duty if you're selected for it. I also contracted with the National Guard so I could get the GI Bill while I was in college. It was a good way to get through college without debt and make sure I had the career I wanted lined up."

"Makes sense. So what do you do now?"

"I basically make Power Points and Excel spreadsheets for a living." He shook his head and let out a breath.

"Uhh... what? I thought you were an infantryman? Doesn't that mean you shoot weapons and... hunt down bad guys, or something?" I sunk in my chair as I realized I had absolutely no idea what he or anyone in the Army did day to day.

"There has been a fair amount of that over the years, especially in the beginning. But some jobs are more office-focused, especially while we're in garrison—not deployed. It's less shooting and more planning. The job I have now is on the battalion staff—I work on planning the training we do in the field, and a lot of what we do is keep track of what training we need to do and when. I'll be moving up to brigade in the next little while, which basically just means I'm moving to a different office on Fort Campbell. I do whatever the guy in charge tells me to do, and then I have my own list of responsibilities too, many of which include changing Power Point slides and spreadsheets."

"That sounds..." I trailed off, not sure what to say.

"Glamorous?" he offered.

I looked at him dubiously.

"You're not wrong. And the guy who's sort of my boss right now is uptight, which makes it even more fun. I'm in this job while another guy wraps up his job and gets ready to move, and then I'll take over. It'll change again in a few weeks. You change jobs a lot as an officer which is a blessing and a curse, but in this case, I'll take it." He took his napkin from his plate and swiped it across the table in front of him and then set it back on his plate.

"Can I get you folks some dessert? Coffee?" The waiter hovered over the table looking back and forth between us. Luke waited for me to respond.

"I wish! I would love to have the bread pudding, but I have *no* room. Do you?" I shared a regretful look with the waiter as Luke shook his head no. Luke handed his credit card to the waiter and he disappeared.

"What about you? Your major and all of that?"

"Business. Minored in communications."

"That fits. But you were always more focused on event stuff, right? I thought my mom told me your job in New York was with a big event planning firm. I don't even know what that means, but I do remember she said it was a big deal."

"Yeah. Every internship I had was focused on events, and that's my passion. The job in New York was event planning corporate events. But my degrees are all more generally business or management." And I was glad for that. I had already burnt out on the life I led in New York, hence the changes I was making, and I liked that my degrees gave me a more general focus even if my experience placed me in one field. I was happy in events, but it gave me an edge to understand other parts of the business world too.

"And the Master's was in business?"

"Yep, MBA."

"You were always such a nerd at heart," he said, shaking his head while his eyes sparkled at me. Yeah, they sparkled, and I remembered why everything felt more intense as I looked back at him.

"Yes. I was. I won't deny that."

The waiter returned with the bill and Luke signed. As we walked out, he placed a hand on the small of my back and every nerve ending in my body zinged and focused on that small area of contact. It seemed like a touch that yes, could have been interpreted as friendly. But it was also a date-date kind of gesture.

He led me out, holding the door as we exited, and there we were in the cooling outdoors, still bright with summer evening sun.

"I thought we'd go walk down by the river, if you want. It's too gorgeous out to be done with the evening, and I still need to hear more about what you've been doing for the last few years." We turned toward the path that led to the river. The best part about our small downtown was its quaint feel and its proximity to the river walk.

"Good. It's not like downtown is so far away from my parents' house, but I just never make it down here. It feels like home, and I have so many good memories in this town, despite how much I wanted to escape." I smiled at him and clasped my hands together as we strolled the path.

"You? Escape? I never would have guessed." He grinned at me. It was always clear I'd be leaving and when. It was just a matter of where I'd go. My dad used to joke I'd steal a horse and ride out of town if no one gave me a scholarship to college.

"Yeah, well you didn't stick around either, did you? I think you would have left town the day you turned eighteen if you'd been done with high school. I always kind of marveled that you did stick around." I felt the air cool as we entered the tree-lined path and heard the bubbling of the river. Rivers in Utah were less *river* and more stream, but everyone called them rivers nonetheless.

"It's not like I was running away." He said this as a statement, but there wasn't much conviction in it. It hung there between us, and then he sighed and ran his fingers through his hair. "Ok, so I probably was running away. I always felt restless here. I think we had that in common." He was quiet then as we walked a bit, and I could tell he was still thinking. "I was ready to do something that mattered and go somewhere that didn't feel like who I was had already been decided. People knew I was Louis's little brother, and I always felt like they were waiting for me to impregnate someone and destroy her dreams too." He cleared his throat and didn't look at me for a moment but then continued. "That's why I tried to get through high school faster, then went to Miller College. I couldn't stand to be in the high school crowd and be judged by people I didn't care about or sit around and spend my days in classes while I waited for my life to start. I remember thinking that really vividly." We met the path that skirted the river and continued walking. Occasionally our arms brushed and my entire universe stalled out at each contact. If this was a play, my nerves would have just re-entered the scene, stage left.

"I can see that. I know there was a shadow cast over you by all of that, which seems crazy now, but I do remember how up in arms everyone was even after they got married and moved to Salt Lake. But you are different from Louis—you always were." I glanced to see if he was listening, to see if he was still bothered by his brother's choices. More than anything, it had scared him. I wondered how he felt about it now but didn't want to press him, so I continued. "I guess in my own way, that was me, too. I felt like I was always compared to my class president sister, the amazing Adriana, and then Michele, who you certainly remember could talk his way out of anything, and then finally I was this poster child for high school without volunteering for it." I breathed deeply and felt myself relax as we wandered the path with the sound of the river swishing around rocks next to us and the sky slipping into pinks and purples as the sun set.

"Yeah? I always thought you were a reluctant hero for the booster club and PTA and all of that. Even the principal, right? Ms. Jensen. Seemed like everyone was always gushing about your SAT scores or your wins at state or your college acceptances, and you just did your thing. I guess they didn't let you do it with your head down, did they?"

We came to a split in the path and he urged me to stay with the one closest to the river by guiding me with his hand on my back again. I sighed a little at his touch before I caught myself. I expected him to pull away when we were on the straight and narrow, but he kept it there a moment longer. I felt my nerve endings light at the thought that he might *want* to keep touching me, even in this small way.

"It wasn't so bad. But I was ready to leave—ready to have a life separate from my siblings and carve out my own path. Inevitably, as soon as I was gone, I missed it terribly. I remember crying over my laptop freshman year, wishing I'd just gone to Miller College and stayed here, living with my parents. They never would have let me do that, of course." I stooped to pick up a rock and toss it the fifteen feet into the river. The satisfying gulp of the water swallowing the rock was muted by the rest of the river's rush.

"Not that I had a say, but I wouldn't have let you either. You were made for stepping outside of this place. You always had such focus and ambition—I can't imagine you would have been happy staying here." His hand was still on my back, and he then snaked it around and placed it on my hip bone as he maneuvered us around a dog that had stopped to wait for his elderly companion who was slowly catching up to him, the long leash extended out between them.

I tried not to change anything about the way I was walking or breathing or talking, but his nearness was basically unbearable in that I never wanted it to end. His hand on my hip felt significant, warm, and like an assault on my nervous system. I felt clumsy, unwieldy, and maddeningly aware of the pressure of his hand and then its absence as he let me go and we walked along side by side again, no longer touching.

Curses.

"I know. I got over it, got my stride, and by the end of my first semester I wasn't looking back much at all. I found my focus again, and about the time Adri was having my second niece, I was realizing I wasn't ready to settle down yet. I do always love coming home though. It's funny that we've only overlapped once." I glanced over at him and saw his hands swinging lightly by his sides. I held on to the strap of my cross-body purse so I wouldn't do something awkward like grab his hand and hold it.

"You know, I think we did overlap once or twice besides our run-in a few years ago at the grocery, but I never managed to see you those other times. I know you're always so busy when you're home." He said this gently, but it was significant —that he'd known I was around but didn't try to track me down. I felt a sting of disappointment.

"I'm sure you are too," I said without thinking. We stayed quiet a beat and then laughed in unison.

"You know that's not true. You're my only friend who has any ties left here. Brian and Sam both moved years ago." He smiled to himself as we kept walking.

I couldn't stop myself. "So then, why didn't you hunt me down? I would have loved to catch up!" It was true. Every time I'd come home from school, and then for holidays or events, I was acutely aware of whether or not he was in town. The first few years I'd often drive by his house, once even stopped in to chat with his mom. After that, I'd managed to stay away, knowing it would only make the feeling of missing him while being surrounded by the memories of our child-hood that much worse. The fact that we'd ever overlapped other than the one time five years ago was news to me. I was watching when his eyebrow quirked up and one side of his mouth slid up into a half-smile.

"Well, I did this time," he said, now squinting a bit before he looked back down at his feet following the path.

I inspected him as he walked with his eyes on the path ahead. I liked the way he must have spent time smiling in the last few years, the crow's feet just beginning around his star-tling eyes. I admired the slope of his cheeks and his sturdy chin—his face was so familiar to me after looking at it almost daily for the first fifteen years of my life, but it was bigger now. It was harder, a little weathered, and impossibly handsome... but I shouldn't have been focusing on that.

I tried not to look at his lips because—danger. *Don't even go there.* His shoulder was even with my eye line and he could absolutely see me checking him out in his peripheral vision because he was still so much taller than me.

"I promise I'm not trying to be creepy," I said before I could think through the path this conversation might follow. I kept my hands tethered to the purse strap across my chest, making sure they didn't start mindlessly working their way over to where they wanted to be.

He chuckled in response. "I don't think you're creepy. Why would you say that?" He looked over at me then and smiled. It was a casual, gentle smile. It had a very un-casual, ungentle effect on my stomach and my heart rate, and I had no idea how to explain myself.

"Uhhh. Um. Hah," I stuttered. I blew out a breath and then smiled a bright, shiny smile back at him to hide my inner turmoil. "I realized you could totally see me eyeballing you, and I didn't want you to think I was trying to proposition you or anything. I just... it's so good to see you right in front of me. It's natural and comfortable and yet somehow totally surreal." I finished a little breathlessly and blamed the altitude.

That was it. The altitude had stolen my ability to walk, talk, and breathe at the same time.

"I know the feeling. It is strangely familiar and, like you said, a little surreal." He walked toward a bench closer to the water, surrounded by saplings and oak brambles, which created a sense of privacy. He sat down and I followed, sitting about a foot away from him. A friendly distance. "And..." he started, but trailed off. I looked up at him, waiting for whatever was coming, and was caught off guard by the look in his eyes. It was like a little spark had lit and they were glowing, or something else indescribable.

"And what?" I asked, my voice a little shaky as I looked back at him.

"Well I was just going to say that if you're going to proposition me, I hope you'll be more obvious about it."

CHAPTER FOUR

He watched my eyes grow large, and then he burst out laughing. "But then I realized *that* might sound creepy, and I think you've been creepy enough for both of us with your incessant staring at me." He raised his eyebrows at me suggestively, and I laughed as I shook my head and looked down at my hands, now in my lap. I hoped he couldn't see my pulse racing in my neck or how my chest was once again flushing red. Before I could think of how to respond, thank God, he started talking again.

"So, college in New York, and then you stayed there, and you'll live happily ever after as a New Yorker forever and ever, amen?" We hadn't talked much about our lives in the last ten years at dinner. We'd emailed here and there, mostly when we heard news from our moms. A congrats on graduating with my Master's, a "glad you're back" after his first two deployments, and so on.

"I do love New York. And yes, other than internships during summers in college and my time getting my Master's in Boston, I've just been there. But no, not happily ever after yet. I'm actually moving next month. I've got an opportunity to move to a smaller company and be a little more creative, and after what feels like a lifetime, I'm finally taking the leap. Who knows though—maybe I'll be crawling back with my tail between my legs within the year, missing the general dinge of the city at all hours of the night." I watched the water sliding past rocks and carrying small insects and leaves with it. Would I regret the move? I didn't think so. I felt so ready to leave the pressure and perpetual dissatisfaction of my current —well, now former—job.

I continued talking before he said anything, feeling the words turn from a dribble to a gush with a mind of their own. "But it's always been love-hate for me and New York. I've loved it ninety percent of the time, I can say honestly. But the remaining ten percent isn't ambivalence. It's hate. It's hard and exhausting and lonely and... sorry." I winced as I realized I was complaining. I hated the idea I was complaining to him, knowing he had just returned from a year of living rough, to say the very least.

He sat patiently and waited for me to go on. "I think I'm just at a point where I've realized I'm a little older than I thought I'd be, and I'm ready for the next phase of life. I think making some changes in my work life and my personal life will get me there... And *wow*, that was probably a whole lot more than you were looking for." I chuckled self-consciously, widening my eyes as I looked out at the river, feeling yet another rush of self-consciousness at my diatribe.

"That was exactly what I was looking for." He smiled encouragingly at me, and I remembered how easy it always used to feel just to sit next to him. "But what do you mean, you're 'older than you thought you'd be?'" His full attention was focused on me, and I had to calm my breathing because the weight of Luke's full attention was no light thing.

I felt a moment of hesitation—how to explain it? "Hmm.

I'm not sure I can explain that. I'm not sure I even know myself. I needed a change and that nagging feeling has been a kind of driving force for me—even though I can't name it. I just know Adriana was in her dream job, married, and pregnant by the time she turned twenty-four. I guess in some ways I feel behind, even though I never wanted the same life my sister had—I never wanted that small town experience. But now I'm realizing putting all my focus on my career maybe wasn't the best idea... or at least, that I need to change something if I want more than my career going forward." I exhaled —even though I'd just let loose, I felt like gasping for air.

"I think I get it. I've felt the same way—or had something like that, that nagging—for a while now," he said quietly. It had been a long time since I had talked about any of this with anyone other than my own mother, much less a peer. My best friend Ellie and I had talked some, but since I couldn't put a name to that feeling, I usually felt frustrated by conversations about what I was looking for, what I wanted to come *next*. I was living the *next* I had worked hard for for years in high school and college, so seeing beyond that felt terribly difficult.

I had definitely not talked about this with another person my own age who was a man named Luke Waterford. I'd always assumed he felt incredibly focused and purposeful and driven and knew what he wanted—that was just how he always was. It was one reason his seeming dismissal of high school was so strange to me—little did I know he'd been more focused than I could have imagined. The same, I always assumed, was true in the rest of his life. He always knew what he wanted.

"You mean... you feel behind?" My voice was small, but I wanted to know if he meant it.

"Not behind, but definitely... like I'm ready for the next step. I spent a long time avoiding that after Louis dove in head first before he ever meant to, but now I'm not avoiding it." His voice was sincere, and I couldn't look at him.

"Well then, one more thing we have in common after all these years." I chanced a look at him again and repositioned my body so my left leg was propped up on the bench, my shoulder and side were pressed against the back of the bench. He rotated to face me and let his right arm rest along the back of the bench, stopping just short of touching me. "Your turn."

"Ah, yes." He paused and took his own deep breath. I waited. "Well, I'm back from Afghanistan. It feels surreal and normal and stupid. I keep vacillating between feeling so glad I can just go get a beer or drive through Starbucks and then feeling really pissed off that no one seems at all concerned at the fact that there is still a war happening, whether we want to call it that or not, and soldiers are dying in it." He swallowed and took a deep breath and looked at me apologetically. "I'm sorry. I don't mean to rant—"

"—*Please* don't apologize for feeling however you feel. Please. First, no one can tell you what you *should* feel. And second, I can only imagine how that must be—to be surrounded by something and then come away from it and feel like no one has any idea what it was like or cares that it is even happening."

"Yeah it's... it's tough. You'd think after doing it a few times I'd know to anticipate it and just deal. It doesn't..." He stopped himself and was searching my eyes for something, his eyes flickering back and forth between mine as he leaned a bit closer. "You just haven't changed. You're still so..." He trailed off again.

"So?" I prompted quietly after he didn't continue, afraid of what he might be thinking.

Naïve? It sure felt that way. What did I know about what he had been through? It felt entirely separate from this moment, and I had no way to access it. Worse yet, I was guilty of going about my life and not thinking about the fact we were at war—that people from all over the country were living in conditions I couldn't imagine, doing a job I was nowhere near brave enough to do. And Luke had done it more than once.

"So kind. You've always been such a kind person, it's almost unbearable sometimes," he said with a voice I hardly recognized. He seemed pained sitting there on the bench saying that.

I opened my mouth to respond, but I couldn't. Once again, I had no idea how to respond to him. I kept shaking my head soundlessly, my eyes wide, trying to reach out for the words to say something. Thank you? Ok? Ouch? You're welcome? What does that even *mean*?

He laughed and the sound broke the tension building in my chest. "I think that came out wrong."

I cleared my throat. "Well I'll admit that being told I'm unbearable is not what I was expecting," I joked, trying to keep the moment moving toward lightness.

"No. *You're* not unbearable. There've just been these moments. I can count them up when I look back over our times as kids, and when I think about them I almost feel embarrassed by how gentle and kind you were to me—even in high school, when I hardly acknowledged you or saw you." His emphatic explanation had brought us closer. His thumb was resting on the bench right next to my shoulder, just barely touching me. He didn't move. I definitely didn't move. I tried to keep my mind on what he just said and not on the searing sensation I felt at that point of contact.

Was it possible for someone's thumbprint to burn a hole into another person's skin?

"I think you've got your rose-colored glasses of nostalgia on. You were kind to me, too. We were close friends for years

—of course we were kind to each other. And what I *just* said about how you're feeling? That's basic human decency."

"We're going to have to agree to disagree on this. I'm not explaining it right." He seemed frustrated with himself and frowned down at the river. With his face turned away from me I noticed the strong slope of his neck down to his broad chest. His collared shirt stretched out over his outstretched arm. I noticed his tan forearms and the hand resting right next to me, just barely touching me.

Was he always warm like this? Were his hands calloused from holding a rifle or whatever it was he'd been doing for the last year? And why could I not stop thinking about his hands?

"So, we got off on a tangent. You're back. You feel... a lot of different things, we'll say, in order to grossly oversimplify. Now what?" He pulled his focus back to me and shifted again slightly. He watched as he brushed his thumb across my shoulder and then caught a strand of my hair between his fingers. I stopped breathing.

"Your hair's long." He smiled while he looked at it in his hand, as if in a trance.

"I guess it is, compared to the last time you saw me." I couldn't process the fact that he'd essentially caressed my shoulder or that he was now playing with my hair.

"I like it." He looked up at me while he wound the piece around one finger and then let it slide out of his grasp over my shoulder when the breeze rustled past us. His hand rested back on the bench, the outside of his thumb still resting against my shoulder.

"Thank you?" It came out as a question. I couldn't explain that. My pulse was pounding, and I was pretty sure the river had begun rushing because there was a definite rushing sound in my ears.

"You're welcome." He nodded to give emphasis. "Now, I

wrap up my leave, and then I head back to Fort Campbell tomorrow and get back to work."

"Will you deploy again?" I asked once I found my voice.

"Probably eventually, but right now our brigade isn't slated for anything. In theory, I should have at least twelve months of dwell time. They've been known to renege on that but since we're past the height of back-to-back deployments, I'll hope for the full twelve for sure, if not more."

I breathed out a breath I didn't know I was holding. Knowing he'd be stateside was welcome news. We sat there a moment, the river bubbling between its banks, and then we both sensed it was time, so we stood and walked back to the path toward his father's car.

"I'm so glad we did this, Luke. It's been fun to hear a bit about your life." My chest tightened at the thought of the night ending, of going another ten years without seeing him or knowing him.

"Yeah, me too," he said quietly, now watching the path carefully. He sounded distant, and I didn't want him to retreat. I only had a few more minutes with him—maybe for a long time—so I kept talking.

"So where is Fort Campbell? I'm sorry, I'm so out of touch with Army bases, I have no clue," I admitted.

"It's in Kentucky," he said, still distracted by something, his attention focused unwaveringly on the ground as we walked.

"The South. Well we'll be kind of near each other I guess. I'm heading to Nashville." I felt a little leap. We'd be in the same part of the country for the first time since high school. Then I noticed he had stopped walking.

"Nashville? Like you're visiting there on your way back to New York?" he asked, almost glaring at me, even as he started moving.

"No. I'm moving there. Next month. In like three weeks, actually. Remember I told you I took a job with a diff—" I stopped talking because I could see he was moving. He was walking toward me with something I could only describe as urgency, and it was exactly that that shut me up. I felt a trill of fear shoot through me that changed to something far more like excitement as I felt him take me by the hips—yes, his warm, strong hands right there on my hips—and pace me backward. I grabbed on to his wrists and moved with him, looking at his eyes and the sheer determination in them.

I definitely didn't see the tree because I was looking at him, but I felt us leave the path, felt the dirt under my feet for a few paces, and then I stumbled over roots, but he steadied me and we took another step or two. Then there I was, backed up against a tree, still unsure of what was happening. He didn't break eye contact, but his hands moved to the sides of my face, gentle and sure, one thumb brushed over my cheekbone, and then he stepped even closer to me, his body a fraction of an inch from mine, and he kissed me.

It wasn't a soft kiss. It was demanding from the moment our lips met. It was hungry and almost like a confrontation, but one I quickly registered I had been waiting for and responded to with equal hunger. His hands slipped into my hair and he angled my face so he could deepen the kiss. I pulled back just a little to gather my bearings before going back in, and suddenly he was three feet away, somehow teleporting there without moving, his breathing ragged as he put his hands on his hips like he was recovering from a sprint. I rested my head back against the rough bark of the hundred-year-old oak and stared up at the dusky sky, and then closed my eyes, still trying to catch my breath.

"I'm..." he started, and I opened my eyes to see he had moved closer now but was still standing at a safe distance. "I can't say I'm sorry because I'm just not. I've wanted to do that since I was about ten. But I'm sorry if I took you off guard." He looked at me for a beat, then looked at my lips again. Then, he was in front of me again. He leaned toward me, and I watched him close his eyes as he kissed me one more time, the touch of his lips light but sure before he stepped away.

"I..." yet again, he'd rendered me speechless. All I could think about was how much I wanted him to do that again. "You're just happy for me about Nashville, huh?" I joked, not sure what else to say.

He smiled and inched closer, resting a hand on the tree next to my shoulder. "Well, yeah." He smiled brightly—even there in the dusk, it was blinding.

"Because... you know how much I love country music and barbecue?" I asked, trying to pin down where his response came from and also trying to do something other than hope he'd kiss me again. Because wow. Turned out Luke Waterford could kiss. I couldn't say I never wondered. Because I had. A lot.

"Actually, I *do* know you love country, or at least you used to. Of course you love barbecue because what good food-loving American doesn't? But I think the response had something more to do with learning you'll be in Nashville, which is less than an hour from where I live." I could see his eyes glittering and a smile playing across his lips and again, I felt my pulse spike.

He shifted his weight and let his hand slide from my shoulder down to my hand. He laced his fingers with mine, sending a shiver through me at his touch. He pulled me with him back onto the path, back toward town and the car. "Come on, it's getting late. I don't want you to be late for curfew."

CHAPTER FIVE

I didn't say much on the walk back or in the car. We were
nearing my parents' house. I had hardly had a coherent
thought since he backed me up against that tree. The fact that
there had been such an incident in my *life*, let alone with this
man, had evidently short-circuited my brain.

"Did I scare you?" he asked quietly, though his voice
sounded loud in the quiet car.

"N-No," I said, unhappy with the way my response
eked out.

Even in the dark I could see him shake his head. "Are you
sure? You haven't said hardly anything since I kissed you."
Hearing him say that made me flush all over again, and I felt
thankful for the covering of darkness in the car.

"I'm not scared of you, Luke," I said, trying my best to
make my voice sound clear and not all husky just at the sound
of his talking about our kiss.

"That's good. That would be the opposite of what I'd
want." He pulled up to my front door. My parents' front door.
Because I could not forget, this was like an alternate universe
version of my high school dream date and I was feeling so

much like eighteen-year-old Alex, all confused and bundled with nerves—it would have been humorous if I wasn't living through it.

"Well, don't worry about that," I said dumbly, unable to say much at all still.

"I'm going to expect you to call me when you get to Nashville. I can help you move in and bring you a potted plant or something. A 'welcome to the South' present." I could hear that he was smiling. It was possible he knew how wrecked my insides were, and he was enjoying it.

Oh sweet baby pineapple, I hoped he didn't know he'd turned my insides into useless goo.

"Sure, I'll call you, but you don't have to help me move," I said, trying to return to the land of the socially functioning.

"Well I'm helping. I happen to be an expert mover. I've had some practice." He opened his door and stepped out as I slid out of my side of the car. He placed his hand on the small of my back and we walked up the steps to the porch. I felt as nervous as I ever had after a date, if not more so. I now knew Luke could kiss, and that he might want to kiss me again—at least, I hoped he did—and that I definitely and completely wanted him to kiss me again. And based on my racing heart and sweaty palms, it was freaking my body out just as much as it was freaking out my fairly reasonable although currently hormone-addled brain.

"I'm glad we did this." I stood facing him, unsure of what to do with my hands or my body or even my stupid lips.

"Me too," he said.

And I thought, in an alternate version of the story, that would be where he would have kissed me again. He would have backed me up against the storm door and kissed my socks off like I'd been wanting him to do since I figured out what kissing was. But instead, the porch lamp flicked on and I saw my dad fiddling with the door, very much like he had done a decade ago at just exactly the right or wrong time. In this case, it fell very clearly into the *wrong time* category. Or maybe it was the right time. I didn't know. I didn't know.

Luke leaned back and offered his hand to my dad as the storm door flew open. "Mr. Moore, good to see you." He greeted my dad with unexpected but unfeigned enthusiasm. He'd always liked my parents, and they'd always liked him.

"Good to see you, Lukey." And my dad pulled him from the manly handshake into the one-armed man pat/hug. My dad was smiling broadly at the sight of him. "All grown up, then. And how was it in Afghanistan? Your dad said your unit was in some bad battles." I winced and searched Luke's face to gage his response. My dad never did have much tact, and it seemed typically pushy of him to go right to what might be the most sensitive subject.

"There were some tough times, but I think we did what we could with the resources we had," Luke said diplomatically, his face flashing with something like regret and weariness.

"Well, good on ya. Glad you're back safe and sound. Glad you're finally manning up and taking my daughter out. Going again soon, I hope?" My dad patted Luke's shoulder again, and I could tell by the glint in his eye he knew he was embarrassing me. It was a familiar look, though I hadn't seen it much since high school.

I rolled my eyes and willed my cheeks not to burst into flames.

"No sir, I head out in the morning. But we've discovered that Alex and I will be living just about an hour apart, so I expect to see her a lot in the coming months." He looked at me, an expression like straight lighter fluid rolling off his face and fanning the flame of my acute awareness of him.

"Alex, I'll see you in a few weeks, right? You have my number?" He said this casually as he took me gently by the shoulders and leaned in to kiss my cheek. It was chaste and brief and all of those things that a friend could do, but my father was catching the heat between us since he'd already offered me up for another date before the first one had ended.

Subtle. That was my dad.

"Yes. You will, and yes, I do. Bye for now, Luke," I said and smiled at him as I followed my dad inside, ignoring my dad's elbow digging into my ribs.

I bit my cheek so I wouldn't say anything else before Luke was gone. I heard the storm door clatter closed behind us as my dad held on to me while we walked down the hallway into the kitchen where my mom was cooking. I heard Luke's door shut, and it occurred to me I should have watched him get in and drive away, but I was evidently incapable of basic social graces at this point, and my dad certainly hadn't made that easier.

"How is handsome Luke tonight?" I heard my mom's melodic voice through the sizzling of shrimp in a sauté pan on the stove. I breathed in the smells of garlic and red chilies and took a moment to relish the scene that had been the hallmark of my growing up years. My mother stood at the stove, her wooden spoon in her left hand, her right poised to gesticulate whenever she spoke. Her apron wound around her still-thin middle and tied at her lower back. Her dark hair, still as long as mine, was twisted elegantly to the back of her head and a few small flyaways sprouted from the corners of her forehead. The silver streaks only served to make her look more lovely. They'd been there as long as I could remember.

"He's looking mighty fine. Grown into a sturdy man, I'd say. Wouldn't you say Alex?" my dad patted me on the back and then walked to the kitchen island where his glass of wine sat. He turned back to me and waited for my response while he sipped.

"He seems like he's doing well, yes," I said, my voice raspy. My mom was eyeing me from her station, poking the shrimp in her pan to flip them. Her right hand was turning off the back eye where linguine boiled, and then she was moving, always doing at least three things at once.

"I see your face is flushed, baby girl. Nothing has changed." Her words were perfect English, and though she'd only spent stints of time in Italy as she grew up, her parents were Italian and I could still hear a slight accent in her vowel sounds. Her smile was knowing as she dumped the pasta water, all but a few tablespoons that she poured into the sauté pan.

"*Si*, mama. I suppose it hasn't." She knew I'd always felt something for Luke, and she and my dad had noticed how I'd very strategically not discussed the time at the coffee shop or how I felt about our impending friend date before I went out that night. I could tell they wanted to ask, but they knew they would only make me more nervous.

"Luke is going to be living near Alex, love. Can you believe that?" my dad asked my mom. His smile was broad, like he'd orchestrated the whole thing.

"*Dimmi!*" my mother demanded. Her Italian came out whenever she was excited or mad or... really a lot of any emotion. And because she was an emotional woman, this happened often. I grew up hearing and speaking the language and loving it completely. Hearing it felt like home to me, and it was a small pleasure to *be* home while she was ordering me around in her first language. Her directive to "tell me" was familiar, and I could think of a hundred times over the years she'd given the order.

"The military base where he lives is in a town about an

hour away from Nashville." I tried not to let the fluctuating tremors of fear and excitement show on my face, but I knew they would see it. I walked to the couch and dumped my purse on the back of one dark brown cushion.

"Compared to a decade, an hour isn't so far," she said.

Ah, my mother. The philosopher and dreamer.

"No, it's not. I'm sure I'll see him."

"He seems fairly determined about that," my dad inserted and rocked back on his heels as he sipped his wine again. He nodded his head at my mother when she raised an eyebrow in question, and at this she pursed her full rosy lips in satisfaction.

"I'm just going to... head to bed. I'll see you guys in the morning." I couldn't make sense of their knowing looks, nor could I think about anything just yet, not having had a moment to breathe by myself and sort through my thoughts.

"Goodnight, baby girl," my dad cooed as though I was but an infant who needed cooing to soothe me. I gave him an exasperated smile and waved them off as I made for my room before they could exchange another round of eerily pleased glances.

What just happened? I leaned back against the door to my childhood bedroom and stared at the textured ceiling. Yet another turn of events to mimic a high school date—I had survived a (admittedly minimal) parental postmortem, and I now had to process internally for a minute in my room, and then I needed to make a call.

Part of me was thrilled at the discovery Luke was, at least on a physical level, attracted to me enough to want to kiss me, and then definitely plan to see me again soon. Another huge part of me was ecstatic that I'd know someone in the vicinity of Nashville.

But as I stood there, trying to sort through what I did feel, a big part of it was a rapidly darkening shade of dread. I felt incredible dread at the thought of trying to be friends and me not handling it, or going on a few dates because it seemed like we should give it a shot, enduring some uncomfortable physical fumblings, and then finally losing touch with Luke for good after he was inevitably assigned somewhere else or deployed again or whatever it was that happened to soldiers. Or worse, after we realized it had been over a decade since we'd seen each other regularly, more than that since we'd known each other, and now we were incompatible, or as we likely subconsciously knew even back then, were better as friends.

Or the absolute worst—we'd date, fall in love, and make plans to be together, but I'd be incapable of actually loving him enough to want to do anything other than stick to my own life plan, and I'd destroy him like I had my ex, Marcus. I'd prove to myself that I couldn't have what my parents had, or what Adriana and her husband Jared had.

I dialed Ellie's number with one hand while slipping out of my jeans with my other. I hopped around as I pulled the leg of my jeans over my ankle and finally whipped them off and sent them to a pile in the corner of the room. The sweet relief of sweatpants layered over my legs while I waited for her to answer. When she finally picked up, I was bursting.

"I just got back from a date with Luke." I didn't even wait for her to say hello.

"That was tonight? Why didn't you text me? How was it? What did he wear? Did you take a picture with him? Because I need to see an updated image of him so I can properly picture him and assess the situation." She was already launching into a full review.

"He wore jeans and a button-down shirt, and he was exquisitely and painfully handsome. I think he may have gotten even better looking since I saw him yesterday. We went to this little place in my town I've always loved, and I got tacos and beer and we did a lot of talking, and he lives like an hour from Nashville, and he kissed me and asked me to let him help me move in when I get to Nashville." I plopped down on my bed and stared at the ceiling, my toes curling at the memory of his eyes before he kissed me and his matter-of-fact non-apology when it was over. *I've wanted to do that since I was about ten.*

"*Whoa,* whoa, whoa, he kissed you? He lives in Nashville? This is perfect! You're going to date him and fall in love and get married and have his babies! Ahhhh!" She yelled into the phone. Yes, my adult best friend was yelling enthusiastically about me having babies.

It was important to know, Ellie was not a hopeless romantic. If anything, she was a painfully pragmatic person who could be dispassionate in her professional life, but on the subject of me and Luke, she'd been theorizing we were meant to be together since I first told her about him my freshman year of college. We were roommates, a cosmic pairing thanks to the gods of housing, and we never separated. We grew close those years, kept in touch while I was in Boston, and reunited when I returned and she was still plugging away at her PhD. We saw each other weekly, if not every few days, while we were in New York, and the impending loss of *her* was something I'd chosen not to fully deal with.

"Ok, getting ahead of yourself much? We are not getting married or having babies. He kissed me once. He is in the Army. He is *Luke*." And I maybe can't fall in love. I sighed.

She could hear my unspoken concern.

"I hear that sigh. I know you're sitting there starting to wallow. Starting to think of Marcus-with-the-goatee and wondering if you're broken. You cannot think like that. It has been over three years since you broke up with Marcus, and it's time to let yourself be interested in someone again." Her voice was stern and I could just picture her face, her long brown hair piled on top of her head in a bird's nest of a bun anchored by two Bic medium-point blue pens, her glasses framing her big brown eyes. I was now talking to Professor Kent, who was bent on me never giving up on my dreams.

"There was nothing wrong with Marcus. He wanted me. He committed to me. I committed to him. So why couldn't I just go for it with him, and what makes me think I'd be any different with Luke?" I felt my anxiety rising in my throat, a kind of panic creeping up from the back of my knees all the way to my neck.

"Stop. Just stop! Marcus was so far from right for you, it's not even funny. You two were a lovely couple on paper, sure. But he was no more interesting than one of my freshman students' persuasive essays on lowering the drinking age. First, I don't think you were ever in love with him—I think you liked him a lot and found him very agreeable, fairly attractive, and acceptably nice at a time when you were lonely and wanted to be with someone. But beyond that, I think you were too young, you weren't ready to turn down a huge job opportunity and go follow him around for his job. And—"

"Exactly! And Luke is in the Army. He's not going to be at Fort Campbell forever. I don't know if he'll even be there a whole *year*. So what am I going to do? Become some slumming girlfriend who follows her Army boyfriend around the country and gives up her own career and choices and *life*?" I spat the words at her before I realized how angry I sounded.

"Alex, calm down. First of all, as you pointed out, it was one kiss and one date. Second, you don't know what's going to happen. Don't disqualify the possibility. And third, Luke is an entirely different person than Marcus, and you are a different person now too." Her voice was soothing, understanding, and made me remember how amazing she was at talking me down. Thank God someone was because me and myself were experts at riling me up and opening the door to the spiral staircase of madness.

"Ok, ok. Thank you, voice of reason." I took a deep breath and rolled my neck from side to side attempting to release the tension.

"Plus, Luke is insanely hot. Founding member of the white hat club hot. And that's me talking based off of a photo from like a decade ago. I can only imagine what he looks like now," she said, her voice a little far off and dreamy.

In junior high, a camp counselor had told me that all "hot guys" wore white hats. It wasn't like the heroic white hat thing —it was like ball cap white hat. After that, I started noticing she was right—and it just so happened that my prime example was my dear friend Luke, who had, late in our eighth grade year, acquired a white baseball cap he wore even after his baseball season was over. It worked for him. So began my reference to the white hat club and anyone who might be a member.

"Oh El, it's painful. He is too good-looking. I'm not even joking. When we walked into the restaurant, the first few tables that noticed us literally stopped talking. One woman paused with her fork halfway to her mouth to check him out. Her buffalo shrimp was just hanging there, abandoned midair in the face of Luke's beauty." I covered my eyes with my hand and sighed.

Great. Now I'd become some sighing woman swooning after her beau even in retrospect.

"I need a picture, stat. I require it. But I do have to ask you —do you think part of the attraction is the history? Knowing that you wanted him so much before, but have never had the opportunity? Or, you know what I mean—the timing wasn't right?" I could still hear the spike of excitement in her voice, like she could tell we'd remember this conversation down the road, or when she was toasting at our wedding. I knew how her mind worked.

"I am positive our history plays into my attraction to him. But I'm also positive that someone with absolutely no knowledge of his existence would be dumbstruck at the sight of him if they weren't on guard." He didn't go unnoticed, that was for sure.

"Damn. Ok, so Luke is a definite contender. What's the plan now?"

"I guess I call him when I get to Nashville."

"Have you two ever talked on the phone? For that matter, have you addressed why you didn't really even speak for a decade?" Her questions were valid, but I didn't want to deal with them. I felt tired, worn down by the adrenaline rushes of the evening and my twisted, fearful heart.

"We haven't. I think we both know what happened. Or at least, I do. We saw each other before I left, and it was great, but then we went our separate ways, and I know for me, I couldn't be the one to reach out to him first again. I wrote him like, twenty letters while he was in basic training. He thanked me for them, but I kind of felt like it was his move."

"Ok, but you did email here and there..."

"Yeah, I heard he went to Iraq. I was home over the summer after my junior year and my dad mentioned it, just tossed it out there like I already knew. I was shocked, I'd had no idea. I knew he'd commissioned the year before, but I didn't know. So I tracked down his mom and got his email address and emailed him. We emailed back and forth a few times, and then it dropped off again when I moved and met Marcus. After that, we ran into each other and it was awkward and quick—I was with Marcus and I think he had a girlfriend, so it seemed weird to reconnect then, you know? Felt like a betrayal of my relationship to Marcus to reach out to Luke because for me..."

"I know, my friend. I know."

~

Luke: *So good to see you last week. Tell me what day you get to TN.*

He waited a cool seven days before texting me. We'd agreed I would call him when I got to Nashville so I wasn't expecting to hear from him. When I saw his text I smiled despite the many conversations I'd had with myself where I'd convinced myself we would just be friends. It was better, it was safer, and it just made sense.

Me: *The 10th. Two weeks from today.*

He might as well know now. Then maybe I wouldn't have to call him, which would save me the embarrassment of sounding incredibly nervous on the other end of the line.

Luke: *Ok. So I'll see you the 10th.*
Me: *What? I definitely won't be settled by then.*

Luke: *Of course you won't. I'm helping you move in.*
Me: *I'm not sure you're man enough.*
Luke: *Hey now, questioning my manhood before you've even experienced it? I call foul play.*

The double entendre there was a bit too much to handle. I chose to ignore it. Also, why had I said anything about his *manhood?* Good grief, woman.

Me: *Fine then. Come and do your worst. Be prepared for the full force of my cat lady tendencies.*
Luke: *You have a cat?*
Me: *Of course. What single female of a certain age doesn't?*
Luke: *So you really are a cat lady. How many? 4? 5?*
Me: *Just the one. But his attitude makes up for his singularity. You'll have to win him over if we're going to be friends.*
Luke: *We already are friends.*
Me: *If we're going to be friends who see each other in person more than once a decade.*
Luke: *Noted.*

~

I spent hours running back and forth between the moving truck and my apartment in the oppressive southern heat, and all that remained were a few larger pieces of furniture. Since Luke volunteered to help, I didn't have to hire anyone to help me with those. Hopefully soon I'd have some local friends, but for now, it was me and Lemon, my angry cat.

I drove as far as I could the night before which had been about two hours farther than I thought I'd get, and then was awake by five and couldn't talk myself into staying in bed, so I guzzled gas station coffee, choked down a Nutri-Grain bar, and made it the last four hours. I arrived at nine that morning and as I met the landlord Lewis, a middle-aged man with gray hair and pleated khakis belted neatly at his belly button with a yellow and purple plaid shirt tucked in, I felt excitement crawling up my throat. By the time he left me and closed the door behind me, I couldn't stop myself from twirling around in the slanting morning sun and letting out a relieved chuckle. It was as nice as the photos. The walls were all bright white, but I didn't mind that. I had plenty of art and photos to hang to distract and add color, and once I got some curtains up, it'd be perfect. The living room faced east so in that first morning moment, it was lit with summer sun. It was absolutely freezing inside as Lewis had made sure the AC was set to a chilly sixty-two degrees for my arrival. I knew I'd thaw out eventually, especially once I began loading in boxes, which I certainly did since Nashville in early July was a bit like sitting in a steam room.

Once we were alone, I let Lemon out, his golden and white tail curling open and beginning his familiarization tour of the place. I wandered through again and ran my hand along the back of the tan couch, smiled at the bright white and yellow chair, and felt the relief at having those few things already in place. Lewis had very kindly received the furniture delivery from the store the day before. I didn't have much space in my studio apartment in New York, so the move necessitated some new items, and I was so glad I wasn't facing moving in those giant pieces.

After I spent a few minutes admiring the space, I started the unloading. I piled boxes on the dolly and scurried back and forth between the van and my blessedly ground-floor apartment with its own little porch and just two steps and a front door threshold to negotiate. It was essentially a single story row house, and so far, I loved it. As I backed my way into the living room once more I eyed the kitchen and smiled at Lemon who was sniffing around the sink, his hind legs still on the light marble countertop, his front paws and face invisible to me since they were tucked down into the basin of the farmhouse sink.

It was the kitchen that made me go for the place, and then the more I looked at it, the more I loved it. There was *space*. It had white cabinets on one wall and a counter running underneath them, and then the fridge on one end. Across from this there was a large center kitchen island with the deep, dreamy farmhouse sink and more countertops. On the far side of the island, there were two tall stools for sitting at the bar now tucked under the countertop. From the sink, where I'd certainly spend plenty of time, I could see directly into the living room since it was all one big room. To the left was the dining area and doorway, and farther to the left was the hallway down to the bedroom and bathroom.

It was so much space, more than double, compared to my studio in New York. It felt like an embarrassment of riches, particularly since my rent, even in this reportedly hip area of Nashville, wasn't even quite ¾ of what it was in New York.

I off-loaded as many boxes as I could stand to before I got too tired and then took a break. I found my boxes of kitchen items where I'd stacked them next to the counter and unpacked those, knowing that having the kitchen settled would ground me. I had white plates because eating on too much color made me feel restless. I wanted to look at and taste the food, not feel like I was eating a pile of flowers or kittens or geometric shapes—whatever nonsense pattern people put on them. All of my appliances that came in a color, including my beloved KitchenAid professional mixer, were bright yellow. I had started adding bright yellow and light blue splashes in my New York place because it was dark and dingy. Here I found that the whole place was bright and these accents fit in well.

Before I knew it, the doorbell rang and I pulled myself away from the small pantry cabinet I was studying and mentally stocking with my favorite pantry staples. I was ready to get everything in its place. My new bed, couch, and chair were in place thanks to Lewis and the delivery guys the day before, but I didn't have my desk or the small dining table or my coffee table, all of which were in the truck. I took a deep breath to steady myself and opened the door.

To that point, I'd managed to be distracted, and I was running on adrenaline anyway, so Luke's arrival was less of a specter than it might have been if I wasn't already up to my elbows in things to deal with. I was wearing a loose, threadbare t-shirt and running shorts. My long hair was pulled into a ponytail and little wisps were falling out in all directions in the wake of the work I'd been doing. I felt grimy and a little sweaty, but I decided the night he told me he was helping me move that I was not going to dress up or wear make up on the day I moved just because he was helping. That felt like a weird betrayal of reality and would definitely be a sign I wanted more than just his help moving. Nope, I was make-up free in functional clothes, and although I will admit to shaving my legs (A girl's got standards. Please.), I will also submit that my hair was in a ravaged ponytail that I was *not* going to check in the mirror before he arrived.

And of course, I swung the door open to find Luke, looking impossibly handsome. In the three weeks since I'd seen him, he'd become even more appealing. He wore olive green shorts and a black Star Wars t-shirt that fitted just like a person would want a fitted shirt to fit. And yeah, I was staring at his perfectly toned chest but jerked my eyes to meet his face when he spoke.

"Welcome to Nashville!" he said with a pleased grin, clearly noticing how I'd devoured the sight of him. He held out his arms and I stepped into them, giving him just a quick hug because being that close to him was dangerous. He smelled like clean laundry and mint and something vaguely spicy. I could feel the magnetic pull of him on my bones and cursed them.

"Thanks. Come in for a sec, and then I'm going to put you to work." I smiled at him as he stepped into my apartment, and I thought my face might crack because my smile was so wide. Apparently, my unconscious was displaying some real zeal at his presence. I tried to talk myself down internally as the bare-naked feeling of having him in my unsettled house hovered over me.

I tried to cover the bolt of nerves that rattled through me by continuing. "I like your shirt. I'm glad to see the years haven't put a damper on your abiding love of Star Wars," I said, trying to distract myself from him by making room for the other furniture we'd be bringing in. He was a Star Wars superfan from the age of four, so seeing him all these years later wearing a t-shirt with a Millennium Falcon on it was delightful. Maybe it should have been a red flag he hadn't grown up, but there was no mistaking that Luke was an adult.

I pushed a stack of book boxes to the side of the little eating nook where my table would go, grabbed one of Lemon's play mice, and tossed it down the hall, out of the way.

"My desire to be Han Solo will never die," he assured me. He stepped farther inside and surveyed the boxes and things lying around the living room, and I chose not to watch him as he wandered. "Looks like you've made some good progress. When did you get in?" He strolled around the living room looking at the boxes strategically piled in different corners of the room.

"About nine this morning," I said as I pushed three stacked boxes of cookbooks to the side of the dining room area.

"What? Why didn't you call me and tell me to come earlier? I would have come." He seemed genuinely hurt I hadn't asked him to be there earlier. It was nearing five o'clock.

I straightened the pile of boxes and then wiped my hands on my dusty shorts. "No no no, don't feel bad. I ended up driving a lot farther yesterday, and I was able to get here earlier. My landlord let in the deliveries yesterday, so I mostly just got the boxes and stuff. I'm living on adrenaline and coffee at this point, but I'm just ready to power through and get settled. I definitely still need your help."

"Ok then, let's do it."

CHAPTER SIX

"I can totally see you in Italy," he said as we sat on the couch gorging ourselves on the pizza that had just arrived.

"I loved it. I loved every second. I will definitely go back. Being surrounded by the language, let alone the food... just dreamy. It's like it's sewn into my DNA," I said as I took another gigantic bite. I was so hungry I could hardly see straight when we finally stopped for the night. Or maybe that was the exhaustion talking. Either way the pizza was manna from heaven, and I couldn't consume it fast enough, though it was finally starting to hit bottom.

"Well your mother is Italian, so it actually is. I bet the Italian men were tripping over themselves to be your *uomo*." His eyebrow ticked up teasingly. I gave my pulse a talking to when it jumped at his using one Italian word. But coming from *his* mouth when unexpected?

Oh hey.

"*Certo.* But it's simply because I'm a woman and not for any other reason. I've decided that Italian men are the least discerning of any general male population I've encountered in that they just enjoy that women exist." I shook my head remembering the many times I'd been shouted at. It rarely felt lascivious though—it was almost always in a kind of cheery appreciation for womankind. It felt completely different than American cat calls.

"I'm not sure you've spent much time around the average soldier, then," he said, his eyes flaring in warning.

"Ah, well no, I don't suppose I have. You're my one and only, so far." I winked at him.

I know, I winked. I was generally less tense around him, but he was still making me nervous. So sue me.

"Well I'm obviously in your thrall, but that's a decades-old story, so I don't count. I'm sure you'll find that simply being female and in the general vicinity will gain you attention. It can be a problem, but most of 'em are decent kids." He smiled at his words. "Man, I sound old."

"You're not old. I understand. I usually feel like a twenty-year-old inside my mind, but then when I talk with actual twenty-year-olds, I realize just how much happens in the ensuing decade and how I'm so not twenty anymore."

"Absolutely," he agreed with a nod and took a big bite of his pizza. He chewed and nodded at it in approval. It was pretty good pizza, especially for not having anything to recommend it other than Lewis had left me the brochure that included a two dollar off coupon.

"Did you ever go to Italy? We used to talk about going together so we could eat pasta together—do you remember that? As though we didn't eat pasta every other day at my parents' house." Snapshots of the many meals we had together flipped through my mind. Especially in the summer months, we ate dinner together every few nights when we were in junior high. We'd play with neighborhood kids, not quite old enough to eschew being outside, and then end up at one of our houses. Usually, we chose mine, as my mom's cooking was far better than his mom's.

"I've never been, but I suspect I'd like it. I like most Italian things. I did a TDY—" he stopped when I tilted my head in question. "Uh, temporary tour of duty, sorry I forget you don't know all the acronyms. I did a TDY in Germany for about six weeks a few years ago and even though I didn't get to see much, I loved it," he said as he took another bite.

"Did you get to travel around at all?" I asked, finally feeling the warm glow of a full stomach creep over me.

"No, not really. I got to leave the post a few times but just to go into the surrounding towns. We're so busy when we're on a training rotation—it's all work and long hours until the end. But I'd do it again just for the chance for a few days in country," he said as he wiped his hands with a napkin.

"I think I've hit my wall. I can't do any more damage to that pizza or I'll pop." I set down the half-eaten slice in my hand. The exhaustion of the day hit, and I leaned back against the couch and rested my head. I closed my eyes and took a deep breath. I felt some of the stress of the last few days releasing its grip on me. Driving alone in a moving van for almost two days straight was totally exhausting, and that wasn't to mention the general anxious feeling I felt about figuring out what life would look like in a new city, entirely on my own.

"You've had a long couple of days, I'm sure. It looks good in here already, though. I bet you'll be all set up by Thursday." His voice settled around me, and I felt myself unwinding the knot of stress that had settled firmly in-between my shoulders.

For a few minutes we were quiet, and I had to work not to

fill the space with chatter. I could feel myself wishing for sleep despite the fact that the silence and his nearness had my body on edge. I could hear my own breathing and his, and let it lull me for a minute, finding that the silence wasn't uncomfortable if I could just calm the crap down. I felt myself slipping into deeper breathing, my body melting into the couch.

I felt something move, just vaguely, around the edges of my slowly slipping consciousness, but when his hand touched my cheek, his finger tracing along my jaw, my eyes opened and my pulse immediately raced.

I'd done an excellent job of ignoring his insanely un-ignorable physical presence all day. I even congratulated myself on not staring at his shoulders and biceps every time we carried something and I was faced with his unmistakably fit body at every turn.

I created little chants for myself. *I will not objectify my friend. I will not objectify my friend.*

"It's strange, seeing you like this," he said quietly as his finger continued tracing the side of my jaw from chin to ear. He'd moved closer to me and sat sideways, resting one elbow against the back of the couch.

I found my voice as I watched him, still resting my head on the couch. "What do you mean?"

"I'm not sure how to explain it. You look exactly like you always did—you look like you, but you're all grown up." His voice was low and calm and a little rough. His finger traced from my chin to my ear and down my neck, then back up. His touch was so light, if I couldn't see his hand moving, I wouldn't have been sure he was really touching me. I tried to keep my breathing even, but I could see my chest rising and falling more rapidly under his attention.

"You're all grown up too, which I believe we've established," I said, my voice steadier than I could have hoped. I blinked a few times and calmed myself, enjoying his soft touch and only mildly terrified by the thought of what he might do next.

"You're even more beautiful than I imagined you'd be," he said, his hand now touching the hair that was tucked behind my ear and hung down to my collar bone.

"Hmm. You imagined me?" I asked with a small smile, eyes on his wrist as it moved slowly up and down, his hand in my hair too close to see without moving my head. I couldn't dwell on his comment, or I would disintegrate into a cloud of stunned delight.

"Yes. Often," he said, his voice dropping lower.

"Really?" I asked.

"Yes. Why? You didn't imagine what I'd look like?" he asked. He stopped his careful exploration of my neck and hair and rested his hand so the tips of his fingers rested at the slope where my neck met my shoulders. He was far more casual about touching me than I felt.

"I'm not sure. I mean, I saw pictures every now and then, so I sort of knew. If you'd just cave and join the modern world of social media, I would've had a much easier time." I gave him a playful glare. "You've always looked like you with varying degrees of... I don't know, experience? Intensity? I guess maturity might be the right word. But you certainly are all grown up now—that's true." I had to bite my tongue to stop myself from continuing the babble.

He laughed at that. "So you're saying I look old again. 'Experience' and 'maturity' are code for old." His fingers started their path again. Ear, neck, collar bone.

"You are so obviously not old, don't start with me. You're only like, six months older than me, right? Plus, men age better than women, so when you look old, I'll look older." I couldn't help but feel a flash of annoyance at the thought of him looking like a ripped silver fox at age seventy while across the world somewhere I'd be sagging and stretched and looking very much my age. I fought against the urge to close my eyes again—I wanted to hide from his nearness, but I couldn't stop watching him.

"I disagree, but I surrender," he said.

"Well, what did you imagine?" I said, slipping back into feeling hypnotized by his voice and his closeness and his fingers still almost imperceptibly tracing along my neck.

He was quiet then, for a minute. I watched him study me, and when I couldn't take the intensity anymore, let myself shut them for another moment.

"I don't know... I can't even remember, now that you're in front of me." His voice had shifted, something in it heavy. As I tried to make sense of what he meant, I felt his fingers trace along the lines of my neck, along my jaw, and then when I felt him pulling my chin toward him, I opened my eyes.

His face was closer now, his eyes searing into mine as I met them. One hand came to rest on top of my hand on my thigh, the other filtered back into my hair. He moved slowly toward me and looked at my lips, then back up into my eyes. I could hardly do anything other than yield to his gentle pull— the sensation of his hand on mine, his other hand in my hair, his face nearing mine, was all too much to process.

He was moving slowly enough I could have easily pulled back or said something, but I let him pull me in. He moved his other hand to my shoulder, now slightly raised up from where I'd been leaning back against the couch, to angle my whole body toward him. Finally, the gap was closed, and his lips were touching mine.

If our first kiss was demanding and hungry, this one was, to continue the night's theme, delicate. He kissed me just once, then pulled back a little and his eyes searched mine. I returned his look, and he must have been satisfied by what he saw because he pulled me closer and kissed me again, this time with only slightly more pressure. His lips moved slowly, carefully, reverently. I let my hands gravitate toward him and felt the short hair at the back of his neck, then slowly ran my fingers through his hair at the back of his head. It was close-cropped and surprisingly soft.

My hands in his hair must have confirmed my interest, as if my total willingness to be pulled into a kiss hadn't done that already, and he intensified the kiss, his tongue and lips moving over mine with enthusiasm. I must have made a sound of approval because I felt him smile. The hand in my hair slipped back down my neck and came to rest on my shoulder. His hands gripped my shoulders now, and he held me in place there a minute longer before he pulled away with a kind of groan. I opened my eyes to see him rest his elbows on his knees and his head in one hand, almost like he was seasick.

I sat up and watched him, completely baffled. That wasn't the effect I'd anticipated. I cleared my throat lightly and said, "Are you ok?" I felt a gush of nervousness rush over me as I waited for his answer.

He kept his head in his hands a few seconds longer and then turned to me with his brow furrowed. "This isn't good," he said, looking genuinely troubled.

His words hit me right in the stomach, and I felt like the air had been knocked out of me. I had invested some serious time over the last few weeks in convincing myself that I only cared about Luke as a friend, that my excitement to see him was because we'd picked up our friendship after so long and not because I found him inescapably attractive on every level.

I hadn't deluded myself quite effectively enough because hearing him say anything like what he'd just said was an absolute punch in the gut. My face must have showed it.

"I didn't mean I didn't like what just happened—don't misread what I just said." He spoke to the floor, his head still resting in his hand.

"Uh, ok. How should I read it?" I asked, trying not to feel as raw and exposed as I did. He slid closer to me so his thigh paralleled mine, took my hand in his and laced our fingers together. My heart beat faster at his touch despite feeling totally confused.

He looked at our intertwined hands. "I can't not touch you," he said in a resigned tone. Then he kissed me again, his eyes open, watching me. I looked back at him, a wide-eyed, but annoyingly willing participant of the kiss. He pulled back and shook his head again, and then finally his seriousness seemed to crack and he smirked. "Damn. I should go." He didn't stop looking back at me, didn't let go of my hand, and made no move to get up.

"I'll admit, I'm confused," I said because I'd never been able to play coy very well, and this whole series of events was hella confusing.

He took a deep breath, blew it out in a burst, and sat up. He looked down at our hands again and said, "I think I thought I could kiss you again and kind of... get you out of my system." He glanced up at me with an eyebrow raised.

"Get me out of your system? What does that mean?" My throat felt tight and I felt incredibly stupid. I felt like an overgrown geek sitting there next to him, lamely letting him hold my hand while he explained why he didn't want me. I pulled back my hand and tried not to let the emotion creep into my eyes.

He hesitated then, his breathing careful and he shook his

head, still looking down where our hands had rested—where his hand was still resting, open and upturned. "I used to be in love with you, Alex." He said it flatly, and like he was sure I knew this already.

"What? When?... What?" I stuttered.

Whaaaat?

"You knew this. You must have. I dropped off the face of the planet in ninth grade when you started 'going out' with Jordan Smith. I was heartbroken. I couldn't stand to be around you after that because I knew you didn't feel the same way, and I just had to get space. Then I figured out the early college stuff, and it was easier when I had a plan." He was looking at me, watching my reaction, clearly surprised to see my baffled face.

"I never knew what happened. I thought it was because of Louis—that you were upset, or embarrassed or... I don't know. I just couldn't get you to come over anymore, or go get frozen yogurt after school, or talk to me, or do... anything. I was devastated," I said quietly.

The silence hung there between us. It still didn't make sense. *I used to be in love with you.* How could he just say that, like it was nothing?

I waited for him to explain how this connected to whatever just happened.

"So you thought you were in love with me, and that applies to the fact that you look like it's the end of the world because you just kissed me again because...? What am I missing?" I felt frustration creeping into my voice. I didn't want to fight with him, but I felt myself gearing up for battle.

"I didn't just *think* I was in love with you. All the crap with Louis just made me... a coward, basically. It doesn't matter. I *was* in love with you. And I was for a long time after that. All those letters you wrote me in basic training...

every time we interacted it came back. You'd think after so long it would have faded. And then we didn't talk much at all for years, just an email here or there, and I finally grew out of it. Then I saw you a few years ago and you were dating someone—and that sucked, but I mean, I was happy for you." He looked at me and then shook his head a little. "Then you were home and single, and I wasn't dating anyone either, and I figured it was the first time in a long time we were in a place to catch up. So I sort of jumped you while we were back home when I heard you'd be nearby—like I wanted to prove to myself we would be friends again, just like before, but holy hell, that plan didn't work." He took a deep breath that filled his chest and then expelled it.

I finally grew out of it. He'd been in love with me, but he grew out of it? I felt an ache bouncing around my hollowed out chest, a familiar sense of loss and confusion.

He gave me another miserable look and continued. "And then over the last few weeks I talked myself into believing that whatever it was I felt that night when I kissed you was just the thrill of reconnecting, of seeing you after so long. I didn't want to risk our friendship getting awkward right as we were reconnecting. I'd planned to be friendly but just that—just friendly today. But I can't keep my eyes or hands off of you, and so I kissed you again, and you kissed me back and—" he cut himself off by running his hands over his face as he groaned in frustration. My heart was racing yet again, listening to him describe much of what I'd been feeling.

"So you tried kissing me again to... 'get me out of your system,'" I supplied, not sure how I should feel about that.

"I was hoping that if I kissed you again it'd feel like kissing a sister, or something, and it'd be awkward for a minute, and then we'd move back into friend zone and live happily ever after as life-long buddies," he explained, looking at me again with his pained, perfectly blue eyes.

"Well this sure isn't awkward at all, so that plan failed," I said, shaking my head at him and crossing my arms over my chest, heat rising to my cheeks.

"It's completely awkward," he said, still shaking his head, and then quietly he muttered, "and I'm totally screwed."

"I'm sorry Luke, I still don't understand. We *are* friends. So you kissed me, and it was good—at least it was for me, but that doesn't mean—"

He sprang at me then, and his lips were on mine before I could finish my thought. He kissed me aggressively this time, his lips devouring me as I responded. I grabbed his shirt and pulled him closer, his hands were in my hair, and my stomach was doing flips at the contact. He broke away again and practically pushed me away.

"Shit!" he said, and he stood up. He moved toward the table where his keys and wallet sat.

I gathered my composure as best I could, still breathing hard in the wake of that mind-melt of a kiss. "I have no idea what's happening right now," I said as evenly as I could.

"I'm just..." He looked at me for a minute and I waited to hear him explain everything—waited to hear him say something to unravel this mess that had somehow appeared out of thin air. He reached for my door knob. "I'm freaking out, ok? I'm going to go, and I'll text you later. Make sure you lock your door." And with that, he was gone.

I expected to cry because I certainly felt upset, but I knew Luke wasn't trying to be a jerk. He seemed genuinely spooked by kissing me, and I guessed by wanting to keep kissing me. As delightfully insulting as that was, I wasn't getting the whole story, and I knew it.

I used to be in love with you. I finally grew out of it. What a thrilling, crushing admission he'd made tonight. What was I supposed to do with that information?

And mostly? I couldn't stop thinking about his lips on mine and his hands in my hair, or his fingers sliding along my jaw. I realized with a sinking sensation that I had no desire to be Luke's friend.

CHAPTER SEVEN

The next morning as I woke from a coma of exhaustion-induced sleep, I checked my phone to see I'd slept until after ten. As a lover of mornings, this was simultaneously delightful, since I rarely slept past seven, and maddening, because I felt the gaping loss of a morning's productivity, and I had a ton of unpacking yet to do. I also saw I had a text from Luke.

Luke: *I forgot to give you the present I got for your cat. Can I bring it by on Saturday?*

Um... ok. I wasn't sure what to expect when he said he'd text—I'd guessed it would be a few days and maybe an apology for running away, but I definitely didn't anticipate his A. ignoring what happened and B. using my cat to do it.

Me: *My cat will not be a pawn in your game to ignore that you ran away from me last night.*

I wasn't pulling any punches–this was nonsense.

Luke: *Straight to that already, huh?*
Me: *Already? Am I supposed to pretend it didn't happen?*
Luke: *No*
Me: *Good. Because I'm not going to.*
Luke: *Ok*
Me: *Ok*

Well this was great.

Luke: *I'm sorry I freaked out.*

I waited for some kind of follow up. Some kind of explanation. Three minutes ticked away, people aged, babies were born, global warming sliced through another section of the ozone, and finally, I responded.

Me: *I'm not sure what to say. It's ok? Of course you can freak out and run away from me whenever you need to, but I hope it doesn't happen again. If there is a next time, I hope you'll stay and talk to me. We've only had, what? Twenty-seven years of experience, give or take a few months to account for the years we were learning to speak.*
Luke: *We had a solid nine-year gap of not speaking, so really, we only have eighteen years of experience.*
Me: *True. Maybe that's it. It has been a while and we're not used to talking eye to eye, especially about uncomfortable things.*
Luke: *True enough.*

Ok. So, acknowledged. Awkwardness abated?

Luke: *Yep. So I guess we need practice.*

This comment was pleasing. Practicing talking to Luke wouldn't be a hardship, of that I was certain.

Me: *I guess we do.*
Luke: *So can I come bring your cat his present on Saturday?*

~

I spent the next few days unpacking boxes and exploring my neighborhood and doing a little cooking. Nothing made me feel like my feet were planted like getting into my kitchen and figuring out what I was working with. I was delighted to have a gas stove again, and my oven's temperature seemed to be accurate. These two discoveries went a long way toward making me feel settled, even though I was far from comfortable in my new surroundings. Fanning out my rainbow of spatulas in a jar of cooking utensils made me feel like I was ready to cook, ready to step into my normal routines.

Aside from these small comforts, and having an apartment full of familiar things, it was all new. And while I was happy with the change on the surface, it was impossible to pretend I didn't feel totally upside-down in pretty much every way possible.

On Friday I went into my new office and met the staff, met my administrative assistant Randy (I shared him with my fellow team leaders Janie and Emily), and got a look at my desk so I could appropriately outfit it come my starting day on Monday. My job in New York had been an account lead, which meant I was the woman in charge for a given event. I walked clients through their timelines, their linen choices, their seating arrangements, their menus, what AV equipment they needed. Depending on where the event was, I coordinated with a venue's liaison, and that person did some of the nitty gritty like selecting burgundy or black napkins and shrimp cocktail or passed hors d'oeuvres for the cocktail hour. But part of what I did to win accounts was create a vision for an event and create bids for companies, hoping my vision for their event would match their own.

I was damn good at this. Almost every account I went after, I got. But I was in the corporate leg of the company, I rarely had time off, and I didn't have much variation in terms of accounts. I became internally exhausted by the Fortune 500 parade and the lack of flexibility or originality. Toward the end of my time in New York, I felt like everything became unbearable. Maybe it was because I knew I was leaving, or maybe it was because I was just so ready for change, or maybe it was because the oppressive heat of New York summer had begun early in June and I felt ready to say goodbye to the city and my life that revolved around work regardless of the day of the week.

My new job was team leader, which meant I'd have several account leads under me. Well, I'd have two, one of whom I'd be sharing with another lead because I was the team leader of the non-profit department. This meant I would be overseeing what my event leads were doing and would work on a more managerial level. I had training in management from all of my schooling years, and I had managed events until I couldn't see straight. Building relationships between companies and vendors was my thing. But if I didn't admit I was nervous to manage another person, essentially a peer in my own field, I'd be lying. It was the next step, and the shift to nonprofit, the move to a new city, and the new job description, was all serving to create an intensity to the experience of meeting my colleagues that made the day feel surreal.

Everyone was incredibly welcoming and kind, and I felt

sure some of the competition and stress that so often accompanied my position in New York might be softened here in the friendly South. So much of that competition had come from account leads working toward the promotion to team leader, and since I was now a team leader in a new company, that should be altogether removed. In theory.

Also, Emily and Janie, my fellow team leaders, mentioned a great barbeque place we'd try for lunch the next week, and I knew I'd have fast friends there.

"We're so glad to have you here with us and add you to the family," Mr. Burney said, shaking my hand in welcome. He hired me based on phone and Skype interviews, and Burney and Wilks' compensation plan was very generous considering they also funded my relocation. I was glad that my first impressions fit with what I was expecting—a friendly, tight-knit place. This was so opposite FixEvents, and it was very welcome.

By the end of the day at B&W I felt eager to begin. I'd gotten a peek inside my small office, which featured a light wood desk, a nice-sized window, and one wall that was floor to ceiling bookshelves. I had two chairs sitting on the other side of my desk, both comfortable and welcoming should I need to host a client or hold a small group meeting.

As I lay in bed that night, waiting for my mind to calm itself, I felt hopeful. I liked what I saw of my job and I prayed it'd feel like home, that it'd feel meaningful and satisfying and like it was enough, or at least the beginnings of it. It had been so long since I'd felt satisfied, happy, and I'd started to wonder if feeling energized and excited by my job, by my life, was possible.

～

Luke knocked on my door at eight on Saturday.

I had done my best to avoid thinking about what our next encounter would be like. That was, of course, impossible, so what it meant was that I'd spent the majority of the last few days feeling unendingly preoccupied by thoughts of his lips, eyes, face, hands, and voice. And the rest of him. And the things he said. Oh and the whole friendship/making out conundrum. And whether he'd run away if/hopefully when he kissed me again.

So... basically I expertly obsessed over him like I did when I was fifteen and he was better, even then, than Justin Timberlake in my eyes. *Oy*.

I answered the door with Lemon draped over my shoulders. Lem was a light orange tabby mixed with something else —my theory was Ragdoll because he was more than willing to hang over my shoulder as I walked around the house. He could even sleep up there, and in winter he provided me a perfectly soft, permanently warm, purring scarf, so it worked for me. So far, the punishing gusts of A/C that cooled every indoor space of Tennessee and could only be subdued a little in my apartment, made Lemon's love of scarf-life a clear way he was earning his keep.

Bright sunshine burst in my door, and I squinted against it as I welcomed Luke. "Come in," I said and stepped back to make room for him.

He stepped in and eyed me and the fluffy mass over my shoulders. "This is Lemon. He's unimpressed to meet you," I said, waving one of Lemon's inanimate paws at him. I felt a small uptick in Lemon's purr as I set the paw down and gave him a pat on his head.

Luke smiled and held up a small potted plant he pulled from behind his back. "Catnip," he said, obviously pleased with himself.

"You come here as a pusher. Trying to drug my cat so you can get on his good side?" I didn't often have catnip for Lemon, but he'd be pleased, and then annoyingly uncoordinated once he got his little feline high going. A warm feeling flooded my chest as I looked at Luke holding out the small terracotta pot. I took the pot and set it on a counter I knew Lemon wouldn't explore any time soon.

"Absolutely," he said, and with one hand on my wrist, he leaned in to kiss my cheek. I closed my eyes as his lips met my face—he must have shaved that morning. His skin was smooth and soft, and he smelled *so* good. He smelled like clean laundry and coffee and minty toothpaste.

"Your cat is out cold. Is he asleep?" he asked as he looked at the lump of fur, beaming at me like it was magic I wielded and not Lemon's natural state of being that kept him on my shoulders.

"He is. That's the only reason you haven't been met with a rumble of disapproval and a glare," I said, holding Lemon's dangling paws. "Prepare yourself," I warned him and then lifted my little fluff up over my head and walked him to the couch. He immediately settled into one of the cushions on the back, gave Luke a withering glance, and then curled into himself to sleep.

"Well, I can't help but feel that went well," he said, waiting for my confirmation. He stuffed his hands in his pockets and looked completely at ease.

"Yes. You've passed the initial 'is he going to kill me or her' test with flying colors," I told him. I grabbed my purse and walked to the door. "I saw a little bakery down the street, and I'd love to check it out. That ok?" I asked, already opening the door.

"I'll never turn down pastries," he nodded as he spoke and followed me toward the stoop.

"I'm with you there, but I can't imagine you eat all that many pastries." I turned and locked my door. He stood about a foot away from me, and it felt like a conscious choice for him to stay at a bit of a distance. A friendly distance.

Ok then.

"True. I don't eat them often. But my normal routine doesn't include eating out all that much," he explained as we walked out onto the sidewalk toward the café. I wondered what a normal day was like for him and felt a pang of longing to know those details about him.

"I have a feeling you're pretty regimented," I said, enjoying the small breeze ruffling my navy skirt around my knees. I took a deep breath and closed my eyes for just a minute to feel the sun on my face. I'd been up and out early for a run, but the day was perfect and not too muggy yet.

"What makes you say that?" he asked, then held the door open for me and gestured for me to enter first.

I walked in and he followed behind me. I breathed in the smell of warm baked goods and chocolate and coffee. Oh dear, this would be dangerous. Far too close to home to be effectively avoided. I mentally resigned myself to embracing a few more pounds in favor of feeding my ever-present but usually-starved croissant addiction.

"Two please," I told the hostess and she beckoned for us to follow her right away to a small table by the window. Luke was behind me, close enough to touch me, but notably *not* touching me. No warm, big hand on my lower back, and I had to work to push the disappointment away. He pulled out my chair, and I sat and scooted myself in as he sat across from me and the hostess handed us menus.

We both perused the menu and I shut mine quickly, already knowing I'd have a croissant and coffee. I'd had baked eggs with a little cream and fresh chives earlier since I'd already gone for a run and gotten cleaned up by seven that morning. I may or may not have woken up when the sun rose that morning at six in anticipation of seeing Luke. I may or may not have had several rehearsal conversations with Lemon in which I was totally normal and charming, not awkward and babbling.

"What are you having?" I asked as I watched him read over the options.

"Coffee. Croissant. And probably more coffee after that," he said. "But you haven't answered my question." He set down his menu and then scooted his chair in a bit more. His knees bumped mine and he reached down to feel what he'd hit. His hand brushed over my bare knee and he pulled it back as if he'd been burned. "Agh, sorry. Didn't realize that was you."

"Yes, that's me. Tiny table. Do you need more leg room?" I asked, feeling our legs threaded together under the table, a remnant of the heat left by his touch just seconds ago lingering on my knee.

It was just a knee. It was just an accident, but there was something suggestive about touching a bare knee. Or at least my body thought so. Maybe his did too based on the way he'd snatched his hand back to avoid a third-degree burn.

"No, uh... no, I'm good." He cleared his throat and looked up at our waiter who'd just arrived with mugs and a carafe of coffee. We ordered and were left to fix our coffee while we waited.

"I bet you take yours black, right?" I asked, watching as he wrapped his hands around the warm mug in front of him.

"I do. You can't be picky about coffee when you never know whether you'll have stuff to put in it. I learned to drink it black during deployments because there was no choice and no time to do anything but guzzle it. After that it made sense to just enjoy it that way so I didn't feel deprived." He was pursing his lips a little then, like he was waiting to say something else.

"And?" I asked.

"And what?" He looked at me with an eyebrow raised.

"You were going to say something else," I told him.

"Hmm. Yes. I was going to say I bet you like yours light and sweet." He watched to see if he was right. I reached down and took a sip of my black coffee and tried not to enjoy the fact that he was definitely staring at my mouth.

"Black," I said.

"See? So much I don't know about you." He grinned.

"True. I am rather mysterious," I agreed.

"So why do you think I'm 'regimented'?" he asked. He took another sip of his coffee and waited.

I held my mug to my cheek, enjoying the warmth and the earthy, bitter smell. "Are you telling me you're not?" I asked.

"No."

"So you are?"

"No. Well, yes, I guess," he admitted. He shifted in his seat.

"It seems obvious. I mean... look at you," I said, nodding toward him with my chin, my hands still wrapped around my mug.

"What does that mean?" he asked, a self-conscious frown tipping the corners of his mouth down.

"Come on, you are pure muscle. People who look like you don't exactly routinely eat pastries by the dozen," I said, knowing my cheeks would be burning red in moments. It wasn't like he didn't know he was attractive, and more so, that I was attracted *to* him. My response to him anytime he kissed me, never mind the now numerous times he'd found me tongue-tied and staring at him, would have tipped him off easily.

"Sure. But I have to be fit for my job. If I'm overweight, I'm out. Or at least, I look like a jerk. So it's in my interest to be this way," he explained in a voice that almost seemed like he felt he needed to defend himself.

"It's in my interest too," I said without thinking and smiled an embarrassed-to-be-caught smile back at him. He brightened at that and started to say something when the waiter interrupted.

"Here we go y'all! Fresh from the oven, so give 'em a minute to cool. Enjoy!" And off he went again. Before Luke could return us to my blatant appreciation of his body, I changed the subject.

"What's it like to be back to work, but not deployed? Is it strange?"

He finished chewing a bite, swallowed, and then said, "Sort of. It feels old and familiar at the same time. It's crazy while you're deployed, and exhausting and stressful, but the work feels important. All those Excels are tracking important information, all of the briefings really matter. But here, that sense of urgency is missing. That can be nice, but I can already tell I'll get restless being back if I stay too long," and then he took another bite of the perfectly crusty pastry he hadn't yet put down.

"If you stay too long? I thought you said you'd probably have a year or so before you deploy again?" I asked, surprised by the way my stomach had dropped at the possibility of him not being around.

"Sure, that's the theory. There are a few options that would see me leaving sooner than the year mark. There's always schools and TDY assignments to take—just stuff to mix up the boredom and nonsense that comes from being in garrison—not deployed," he explained. He sipped his coffee and eyed me over the cup.

"Ah, gotcha. Well..." I trailed off and realized I might sound strange if I just stopped talking even though I had nothing more to say, so I quickly finished, "I'm glad you have ways of making things more... interesting for yourself." I broke eye contact then, feeling ignorant yet again.

Interacting with this *friend* always made me feel clumsy and foolish. In an effort to channel the feeling away from the creeping flush of my cheeks, I focused on my croissant. I brought it, still warm, to my mouth and took a bite from one of the ends. Little wisps of pastry layered with butter-inspired air compressed between my teeth with a satisfying crunch and then give, the center layers soft and tender, just the way they should be. I closed my eyes so I could taste the perfection I was now chewing without the distraction of sight.

"You approve of the croissants, I see."

I didn't speak but instead took another bite, smiled as I chewed, and after returning the little pastried perfection to my plate, held my coffee mug to warm my hands again.

"What have you been doing these last few years?" He sounded conversational, but something in the way he said this sounded loaded. We'd covered the basics weeks ago on our night out back home.

"Like for work? You know I worked for the event planning agency and did mostly corporate events. Mostly fun, but eventually exhausting, hence the move here." I took another bite of the croissant and smiled as I chewed. God bless the French.

"Did you date?" he asked bluntly, but avoided eye contact with me and sipped his coffee. I felt a flash of dread at the now unavoidable exes conversation.

I definitely wanted to know what his history was, to fill in the gaps a bit, but I didn't care to share my own experience.

He knew I had been with someone when we'd run into each other at the grocery store while I was home for Christmas five years ago, just before I'd gotten engaged, and we'd both been dating people at the time. But yuck. Who wanted to discuss these things with... well, with Luke?

Not it!

"A bit." *I know. I know!* I wasn't trying to be evasive, but I suddenly felt painfully aware of my awkward dating history.

"So, no one serious since high school except the uh... the guy a few years back?" he pressed.

"I didn't have a boyfriend in high school, which you maybe knew. I did date a guy, Marcus, while I was in Boston. It got serious." I watched for a reaction, but his face was a mask of neutrality. Or maybe it wasn't a mask. Maybe he wasn't at all bothered by that news. Why would he be?

"How serious?" I guess he was curious enough, though.

"We were engaged." I let out a shuddering breath after that, then hid behind my coffee mug while I waited for his response.

"Wow. That's... wow. But I guess it didn't work out?" His voice was gentle now, less prodding, but I still felt frustrated by his persistence. I didn't normally have much of an issue sharing the details of my breakup with Marcus, but somehow telling Luke made me feel all twisty and irritable.

"Well, no, obviously not. He wanted me to stay with him in Boston, and I had an offer in New York. It was my dream job, and he knew that. In the end, I couldn't imagine sacrificing my plans in favor of his, so we parted ways. He was upset, but it was an amicable split. We lived together for a year before we broke up, so that was awful, but since I was moving away anyway, it made the transition better than it would have been otherwise. I also learned I'd never do that again—live with someone, so... that was good." I shoved the last third of my croissant in my mouth and chewed it so I would stop talking, so I would feel better, so I could crush something in my teeth.

"It sounds like he didn't get you, maybe." He was leaning on the table now, his arms crossed in front of him, looking at me.

"No, I don't think he did. And maybe I didn't know myself either—at least until the time when I did, and I knew I couldn't marry him and change everything for him. I wasn't ready for all of that yet. I don't think I loved him, and that was part of it." I lifted one side of my mouth into a reluctant half-smile I hoped conveyed the mixture of regret but not desolation I'd felt afterward. I'd been upset about ending the relationship, but also relieved. I was mostly just relieved when I got to New York, excited by my job, and glad not to have to factor someone else into all of my decisions. I felt sad that I thought I'd loved Marcus and embarrassed a little by the realization that I hadn't loved him, but I wasn't even mildly depressed. In the end, that lack of depression had me more concerned than the breakup itself.

"Well, then it's good you split." He punctuated this statement with a nod.

"What about you?" I asked, eager to shift things away from me, but anxious to hear what might be coming.

"Not much to tell. Nothing special," he said without expression. Really, there was no expression on his face. Fine then.

"You're going to have to elaborate." I tried not to convey my annoyance at his non-answer. He'd been the one to start the conversation, so his avoidance, or vagueness, was just not ok.

"I didn't date in high school—just avoided that whole issue so I didn't fall into the same situation Louis did. Not that

I would have, but I just focused on school so I could get out on my own. I dated on and off over the years, but anytime I found someone I might be interested in something more than casual dating with, it was about time for me to move or deploy or whatever. It was always easier to cut ties. So I haven't had a long-lasting relationship. Certainly no engagements to speak of, and no roommates either." He ate the last bite of his croissant, his eyes never leaving mine. I swallowed some coffee and set my cup down gently.

"Well, what a pair of losers," I said with a forced smile, trying to shift the conversation to something else. I pushed my fork and spoon a few inches away, then turned my attention to my lap where I folded my paper napkin in accordion folds. I tried to laugh but it felt forced so I kept quiet and my eyes stayed glued to my napkin.

I felt a strange and convicting sense of relief at hearing he hadn't ever been serious with anyone. Was I glad he hadn't found someone? Was I the kind of person who wanted to hoard people for myself? That was an ugly thought. But maybe it wasn't everyone—I only cared that Luke hadn't found someone serious, someone special.

I shook my head at myself and changed the subject. "How's Louis?"

Luke sighed, looking deflated. "He's ok. Tessa is awesome —they keep my office space wall-papered with her artwork. She's thirteen now, so that has transitioned to photography. And Louis is... fine. I don't know what other word to use."

"I can't believe she's thirteen." I smiled at the memory of the last time I saw her—she'd been eight or nine, and couldn't stop talking, even when Luke's mom told her to say goodbye and they pulled out of the parking lot where we'd run into each other. I don't think her mouth ever stopped moving. "And Jen?"

He cringed before speaking. "She's in Sandy or some-where south of Salt Lake. Last I heard she was working as an aesthetician. I haven't actually seen her in two years, since Tessa's eleventh birthday. She was quiet. She ignored Louis, didn't speak to him the whole party, and glared at him when-ever he came into view. I think she's still really angry with him."

"I'm sorry." That he'd be upset by his brother's unhappi-ness, and Jen's too, was no surprise to me.

"Yeah. I am too." He gave me a reluctant smile and eyed me as he sipped his coffee. I smiled at him too but couldn't think of what to say now. I didn't really feel like talking about my own siblings, even as much as I loved them. I wanted to know more about what his life was like, and who he was now, and recover the conversation in the wake of the mess that was and always had been Louis and Jen.

"I have a favor to ask you." He hadn't stopped looking at me and when I met his eyes, I had that familiar feeling of being the prey.

"What?" I asked, licking small remnants of the pastry's flakey layers from my lips.

"Well first, I need you to forgive me for running out of your house like a burglar the other night." He stopped for a minute and looked at me pointedly, like he was not only apol-ogizing, but apologizing again for taking so long to address it in the first place. "And second, I want you to come with me next Saturday to this thing." He reached over and grabbed my hand where it rested next to my coffee mug. I felt my pulse quicken and my mind fog at his touch.

"Thing?" I asked.

"It's kind of a hassle, but it would be doing me a favor. If you could come. Which you don't have to do. But it would be great if you could. But it'll probably be boring." His speech was stunted, starting and stopping. He squeezed my hand and then his slid back across the table, and his thumb and pinky drummed back and forth while he watched me.

He was nervous asking me. So far, he'd been calm and confident as usual, but here was a breech in his front. He was as close to babbling as I'd ever heard him, and I couldn't say I wasn't charmed.

"What kind of thing are we talking about? You've made it sound totally amazing, so I can't see myself saying no, but..." I trailed off and waited for him to fill in the blanks. He shook his head at my sarcasm.

"It's a military ball." He said it quietly, just loud enough for me to hear, almost like an apology.

"A ball?"

"Yeah." He grimaced as he confirmed, like the reality of a *ball* would suddenly make me run screaming from the room.

Did he not realize that women—at least this one—loved the idea of going to a ball?

"What does that mean?"

"Uh, well it's formal? So I wear my blues uniform and you would wear a dress, if you come, which you don't have to, and we'd go. They serve dinner and there's some ceremonial stuff that happens, and then we'd leave as early as possible because there's always a weird combination of tedious slide shows and drunken lieutenants attempting to dance to hip hop." He rattled this off and sat, waiting for my response, his hands now clasped tight around his mug in front of him.

"A dress? Like I wear a ball gown?" Naturally my biggest concern was what I would wear because I had to choose not to focus on the already intimidating reality of going on a very formal date as Luke's not-really-date to a military anything. Holy crap.

"Yes?" he asked with a wince, like each question I asked was taking me closer to saying no.

I sat back and crossed my arms. Of course I was going to say yes, but I was enjoying this very brief moment of his nervousness. I was constantly feeling the effects of *him* and all that did for me was make me sweat and hyperventilate. I needed to savor this moment for just a minute.

"Ok," I said, staring at him without a smile.

"Ok?" he asked.

"Ok," I said again with a nod.

"Ok, you'll go with me?" he asked again, leaning forward over the table.

I leaned forward too, and now our heads were about six inches apart. "Yes, of course I'll go with you. Do you think my social calendar is already full after being here for five days?"

"No, but... I don't know. It *is* a hassle. You'll have to get a dress, unless you have one. And I mean it can be fun, don't get me wrong, and going with you will definitely make it bearable, but—"

"Bearable. Yes. That's what every woman wants to hear—"

"Of course it'll be more than bearable with you. But it *is* work for me, so I appreciate you doing this." His expression was serious, and I realized he was dreading the event, so I softened my face.

"I'm happy to."

CHAPTER EIGHT

Luke was going to pick me up at five. The cocktail hour started then, and he said he wanted to be a little late. I had no idea what I was in for with this whole event, but like any good modern woman, I'd done some researching. I discovered I needed an actual, floor-length gown, not just a cocktail dress, unless I wanted the scorn and judgment of all the seasoned military wives and girlfriends in the room to reign down on me. *Noted.*

Also? Terrifying.

I found something at a mall in town, and in the end, I felt good in it.

Well, that was a lie.

I felt damn good in it.

The dress was a deep navy silk lined with gold silk on the inside. It had a high scoop neck front and then a low back that draped down to just below my natural waist. The front smoothed over my curves and then was cut on the bias so the skirt swirled around my hips. The silk was heavy enough that it felt comfortable instead of like it was accentuating every very real bump and lump (see: croissants). On the left there was a slit to my mid-thigh so when I walked you could see the gold lining. I wore sparkly, dangly earrings, my hair long and down pulled over to one side of my head so it hung in curls over one shoulder. My make-up was a bit more intense than I'd normally do, but if you couldn't do it up for a ball, then when could you?

Aside from my general excitement, I thought about how strange it was to be attending an event like this. For the last four or more years of my life, I'd been on the other side of things, managing events. I always wore a black suit and low heels or flats, depending on the event. I was always saddled with a walkie-talkie and at least one extra cell phone as well as a belt that had a fanny-pack like pocket on it for my arsenal of fix-it items to stave off small disasters. I so loved the rush of keeping things together and pulling off an event. I couldn't wait to see this place where we were going, a space I'd likely encounter in my working life in a very different way in the coming months.

I was trying to calm myself down and convince myself I'd be fine and know what to do when I heard the doorbell. I swung open the door and didn't look up right away as I fumbled with my purse, making sure I had gum, lip gloss, phone, etc.

Luke made a sound I didn't recognize, and I looked up to see him standing there, mouth open, hand frozen as if he was still reaching for the door knob though the door had swung all the way open and away from him.

I smiled at him and stepped closer, then gave him a kiss on the cheek, my hands resting on the center of his suit jacket where brass buttons glinted. His head turned toward me and he kept watching me, still frozen at the door.

"Do you want to come in for a sec, or should we go?" I

asked him, trying to convince myself the look in his eyes wasn't regret. He hadn't spoken or made another sound.

"I think we have a minute," he said, his voice raspy and low. He stepped in and closed the door. "I don't mind being a few minutes late..." his voice faded out and he didn't finish his thought, so I turned back around to face him. I'd walked to the counter to take one last drink of water from my glass. I turned to find him frozen again, mouth agape yet again, looking utterly bewildered.

"You ok?" I asked.

"Your dress. The back... there's no back," he said, almost accusatorially, except his tone was more stunned. His hand was still jutting unnaturally out to the side, like he hadn't yet realized there was no door handle in his grip.

I felt myself flush with self-consciousness. "Oh, yeah, kind of not. I put it on and it was so comfortable I thought it'd be ok, but if you think it's inappropriate, please just say so and I'll change." I twisted my purse's strap in my fingers and felt a familiar heat on my cheeks. I continued, the urge to ramble away my explanation completely unavoidable. "I searched online and it said I needed a long dress, not a cocktail dress, and nothing was quite right but then I saw this..." I said quickly, trying to explain. I smoothed one hand from my waist, over my hip. His eyes followed the movement of my hand.

"Is it too..." I trailed off, not sure what to say. The dress could have been risqué, sure. The back was open to my lower back, but it fit so well, and the rest of it was pretty modest— the slit to the mid-thigh, not the hip or anything too crazy. It felt like a sophisticated way to show some skin. But I felt significantly less sure about it as I waited for his response.

"No! No. No. No. No," he chanted, looking hazy and irritable.

"No, what?" I was anxious for him to clarify.

He took the two steps toward me and grabbed my hand with his free one as he shook his head. His palm against mine felt like a shock, his hand warm against my nervous, cool one. I realized other than briefly toughing my knee and grabbing my hand the weekend before, he hadn't touched me since he kissed me the day he helped me move in. My cheeks turned a deeper red with that awareness.

"You look absolutely stunning. Did you see me? I was literally stunned just now," and he gulped and let himself look me over once more before returning to my eyes. "The only problem with the dress is that everyone is going to be staring at you all night, and I will have to not beat them up when they do," he said with a smile and a kind of wince.

I felt panic rising. "I'm not sure that's what I—"

"Because you are painfully beautiful. Not for any other reason. The dress is perfect. You are perfect. And I am an idiot for not clarifying that because holy *shit* Alex... ah, sorry. Crap. Please don't worry." He was pleading with me, and I realized he was as nervous as I was.

"Ok!" I laughed nervously and let his hand go, still feeling awkward and totally unable to ingest what he'd just said. If I sat there and let his words fully register, I'd probably swoon or at least get a little drunk on their potency. I moved toward the door and gave him a look I hoped wasn't too embarrassed or overwhelmed. "Ok. I'm not worried. Let's just go."

In the car we sat quietly, music too quiet to hear in the background. He drove with fierce concentration, and I tried not to watch him. He was shaking his head, a smile playing on his lips.

"What?" I finally asked, unable to pretend I hadn't noticed.

"I was just thinking about what an idiot I am," he said, still shaking his head, eyes on the road.

"How so?" I asked, glad he was talking and not just staring and driving.

"What I said when I saw you—I think I implied people would be looking at you *because* of the dress. And it's a good dress," he glanced at me out of the corner of his eye, then quickly turned his attention back to the road. "But people would be looking at you if you were wearing an old bathrobe. I hope you realize I'm not suggesting the dress is what makes you... you know." I watched as a red flush crept up his neck and into his cheeks. As though Luke wasn't good looking enough already, he was blushing. It was adorable. I looked the other way, out the window, and I smiled to myself.

"Well thank you. You certainly look handsome in your uniform."

"They say ladies love a man in uniform," he said with a laugh, not moving his eyes from the road now.

"Fact," I stated.

And it was. Because seriously. If this man was any more handsome, he'd need to be fined. Or charge a subscription fee for monthly views. Or something. The shining brass buttons of his dress coat and the weighty looking medals and ribbons decorating different spaces on his chest made him even more alluring. Knowing each one of those things meant something, signaled some accomplishment or effort, was fascinating. I couldn't wait to ask him about them.

We arrived at the Gaylord Opryland Hotel, a hulking white face with a parking lot that stretched for what felt like miles, and once we found our way through the maze of a hotel to the conference center area, we entered the ballroom. The place was a mixture of resort and hotel—it smelled a little like Las Vegas, and something about it reminded me of it too, but it lacked the camp and glare of Vegas. It felt strange and delightful as we walked through the indoor gardens. The ballrooms weren't as unique as the hotel itself, but they were full-sized, and I felt a little rush of pleasure at seeing the space and knowing I could definitely use it well for the right event.

Luke nodded to a much younger soldier who stood at the door and stopped to check us in.

"The receiving line started about fifteen minutes ago—it should be about done but you might be able to catch the tail end of it if you want, sir." The soldier watched for Luke's response, and Luke smiled back.

"Good, so glad we didn't miss it," Luke said with heavy sarcasm. "Thanks Benson." Then he patted Benson on the back and moved to open the door for me. As I passed him, he placed his hand on my back.

My bare back.

His strong, warm, gorgeous hand was on my back, directly on my skin.

Nothing was happening in the universe of my brain except the recognition of small explosions on the surface of skin where his hand touched me. He wasn't hesitant about touching me, and that might have been the best part. He ushered me forward with purpose, apparently entirely unfazed by the contact, and I couldn't even enjoy the opulence of the ballroom or the soldiers and their lovely dates and their lovely dresses that we passed because all I was thinking was how good his hand on my back felt.

Help.

I felt the pads of his fingers on my spine, steady and reassuring. Or, I assumed it would have been reassuring if it hadn't made my entire sensory system stage a coup against my centers of rational thought and turn to mush. I imagined I was beet red and the aura surrounding me was something called *extremely loud and incredibly aware.*

He weaved us through a small crowd and came to rest at the end of a short line. I could only stare at another uniformed back in front of me and notice how cold my skin felt when Luke removed his hand. He slid it away gently, and it felt like a cruel caress.

"This is the receiving line. Everything about military balls is very formal and rooted in tradition, so there'll be a lot of obnoxiously formal stuff we do. Most of it is explained in the program at dinner, but first, you get to shake clammy hands with the Battalion leadership." He gestured with his chin to the semicircle of handsome slightly older men and their polished wives shaking hands and smiling brightly at a line of people in their finest. I must have looked confused because he continued. "Essentially, my bosses. Or, really just Lieutenant Colonel Wilson is the boss, and Sergeant Major Smith is his right-hand man. That one on the end is Major Flint—he's the Executive Officer, or we call him XO." He nodded toward the severe man at the end of the line whose serious face was nodding at each person whose hand he shook, his lips not moving.

"Oh ok. Yeah, I think I probably knew that, somewhere in my mind. I think I read about the receiving line, but I've only done them at weddings." I found my voice, found the ability to respond, and tried to get a grip on my fluttering nerves.

"Well just think of Lieutenant Colonel and Mrs. Wilson as the happy couple, and you'll be fine." He smiled at me but unfortunately did not touch me. Apparently, all I could think about was when he would touch me again like some hormone-addled teen.

The couple in front of us turned, and the man said, "Hi, I'm James. This is my wife Megan." He took my hand with a firm grasp and shook it, then handed me off to his wife. She smiled at me.

"I'm Alex," I said and smiled back.

"It's so nice to meet you Alex! I just love your dress. You look fabulous." She beamed at me, and I let her silky southern accent pour over me. She had one of those voices that was smooth and feminine. Paired with her light accent and something about the look in her eye, I immediately liked her. "I'm already sweating like a whore in church, but what can I say? Sometimes you've just got to go sequins!"

I laughed at her unexpected comparison and felt compelled to respond. "Well sequins, nervous sinner sweat or no, were a great choice. It's an amazing dress." I wondered if women just spent the whole night fawning over each other. The men all looked gorgeous in their uniforms, but aside from a few variations in ribbons and style, they largely looked the same. But the women—wow. Each dress was unique and expressive and interesting. Megan's dress was bright red with sequins covering every inch. Her blonde hair was pulled up into an elaborate updo, and she looked like a disarming version of a Texan beauty queen.

"Well thank you, Alex. But tell me, how long have you known Luke?" she asked, and I realized that James and Luke had been quietly having their own conversation. Despite my heightened awareness of Luke, Megan had captivated me.

"All my life," I said and turned to glance at him. As our eyes met his hand returned to my back. My stomach's inner ice skater did a triple Lutz.

"Alex and I grew up together. She just moved to Nashville, so she's humoring me by being my date." He lightly rubbed his hand around on my back as if to console me for having to fulfill this role. I swallowed and heard the sound echo in my ears.

"Yes, I'm sure that's a terrible hardship for her," Megan said and winked at me. Goodness, she was pretty. She could wink and make it look fun and conspiratorial, not creepy.

She turned around with a flourish just in time to start shaking hands, and then it was our turn. Luke stepped behind me and I went first through the line like I'd seen Megan do, shaking a hand, introducing myself, and on to the next person. I tried to smile naturally, make normal human small talk in the seconds I interacted with each person in the line, tried desperately to commit to memory the names of the wives since the men had their names on their uniforms and did my best to ignore that my hand was sweating.

"Well, that was a short one. Be thankful." Luke breathed out a large breath, and I could see his shoulders relax just a bit. I hadn't thought about the fact that he might be nervous about the ceremonial portion, too. Was that it?

"It wasn't bad. I'm sure I'll never remember their names, but they won't remember mine either, so that's fine." We arrived at a table, and I saw Megan and James were already sitting.

"Perfect! I was hoping you'd be with us." Megan clapped her hands and patted the seat next to her.

Luke pulled out my chair and helped me scoot it back in as I sat down. I felt keenly aware of his movements, as usual, and had a sharp sense of longing as he sat down next to me. He seemed stiff and almost restless, but he gave me a reassuring smile each time we looked at each other.

"What happens next?" But as soon as it was out of my mouth, I heard, "Post the colors!" in a commanding voice. I saw Lieutenant Colonel Wilson standing at the head table, and everyone else stood. I watched a group of soldiers process in holding the flag, and then they stopped. The room was silent as their shiny shoes clicked against the ballroom floor in unison, then silenced as they stepped over to carpet. They set the flag, faced the Lieutenant Colonel, and he nodded, so they left.

From that moment on, I was enthralled. Everything that happened was imbued with meaning. Every speech, every toast (My favorite was "To the Ladies!" one devastatingly adorable lieutenant shouted), every moment was carved out with purpose.

The Fallen Comrade table just about brought me to sobs. They explained the significance of each element—the small, isolated table for the soldier's frailty, the red rose for his shed blood, the white table cloth for the purity of his service and sacrifice—God, I could hardly bear it. It was such a strange moment to feel the weight of this reality in the midst of the ceremony and feel that it all mattered. What Luke and these men and women were doing was incredible and weighty and valuable and terrifying. I felt grief bloom and heat my chest, both for the possibility of something happening to any of these beautiful people surrounding me and with surprising sense of longing. There it was again—the desire to have something mean something for *me*, too.

I'd flicked away the tear that seeped out of the corner of my eye when they were explaining the symbolism of the table, and Luke grabbed my hand and brought the back of it to his lips. I watched as he gave me a gentle kiss and then kept my hand in his for the rest of the formal program.

I had room to breathe once dinner was served. We talked with Megan and James, and Ally and Jose, and Cindy and Grant, our other table companions, as we ate. I found I genuinely enjoyed these people, which was a delightful discovery, and made the evening so much less awkward than it might have been if we'd been seated with awful people. Not that I'd expected them to be awful, but after my brief stint searching the dresses and some of the comments I'd seen, I wasn't sure how things would go.

Before dessert was served, Megan scooted back from the table and declared "bathroom time, ladies," grabbed her red clutch from the table, and turned toward the doors. I felt compelled to join her, so I grabbed my own small purse and began to slide my seat back. Luke hopped up and pulled my chair the rest of the way out, and I reached up and put my hand on his shoulder to give it a small squeeze in thanks as I walked by him. When I looked up to smile at him, I was hit with his smoldering gaze.

Yep. It was smoldering. I'm not sure how he did it. I didn't see him drawing in eyeliner or adding contacts, but somehow his eyes were darker, bluer, and more magnetic. He smoldered. I huffed a little without sound, not sure what to say or do, and followed Megan.

CHAPTER NINE

Once the necessities were taken care of, we all stood washing hands, reapplying lipstick (wearing a ball gown made one particularly aware of one's lipstick) and chatting.

"Luke is so adorable. He's so polite and nice to everyone. I'm so glad you're here with him." Ally smiled at me sweetly. She was a petite woman in the truest sense—maybe not even a full five feet tall. Wearing platform heels that gave her a good three inches, she was pure muscle. She was feminine and curvy in her silky deep purple gown, but it was all muscle under there if her shoulders and arms were any indication. Her husband had bragged about her growing up as a competing gymnast during dinner. Her voice was just exactly what you'd expect from a tiny gymnast—it was almost child-like, and it matched what I could already tell was her genuine kindness.

"You guys are so sweet together." Megan smiled at me and watched me as I finished swiping on my lipstick.

"Thank you. We're good friends," I said to the counter as I sifted through my tiny purse, avoiding eye contact and the accompanying awkwardness this conversation could present. I set out each of the items: phone, a few sticks of gum, driver's license, credit card, forty dollars in cash, hair tie, bobby pin, safety pin (always be prepared), lipstick, lip gloss.

"Friends, huh? So you're not his girlfriend?" Megan said this, her southern accent dragging out the sooooo and betraying her skepticism.

I cleared my throat and met her eyes in the mirror. "No, just good friends." I definitely didn't feel like we were just good friends anymore. A few rounds of making out changed things, or at least it did for me, but I couldn't tell what he was thinking, or what he wanted, and I wasn't about to call us a thing to his friends when I didn't know what we were.

"Mmmmkay. So him looking at you like he wants to take you on the table, audience be damned, is just my imagination?" Megan crossed her arms and leaned back, her besequinned hip jutting out, everything about her posture speaking her disbelief.

I opened my mouth to say something, but I couldn't find words and a little garbled nervous laugh jumped out instead. I felt embarrassed by her assertion but also a definite thrill. Had he looked at me like that? I found a not-small part of me hoping she was right.

Finally, I found my voice. "Ah, uh... no? Er, uh, yes? It's your imagination?" I busied myself with reloading my purse, one thing at a time, so I didn't have to look at either of them.

"Honey, that man wants you. And I do not mean in a friendly way. I mean in the most delicious, unfriendly way possible." Megan smirked at me when my eyes jolted to meet hers. She raised her eyebrows to punctuate her point.

"I think she's right Alex. He can't stop looking at you. Plus, the guy is so darn polite and sweet, how can you resist him?" Ally's tiny voice reinforced Megan. Megan put her hand on my arm and tugged a little so I looked at her directly instead of through the mirror.

"Do you really not like him like that? Do you really just want to be his friend?" The look in her eyes was one of concern. I'm not sure if she was concerned for me, or Luke, or her own disappointment at not witnessing a childhood sweetheart love story, but it was unmistakable.

I sighed and felt my shoulders drop, my perpetually good posture losing its will to keep my shoulders back. My mother would be shaking her head if she could see me.

"I do. Of course I do. I've been friends with him for basically my whole life. But it's confusing and complicated, and I'm not sure what he wants. I will acknowledge that he finds me attractive and, I mean, look at him. I *obviously* do, but... I'm not sure it's worth the risk." I felt the kick of my k at the end of my sentence snap through the empty tiled bathroom as an instrumental version of "Shake it Off" played just above the silence.

"Mmm," Megan said like the nonverbal declaration was the final word on the matter. She looked at me, even narrowed her eyes and squinted at me, but didn't say a word. Her eyes jumped to Ally's, then back, still assessing me. "Let's get back."

I resisted the urge to ask what she was thinking. I didn't really know her, even though I liked her. I felt a little judged, but mostly curious. I also felt a low humming in the back of my mind—was it really not worth the risk to date Luke? I hadn't let myself think about what it would actually mean. I'd felt the thrill of kissing him and the general pleasure of being around him, but I hadn't let my mind trot down the path of what an "us" would look like.

Luke saw me coming back to the table and stood up, then scooted my seat in as I sat down. It was nice. It was one of those traditional manners-y things that seemed dumb when I learned them in cotillion class in junior high—that the man always stood when a lady at his table stood. It was a great way to play a game—stand every twenty seconds and see how many of the guys remembered the rule. But here, in adulthood, next to an actual man, it felt like a very small way he was showing me he noticed me. Like pretty much everything else he did, it sent a small flock of hummingbirds adrift in my belly.

"You ladies solve all of the world's problems?" Grant asked as he picked up his fork. I looked around and saw they'd served dessert, but everyone had waited for us to return.

"Oh, of course. There's peace in the Middle East, we've ended famine worldwide, and we've outlawed chain email forwarding by baby boomers. Our work here is done." I smiled at him and picked up my fork and dove in to the little cake. It was red—probably velvet.

I was a sucker for red velvet anything but approached it with a sense of mild skepticism whenever I had the chance to eat it, especially the cake variety. My own recipe was flawless and delicious and what I wanted red velvet cake to taste like at any given time. Anything else paled in comparison, but I always hoped I'd be pleasantly surprised. This one had buttercream, not cream cheese frosting—they'd made it too sweet, likely neglecting that pivotal drop of white vinegar to counteract the dye and sweetness. They'd used unsalted butter but didn't properly salt the frosting. I pulled my fork from my lips, clean of all frosting and cake crumbs, and set it down gently, trying not to betray my mild irritation. Why bother with red velvet cake if you couldn't do it right?

I saw movement out of the corner of my eye, so I glanced over at Luke as I sipped my piping-hot cup of decaf coffee. He was shaking his head and trying to suppress a smile.

"Do you have something you'd like to say?" I asked, my eyebrow arched.

"This is one of your things, right?" He nodded with his chin toward the cake.

"I have no idea what you're talking about," I said and looked around the table to find everyone watching us. I shrunk a bit in my seat.

"Yes you do. This is one of your things. I didn't know cake was one of them, but I can totally tell." He smiled triumphantly as he looked at me and could tell he was right.

"It's not all cake. Just red velvet. Maybe a few other specific kinds too. But red velvet is the biggest one." I said this quietly, not wanting to share this part of my weirdness with the table.

"What about it?" Megan asked loudly, demanding we include everyone.

"Alex loves food—loves it in a way that is primal. She has certain foods that she cooks a certain way, and those recipes are essentially sacred to her. So when she eats one of those foods and it doesn't live up to her perfect recipe that she alone can make, she can't eat anymore, and then gets this torn, end-of-the-world look on her face." He was teasing me, but it was surprising to hear him explain this oddity of mine so well. He was exactly right.

"Ohhh, you're a food snob!" Megan seemed delighted by this news and took another bite of the abomination someone was trying to pass off as red velvet cake.

"No, no, no. I'm not. I like all kinds of food. But when it comes to things I, or my mother, or someone I love, can make well, I definitely am. It's not just my own recipes—there are dishes from restaurants, that friends make, stuff like that, that are the best so any cheap imitation of them is just that. It's a trait that has been ruining meals for me since I was about five." I rolled my eyes at myself.

"So, red velvet cake. What else?" James asked as he took another bite of his cake.

"Hmm. Lots of Italian food. Those are the biggest culprits. My mom is second generation Italian, and I lived in Italy in college for a while. Most Italian dishes are ruined for me unless my mother, father, or some long-lost Italian relative is cooking it for me."

"She is the same with blueberry muffins. I remember that one from when we were kids. And vanilla ice cream." He took a sip of his coffee and watched me.

"True. But the vanilla ice cream isn't my recipe. That's yours." I realized I was staring at him, staring at his hand wrapped around his coffee cup, and I looked up to see him still watching me. I felt my pulse kick up and willed my body not to get excited by the memory of stupid vanilla ice cream.

"I love that you guys have known each other for so long. It's so sweet!" Ally couldn't contain the exclamation, and Luke and I laughed quietly at her enthusiasm. Before we had to say anything else, the formal speeches began, so we all turned our attention to the podium.

As the night progressed, it became clear to me why Luke had been reluctant, but determined, to have a date. Every other captain, at least that I could tell, was there with a date. I didn't know anything about rank, but he pointed out the two bars, essentially a vertical equals sign, on his shoulders and told me what it meant, so I kept an eye out for his fellows. In most cases, the women with his peers were wives, not just girl-friends, like Megan and Ally. I'd assumed he had single friends he spent time with, but his closest friends he'd introduced me to were all married, one engaged. Most of the younger soldiers were there with spouses as well. There were two female captains without dates, and I wondered if it was difficult to find partners as women in the military. Truly, everyone else had dates, and nearly everyone I was introduced to, regardless of rank, was married.

Despite my being not even a girlfriend, we had a fantastic time. Megan, Ally, and Cindy made me feel welcome at their table, and by the end of the night I felt like we were actively friends.

When the speech and awards were over, my wine glass was empty, and the emcee announced dancing would start soon. When the music cranked up to an obnoxious decibel, Luke leaned over and said, "I think if we just circulate for a few minutes and maybe dance a song or two, we can leave without being the first ones and I'll have done my duty."

When he spoke to me, he placed his hand on my leg, and I felt his touch burn its way through the midnight silk of my dress. I was sure I'd see a mark there later. I forced myself to keep my eyes forward despite the incredibly alluring feeling of his lips brushing against my skin as he spoke directly into my ear over the blaring music already playing. A few couples danced enthusiastically to something hip hop and impossible to dance to, and he stood up then and pulled me up with him, his hand moving to guide me on my bare back yet again.

It wasn't the first time he'd placed his hand on my back, obviously, but I couldn't get used to it. It felt intimate and sensual and not at all friendly. That was only because of my wardrobe choice, though. Right? I was chanting in my own mind that he had brought me as a friend, a functional date, and I needed to keep that in my thick skull, front and center. I felt the slightest buzz in my head from the wine I had—not much, but I hadn't eaten all that much, either—just tasting things as we all talked over dinner, and then the horror that was dessert wasn't filling, of course. I took a deep breath to ground myself as I walked with him.

He led me around to a few different tables to chat, doing his duty, and then led me to the floor just as the song shifted to something melodic and slow. I let out a breath, mentally thanking the DJ for letting me escape certain embarrassment by attempting to dance to hip hop in a ball gown (or at all).

He steered me with the hand on my back and pulled me in so I was practically crushed up against him, his other hand taking mine and linking our fingers together. I rested my free hand on his shoulder and tried to keep breathing and not fall over. Luke Waterford up close like this, in his uniform, pulling me *that* close to him—sweet caramel cheesecake, it felt decadent.

"Thank you for coming. This has actually been fun," he said, his breath whispering near my ear. My temple rested against his jaw. I relaxed a little in his arms as he spoke, trying to remember this was just Luke. My longtime friend Luke, just chatting with his friend Alex at a work function. Right?

"It has been fun. I like getting to peek inside your world a little," I said with a smile he couldn't see. I meant that. The Army was fascinating and so different from my experience with corporate events life. Everything was at once more formal and much more personal. And that feeling that every-thing had a purpose or meaning behind it was completely alluring.

"Most of the Army isn't at all like this, but I'm glad you've gotten a taste of it," he said, guiding us around the little dance floor, steering around other couples deftly.

Of course he could dance. Of course.

Just then the young lieutenant who'd made the toast *to the ladies* rammed into me, and Luke pulled me closer.

"Holder, get a grip," Luke said in a low voice.

"Sorry, sir. Feeling good! And daaaaaaamn your date is fine!" The lieutenant's date covered his mouth and jerked him away, stumbling and laughing right along with him. She seemed to be having as good a time as he was.

"Looks like he's enjoying himself," I said with a smile and pulled back just a touch. Not that I didn't enjoy being plastered to Luke, but I might combust if I stayed there too long.

"I think getting drunk at a ball is an unwritten rite of passage for lieutenants, though once it's *not* you, it's incredibly annoying."

"Yes. Kids these days," I said, lightly shaking my head. I ran my fingers over the stitching on his light blue shoulder board and thought again how appealing the uniform was. Each detail was so purposeful. I didn't know what each element meant, though I knew those little boards indicated rank. The light blue color was repeated in a cord that ran from under his arm to over his shoulder on his right side—the Infantry cord, he'd called it, indicating his job as an infantryman. Luke had told me the little yellow stripes on one of his sleeves each signified six months of time deployed. He had five of them.

I held on to him as we danced a minute more, and the song was done. Another slow one followed, and he pulled back just enough so he could look in my eyes and said, "Want to do one more?" as though I would say no to being right there, surrounded by him.

"Sure. We can pretend we're at prom." I grinned, trying to focus on something other than how comfortable and yet insanely uncomfortable it felt for him to be holding me, his right hand resting on my bare mid-back, his other hand clasping mine.

"Ah prom. I almost died when I saw you at prom with John Allen." He squeezed my hand and cleared his throat.

"What? You went to prom?" I didn't remember seeing him. I had actively looked for him because I knew he'd look adorable in a tux. I'd been anxious the whole night to see him, to see who he brought.

"I did. I actually..." He stopped a moment, shook his head slightly and then looked at me with chagrin. "I wanted to ask you, but by the time I got myself psyched up to do it, John had already asked. So, I decided I would go and at least get one dance with you." He looked at me, waiting for my response, which was already playing on my lips. I couldn't help the small glowing feeling I felt for my eighteen-year-old self.

"But you never came and found me. I never even saw you." I hadn't seen him, and I had been looking from the moment we walked in to the building. I had hoped he would ask me, praying maybe he'd reappear in my life in some romantic gesture years after we'd stopped talking, but John was a good friend, and I knew he wouldn't try anything crazy or expect me to go to a hotel with him after or any nonsense like that, so I'd said yes. At that point in the year I hadn't even seen Luke in months except in passing in the neighborhood, and although I'd hoped, I didn't believe he would show up. So, I said yes to John.

"Yeah, well I got there, and I saw you guys dancing, and I just couldn't do it. I remember thinking you looked too pretty. I mean, I'm sure *pretty* wasn't what my high school inner monologue called it, but I was totally paralyzed, and you seemed so comfortable and happy. I just couldn't do it." He pulled me an inch closer, if it was possible, and I felt the heat of his body through his suit, through my dress. "So, you're right. This one's for you, eighteen-year-old Luke."

"I should have told John no." I looked at him, hoping he'd understand how much I had wanted him back then.

"It's probably best you didn't. That you went with him," he said quietly, but before I could ask him why he thought so, the song ended. "You ready to go?"

"Sure," I said with a nod. He released me but took my hand and pulled me with him.

"Can you wait here for me, for just a sec?" he asked as we approached our table.

"Of course," I said and sat in my chair for a minute to give my feet a rest. My heels were comfortable, but any shoe other than tennis shoes were uncomfortable after that long. Cindy, the woman who sat nearest to me, was beaming at me.

"I'm so glad you came with Luke. We love him. It's about time he found someone," and she smiled over at her husband. She hadn't joined me and the other girls in the bathroom, so she wasn't privy to my awkward explanation of our friendship.

"Oh... uh, yeah. He's great. We've been friends since we were kids," I said, crossing my legs and twirling my clutch's little leather strap handle around my finger. I took a sip of water and watched as Luke shook hands with the people at the head table across the room.

"How lovely. What a great love story," she said, leaning over to her husband to say something. I sat there, silenced, very glad Luke wasn't sitting next to me to hear her comment and relieved she didn't seem to require a response.

"Isn't it though?" Megan added and looked at me meaningfully. Luke walked up then, and I shook off the unsettled feeling Cindy's comment had created and stood. I gave Megan a quick glare of disapproval, and she laughed at me.

"Ready?" he asked and held out his hand.

"Absolutely," I said and took it. "It was so nice meeting

you all." I smiled at them.

"I'll call you girl, we'll get together," Megan said, and I knew she would. This woman, I could tell, was a woman of her word. I gave another small wave and heard James and Jose say "Luke" and "See ya, man" and Grant say "Sir, have a good evening" and then we were off.

"Sorry I left you there for a minute. I needed to give my regards to the colonel. I figured if I left you here it'd give me an easy exit strategy instead of us both having to endure a long, awkward story neither of us wanted to hear," he said as he pulled my hand up and placed it in the crook of his arm. I held on, enjoying the firm roundness of his bicep underneath his jacket and shirt.

Ok, don't think about his biceps.

On the drive home, we talked over all of the events of the night, and he explained who some of the people we met were. He mentioned the people he worked with and those he spent most of his time with. I asked him about a few of his friends.

"What about Sergeant Harrison? He seems so severe. Where was his wife?" He was one of the first people Luke introduced me to during the mingling section. He wasn't at our table, presumably since he was there without a date.

"Jake's not married. He's a friend though. We spend a fair amount of time together even though it's technically fraternization, mostly at the gym. We're some of the only older guys who aren't married so I guess it sort of fell that way and we don't talk about it at work," he explained. "He's a man of few words."

"I can tell. What about that stern looking man—super tall? The one at the end of the receiving line? I know you told me his name..."

"Major Flint. Yeah, that guy... if I have job stress, he's the reason. I think I told you he's the XO—the executive officer.

It's like the right-hand man for the commander. And he is a hard ass if there ever was one. I think because he's miserable he expects all of us to be too." Luke shook his head but kept his eyes on the road.

"That's a shame. I wonder why he's miserable. I guess he's not married?"

"No, he's not. Might be divorced. Of course, there's always rumors about him being gay because he isn't married, but who knows. No one knows anything about him other than that he is a demanding asshole and if he's not being an asshole then he's awkward." Luke's voice was surprisingly hard. "Sorry. He laid into me last week about something, and I guess I'm still annoyed."

"Understandable," I said, not wanting him to feel like he should censor himself around me.

We continued chatting until he pulled up in front of my place. He parked but didn't turn off the car. I felt a surge of nervousness shoot through me.

"You should come in. At least change your clothes before you drive all the way back," I said, twisting my fingers together with the strap of my purse. He turned off the car and got out and met me by my door before I was out all the way. Once again, his hand was on my back, guiding me up to my front door. I was thankful he was coming inside so we could avoid the very loaded doorstep scene, although of course, his coming inside felt heavier. I opened the door and there we were, inside my apartment. I flipped on the living room light.

Reality crashed in. We'd just been on an actual date—maybe friends in title, but it was still a real date. I was introduced to his friends, his boss, his coworkers. We danced. I felt a connection with his friends, and even with the whole atmosphere. Now there we were, in my apartment, alone.

CHAPTER TEN

"Do you want something to drink?" I asked, more like croaked, setting down my keys and flipping on the kitchen lights as I walked to the fridge. "I have water, wine... and milk. Not a huge selection." I felt my stomach tie itself in knots of anticipation. I opened the fridge and grabbed the water pitcher, then pulled open a cabinet to find two glasses.

"Water, please," he said, and stepped toward the kitchen, and kept coming until he stopped and leaned against the side of the counter, watching me pour our water.

I filled one glass and handed it to him as I picked up my own glass and brought it to my lips. He kept his eyes on mine while he took a sip of water, then took a step closer to me and set it down. For a moment, we just stood there, and I felt like my heart was going to beat out of my chest. I might have even been a little lightheaded.

This was ridiculous.

But looking at him standing there in my kitchen in his dress blues was a special kind of torture. I held on to the edge of the counter because I could tell my ability to *not* reach out and grab him was failing. He slid his hand along the edge of the bar and stopped just short of my left hand.

I heard Megan's voice in my head.

Honey, that man wants you. And I do not mean in a friendly way.

He was still looking at me—I could feel it. I was looking down at my hands, unable to speak or meet his eyes. I felt like I was shaking, my whole body humming and aware of him. Finally, I couldn't resist the pull of his stare and I looked up. I looked back into what felt like pools of blue flame and opened my mouth to speak but had no idea what I was going to say. Before words could form, his hand covered my own, brushed up my arm, came to rest on my shoulder, and he pulled me toward him just a little so I was facing him. He let go of my shoulder and slid his hand from my side to my back as he stepped closer. The feeling of his warm hand on my bare back again made me shiver.

He closed the distance between us and kissed me, his lips gentle for only a moment until my arms wrapped around his neck. One hand in my hair, one sliding up and down my back torturously slowly, he tilted my head and kissed me and kissed me and kissed me until, if you'd asked me, I couldn't have spelled my own name. He was holding me close, pressed against his uniform, and his hands slid over the smooth silk of my dress in every direction. I pushed back just a minute to catch my breath and he took a step back from me, breathing like he'd just finished a race. He looked around like he'd forgotten where he was and looked at me with an unreadable expression.

"I should change my clothes and get out of your hair," he said, his voice gruff and jarring in my silent apartment.

"The bathroom's just there down the hall," I said, pointing the way, still recovering from the kiss and congratulating myself for not saying, *But I like you in my hair* and attacking him.

He turned and walked to the dining table and grabbed a small bag I hadn't noticed he'd brought in. He disappeared into the bathroom and I let out a breath. "Holy crap," I said to myself, and then to Lemon, who was unmoved by the full-on but all-too-brief make out session he'd just unwittingly been a party to.

I changed in my room while he used the bathroom. It was a relief to take off the dress. Even though I felt good in it, it was a lot of work to stand up straight and keep my stomach sucked in and shoulders back and meet new people and be all sparkly and date-like. The feeling of his hands smoothing over my bare back was addicting and the light silk of the dress made it all too easy to imagine what it might be like to, say, not be wearing the dress, so it was time to ditch it or jump an irrevocable hurdle from which our friendship might never recover.

It felt like I could let myself relax a bit as I pulled on my tank top and boxer shorts. Out of the dress and feeling more grounded, more like myself, I came out of my room and padded down the hall to grab my water and found him in the kitchen already. He was talking to Lemon who was still perched on top of the fridge like a feline overlord surveying his territory. Luke turned to me and his eyes flashed with frustration before the look cleared and he spoke.

"We have an agreement, me and Lemon. I just think you should know that."

I laughed at his very serious face. "I'm so glad," I said. I picked up my glass so I would have something to do with my hands and walked around the bar to the couch.

He'd changed into jeans and a white t-shirt. Considering he had just been in his formal uniform, you'd think it would be impossible for him to be more attractive, but somehow, he'd done it. He looked relaxed, and seeing him walk into my living room barefoot was nothing short of totally pleasing. The fact that I could tell he was decidedly *not* relaxed made me nervous. His hair looked ruffled and his eyes a little wild— he seemed caged, and I could see tension in his shoulders from where I sat.

"You can absolutely run away from me right now if you need to, but I'd love it if you would come and sit with me. We can talk, or watch a movie, or whatever you want." I said the last part quietly as I realized that last part wasn't quite true— not *whatever*, but I suspected he knew that since he was consistently the one trying to create space between us, even though he was also the one making that space disappear into lip-smashing oblivion.

"I'll stay for a bit," he said, choosing to ignore my runaway comment. He plopped onto the couch next to me and set his water next to mine.

"Your commander said something about the next 'rendezvous with destiny' and I'm guessing that's a deployment?" I asked, trying to shift the conversation to something he *would* be comfortable with.

"Yeah, that's a phrase General Lee used in World War 2, and it's stuck around the Division at Fort Campbell ever since. Shouldn't be for a nice long time though," he said.

"I love all of the history and ceremony. The ball was such an interesting glimpse into military culture. I know it's mostly *not* like that, from what you've described at least, but thank you for taking me. It was lovely. Your friends were great too." I tried not to gush too much, but I'd loved the experience. It was likely due to being with him, but even just observing the traditions was both fascinating and... inspiring, or something I couldn't quite name.

It was like I felt more proud of everything while I was there.

"I'm glad. I know Megan and Ally will probably track you down soon but don't feel like you need to give in. They're persistent but, you know, you can always say no if they try to get you to hang out or whatever." He fiddled with a seam of the couch cushion like it was his job, studiously avoiding me, and I felt my stomach drop a bit. Did he not want me spending time with his friends' wives? Was that too much, too soon?

"Thanks. I liked them," I said quietly to my hands. "It seems like there's a bond with all of you guys. I guess that happens in the Army in a way it doesn't in a normal job," I said, wanting to gather back that feeling of hope that had just fled at his comments about Ally and Megan.

"Yeah, living with people for a year straight, and sharing in the training and all of that, it definitely creates a bond. Sort of like a team, but more personal in a lot of ways when you see people doing their jobs in crazy circumstances, sometimes scared shitless or crying at a memorial service or just so damn bored of the routine they can't think. That changes things." His voice was rough and he watched me.

"I'm sorry for the soldiers who were killed. I can't imagine what that's like," I said quietly. I hadn't known what to say when they showed the slide show of the five soldiers in their battalion who died in the most recent deployment. Five men between nineteen and twenty-seven. Five sons. My feeble acknowledgement felt just that—weak and not enough, but I didn't know how else to do it.

"Thanks. There's no getting around it. It's awful, and it doesn't stop being awful. I'm glad some of the families could come tonight."

"I was surprised they would, I guess. I thought maybe it would be worse for them, being there," I said. I had been shocked to see that two wives and two sets of parents had come to the ball. They owned the terrible and venerable title of *Gold Star Families,* and I wasn't sure how to look at them without pity even though they seemed to be an astounding mix of proud and sorrowful and determined.

They were amazing.

"I think for some people it helps them feel like they're honoring their soldier, and they like to see that the unit hasn't forgotten them. Remembering that sacrifice, that loss—it matters." His voice was gruff and low.

"It does. I see that." I felt the weight of the evening in my sternum, settling there on top of my lungs. It had been a meaningful night in a lot of ways. I flipped between feeling overwhelmed by how much I liked Luke and feeling impressed and drawn to the idea that a person's life and work could have that kind of significance. I felt that pull and longing so much so that, during the Lieutenant Colonel's speech, I actually felt like I'd gotten the wind knocked out of me. I didn't know what to make of that, except I was ready to start my own work and try to chase that meaningfulness in my own life. I shook off my thoughts and looked at him. He was staring at something across the room, just staring. I thought maybe he didn't want to keep talking about those losses.

"So, you are here for about a year? I bet everyone is glad for a break. It sounds like this last deployment was hard," I said.

"Not really, unfortunately. There will be trainings that come up and different things we can elect to do. I'm heading out Monday for a bit for some training," he said, still not meeting my eye.

Um... ok. This was definitely news. I tried to sound casual, like it didn't bother me he hadn't mentioned this before now. I tried not to feel like I had a right to know where he was and was planning to be. "Oh? Where are you off to?" I bit the "and for how long?" back and waited for his response.

I kept my breathing calm and tried not to cry. It felt like a crazy reaction to something I knew nothing about, but I felt like I'd been slapped.

"I'm heading to Arizona. I'll be leading some guys testing some new equipment," he said, looking at his hands as if they were the most interesting thing he'd ever seen.

He seemed to be expecting me to get upset, or say something, but as upset as I did feel, my pride kicked in. I couldn't let him see I was affected by his news, especially in the wake of his choice not to tell me until now.

"Well... that's great. I hope it's interesting, or fun," I said and got up from the couch to move because I had to. I couldn't sit there, that close to him, and not betray my growing sense of hurt.

"Yeah. It should be good," he said, and he stood, grabbed his water, and brought it to the counter. "It's late, and I should probably get on the road so I don't fall asleep at the wheel."

"Good idea. Do you want me to brew you some coffee?" I offered weakly, more than ready for him to go. He took up too much space now that I knew he was going to be gone.

"No, I'll be fine. I'm wide awake, just don't want to get tired before I'm driving, you know?" He walked to the dining area and picked up his bag and hooked the hanger of his uniform over one finger. I moved to the door and pulled it open.

"Thank you for taking me tonight. It was fun," I said, my smile bright. I felt the knot in my belly grow heavy.

"Thank you for coming," he said as he stepped around me. I stood there, holding the door knob with a heavy grip, waiting for him to go. Instead of passing through the doorway he stopped and faced me. "Really. Thank you," he said. He rested his free hand on my arm and leaned in. Despite the jumble of hurt and confusion I was feeling, my heart sprinted when I felt him getting closer, and then his lips touch mine. It was just a quick peck, not even a hint of lingering, and then he moved back, away, and was walking out.

"Drive safe," I said in a rasp and shut the door before he even made it to the sidewalk. I didn't slam it—in fact I made sure it couldn't possibly be construed as a door slam. But as soon as it was closed I felt like shriveling up and crying.

If this had been just a date with some guy, some nice guy I met at work or at the bakery or church or whatever, I wouldn't feel upset. But this was Luke, and I was royally confused.

He purposefully pursued me, or at least it felt that way. He asked me to coffee back home when we ran into each other at the grocery store. He asked me to dinner. He kissed me. He texted me. He insisted on helping me move. He kissed me again. And sure, I wasn't taking any responsibility for myself, but that wasn't the point. The point was that the last few weeks of not only reconnecting with an old friendship but starting what felt like a fledgling little stab at a relationship, or what could become one, was important to me.

Some unexpected hope had taken root in me, and I knew I wanted him. Maybe, I'd even always wanted him and that was why no one, so far, had measured up. I'd always loved Luke, and though it terrified me to think of hurting him like I hurt Marcus, I was getting used to the idea that maybe it would be different with Luke since everything had always been different with him.

But now he dropped this little bomb and it felt like maybe it was one that signaled he wasn't as affected by what we had going on as I was. In fact, that was clear. Between his frustration with our interactions and now his leaving for training with very little warning, he certainly wasn't pursuing me anymore.

I busied myself with putting our water glasses in the dishwasher, wiped down the already-clean counter, and rose on my tiptoes to jostle Lemon awake. "Come on Lem, let's go."

He dealt me a sleepy glare but stretched out his hind legs, his tail straightening and nearly touching the ceiling, and then he dismounted with a nimble hop to the counter, and down to the ground. He sauntered down the hall into my room, and I could hear him jump onto the comforter of my bed in my darkened room. I stopped in the bathroom to brush my teeth, wash my face, and felt triumphant I hadn't cried yet.

Good. I'd certainly cried over Luke enough as a teenager, and he had no clue. I wasn't going to act like some wounded chicklet who couldn't be alone.

I snuggled into bed, my house dark other than my bedroom lamp. Lemon's low rumble of a purr hummed from the middle of the bed, his fifteen pounds of cat weighing down the comforter more like forty. I looked at him, peaceful and oblivious in sleep, and decided he was wise. I clicked off the light and scooted down into my bed and closed my eyes.

Of course, Luke was staring back at me from behind my eyelids looking gorgeous and blue-eyed and unavoidable as soon as my head hit my long-awaited pillow. "No," I said aloud because sometimes I was really a cat lady who talked to herself.

Ok, often.

But times like this deserved the power of the tongue behind them—he needed to be banished from my mind, or I'd end up having some illicit dream about him and never be able to look him in the eye again, especially if I was now heretofore planning to be relegated to the friend zone. I started counting back from 100, just imagining the numbers in my mind. I tried to focus on that and only that—it was a tool I always used when I couldn't sleep and needed to shut my mind down.

I felt myself relaxing a bit. 34... 33... 32...

Buzz. I ignored it.

30... 29... 28...

Buzz.

38... 39... 40... Damn! There was no avoiding it. My mind was pinned on my phone, face down on the bedside table so the light wouldn't disturb me, as though the buzz from a text wouldn't do the trick. It didn't take long—I gave in at the tail end of the third buzz. I grabbed my phone, not without a fair amount of huffing and puffing, my feigned annoyance at Luke for texting me when he was home since I absolutely wanted him to.

Luke: *Made it home.*

Well, super. I didn't respond.

Luke: *Thanks for going tonight.*

Nice effort, friend. That's what I wanted to type, but I didn't.

Me: *You're welcome. It was fun. Night.*

I tried to keep it short and sweet without sounding short. The last thing I wanted was for him to know he'd upset me by not treating me like his girlfriend. We hadn't talked about that, and it wasn't fair for me to expect it. As a friend, I'd be bummed to be without him for a few weeks or however long, but I definitely wouldn't be pissy or hurt.

So, ok. Function as a friend. Ignore the fact that we'd just made out like the world was ending. But then another buzz.

Luke: *I'll miss you while I'm gone.*

Ok. That was... confusing. Perplexing. Totally unclear. What the hell?

CHAPTER ELEVEN

Me: *You all packed up?*

I didn't respond to his last text the night before. I had no idea what to say. But I didn't want him leaving with that as his last thought. I didn't want him to think I wouldn't miss him, but it felt like too much to say it back. So, there I was, trying to chat with him and get up the guts to say something so he'd know it wasn't all totally neutral territory for me.

Luke: *Yep. Ready to roll out bright and early tomorrow.*
Me: *I realized you never told me how long you'll be gone.*

That was one thing I was dying to know. Was training for "a bit" a few days, a few weeks, or even a few months? There was what felt like a dramatic pause. I pulled on my dress, fitted my feet into my heels, and patted down the ensuing static in my hair. I put my coffee cup and plate in the dishwasher, added some fresh water to Lemon's bowl and gave him a ruffling pet, went to the bathroom to check my makeup... I swirled around my little apartment several times before he came back.

Luke: *Six or eight weeks, probably.*

Yeah. *Yeah.* I shook my head as I stared at the phone.

"Yep!" I said aloud. It was long enough that he should have told me, even as a friend. He should have said something, and if he was going to keep kissing me, he definitely should have said something. I'd been holding out hope it was more like ten days and in that case, maybe I could have understood.

Six or eight weeks? People fell in love in six weeks. Women went from not pregnant to full on morning sick in six weeks. HBO shows were half way through their seasons in six weeks.

Me: *Wow. Well, good luck. I hope it goes well.*

I felt myself locking down that pulsing, sinking feeling in my chest.

Luke: *I'll have my phone for some of the time. You should text me and tell me how your job and everything is going.*
Me: *Well, I'm very busy and important and you know my social calendar is chalk-full, but I'll see what I can do.*
Luke: *Good.*
Me: *It goes both ways though. You can text me too.*
Luke: *I will.*
Me: *Safe travels.*

I started to type "see you in six weeks" but realized even that was presumptuous.

≈

Luke: *Did I tell you about Prince's Hot Chicken?*

Luke was faithful to his promise to text me. He did about every three days.

Me: *Um, did you need to? You know I've already been, right?*
Luke: *I should have known.*
Me: *You should have. That may or may not have been a deciding factor in making this move. You know I love a good meat and three.*
Luke: *Was it all you hoped for?*
Me: *The stuff of dreams.*
Luke: *You'll have to take me when I get back.*
Me: *Wait, you haven't been yet?*
Luke: *No. I'm always doing something else when I'm in Nashville and never have made it.*
Me: *Like putting on your audience-shocking shows at world famous Tootsie's?*
Luke: *Yes, just like that. Me and Merle and Willie. I'm going to grow out my hair into braids and start smoking incredible amounts of pot just as soon as I retire.*
Me: *I'd love to hear that trio, though Merle is unfortunately gone too soon. But I support your mission to grow pigtails. The pot? Not so much, but a man must find his own path.*
Luke: *Well one path I'm going to find is my way to Prince's, ideally with you as my guide.*
Me: *Twist my arm.*

≈

I made some friends. I made some real live Nashvillian friends, and some of them weren't even transplants. It was amazing to have locals to hang out with because they knew all the secrets. In New York, no one was really a local. They maybe had a kind of seniority, but it was rare to meet someone who was born and raised in Manhattan. Finding native Nash-folk wasn't as hard, and I found them delightful. Their easy accents, their love of food, and their amazing tolerance for the end of summer humidity was teaching me things.

It had been three and a half weeks since he left, and I was missing him with an annoying ache I didn't have the right to have after such a short time reconnecting—or maybe I did have the right, but that was still so freaking confusing. I'd never missed anyone like this... except Luke. I remembered this feeling—from high school, when he disappeared on me. After he went to basic training, and again when I left for New York. Whenever I'd had subpar vanilla ice cream over the last decade, and he wasn't there to scoff at it with me.

But I was making friends, and they took up at least one weekend night so that helped my social isolationist tendencies. I could have easily become a hermit who only emerged during the week to go to work, avoided talking to anyone I didn't have to, and then returning to her pale gray existence. It wasn't a healthy thing, it ultimately didn't make me happy (though sometimes I felt like abandoning my couch to socialize was a cruel punishment), and I was glad I was being forced away from that desire.

On Friday of the fifth week after Luke left, I was out with friends at a honky tonk, having a beer and some appetizers before I headed home after what felt like an interminable week. We'd taken on a new event at work and I was excited for it, but the initial learning curve of the new office, navigating the office's rhythms, and then trying to learn the dynamics of my new team, was exhausting. But there I was, out and actually having some fun with my fellow team leads Janie and Emily and a few guys they normally hung out with. They'd adopted me into their little group, and I was glad for it.

Luke: *Hey, do you have a minute?*

He popped up when I least expected it. There was no regular time to his texts, so I suspected he grabbed a moment when he could. I'd admit it left me checking my phone even more than usual. I chose to ignore that and cast it off as a mild demonstration of concern for his safety rather than a perpetual preoccupation with wondering how he was, what he was thinking, how he was doing. I was a grown woman after all—so it was just concern.

Me: *Sure, what's up?*
Luke: *I have a few minutes and wanted to see if I could call you.*

Just reading the message made my heart rate increase. My first thought was excitement, and then I felt scared, like he might need to call me and tell me bad news. I tried to lock down my imagination.

Me: *Sure! I'm out with some friends but call me in like 3 minutes, I'll run outside.*

"Hey, I've gotta take a call—I'll be outside for a sec, but I'll be back. Don't eat my nachos!" I said a little too loudly as the song that was playing ended.

I stepped out into the stuffy night air, still warm and stale and thick at the tail end of August, and answered my phone as it rang.

"I think that was exactly three minutes," I said, feeling my smile grow as I heard him answer.

"It was. I was counting. How are you?" he asked in his smooth, deep voice. My heart's race went full throttle.

Silly what a nice voice could do.

"I'm good. It's nice to hear your voice," I said, trying not to sound breathless the way I felt.

"Likewise."

"How's the training going?" I asked, feeling painfully aware of the fact that we'd never had a conversation on the phone before, at least not in the last decade.

"It's good. I'm ready for it to be over with, but it's been useful, I think," he said. He sounded tired.

"You sound tired." Ever the conversationalist, me.

"Yeah, I am. Long days here. I'm up at four and in bed midday because it's so hot, and then we stay up late for more. I'll be heading back out in a bit."

"Are you kidding? It's almost nine here which means it's almost seven there, right? You need to stop talking to me and rest. I can't believe you're working that early *and* late," I chided him, laughing, but also feeling a competing sense of concern for him and delight that he'd bother to call me when he was so clearly not overflowing with free time.

"I know, and I do need to, but—"

"Alex, get back in here! The guy Emily is obsessed with is coming up!" Rick yelled to me from the doorway, beckoning me in. I gave him a thumbs up so he'd know I'd heard him. He flashed me a wide, bright smile and lingered for a second before turning back inside.

"I'm sorry. I don't want you to—" he started.

"It's fine. They're all just being obnoxious."

"No, no. It's fine. I need to get ready to head back out. We're working through the day tomorrow so it'll be a long one."

"Ok. Yeah, I hope things go well tonight and that you get some sleep at some point."

"Have fun tonight... be careful," he said, but it sounded like maybe he wanted to say something else.

"Of course. Thanks for calling. I hope tomorrow goes well," I said.

"Thanks. Talk to you soon."

"Ok, bye," I said and hung up.

I looked around at the Elvis statue and the glittering neon signs of Broadway and felt hollow. I felt so happy to hear his voice and to realize he'd taken the time to call me. Now I felt empty and sad and... yikes.

Danger.

I shook my head to shake off the disappointment and marched back into the bar to our table where my new friends stood. Rick nodded to my phone and nudged my shoulder lightly.

"Who was that?"

"My friend Luke."

"*Friend* Luke?" he asked, eying me closely.

"Yes, old friend Luke. We grew up together, and he's out here at Fort Campbell," I explained. I studied Rick as he stood there, looking a little perturbed. He was in accounting at the firm and had that cute smart guy thing going on—good with numbers, I assumed. His light brown hair hung a little into his green eyes, a good nose and an angular face meant he was, by all rights and every woman who'd run into him so far tonight, very handsome. But... need I say it?

"What a small world." He seemed genuinely surprised by

the coincidence. His eyes swept over my face, stalled on my lips, and only left them when I grabbed my beer and took a drink.

Ok...

"Yeah, crazy."

"Listen, would you—" Rick started, but Emily cut him off.

"*Look!* You guys! He is *Adorable! Seriously!*" Emily yelled as the band she loved, Lazy Echo, started to play. She talked endlessly about how much she loved this band. Her comment was well-timed, as was the start of the music, which was far too loud to talk over.

So far, Rick and I had only hung out a few times in a group setting. He was nice enough, charming enough, and I liked talking to him well enough. He tended to pay me a lot of attention, more so in the last few weeks. It had started to make me a little nervous now that I noticed it, and I thought maybe he was being more obvious so I would. But I knew there was nothing ahead for me and Rick, regardless of his attention.

I was more than half way to being in love with Luke after just a few interactions, and I felt stupid and embarrassed and hopeful. But I also felt determined not to build my life around this guy who didn't seem to take me into account for much of his, even if he was a loyal texter.

I looked down at my light, tasteless beer and as the music crashed around me, I thought about what it'd be like if Rick asked me out. I felt like going out with someone else would be a kind of a betrayal. Not to Luke, who had zero claim on me, particularly after making absolutely no effort to acknowledge some state of relationship beyond friendship, but more so to myself and my own feelings.

My hopes, really.

Because yeah, I wanted to be with Luke. Absence was definitely making the heart grow fonder, whether or not that fondness was returned. It was also causing me to recognize my feelings for Luke were different from anyone I'd ever dated, even Marcus.

I'd never worried about Marcus or thought about him when I wasn't with him. It was a placid, easy relationship. It was even-keeled. It didn't knock me off-kilter and leave me wanting, longing, burning like whatever this was with Luke did.

But Rick was cute. He had a job. He was apparently available and clearly interested. For now, I was thankful for too-loud amps and over-enthusiastic fans to buy me some more time to think about it.

That Tuesday at work, Rick cornered me by the community Keurig.

Ok, not actually cornered me, but I was alone in the little galley kitchen break room, and he came in and just stood there watching me insert my little pod of Peet's coffee for my afternoon caffeineation—if I didn't get it in soon, I'd miss my three pm cut-off, so I was all business. My team had just nailed a bid for a January event that I'd pushed them on, and I was taking a celebratory break in the wake of the signed contract arriving in my email. The account was a long shot and the agency had submitted bids to them for the last three years and had never won—until this year. I was bouncing around on my toes, charged with adrenaline and satisfaction.

I planned to pair my coffee with a maple pecan granola bar I'd made over the weekend, and I was on a mission. My celebratory caffeine-and-snack break had been motivating me to finish all of the items on my morning to do list. Wrapping that up by reviewing the signed contract for a much-desired account that happened to be my second big win of the month just sweetened the deal.

As I'd pressed the sticky mix of granola, toasted pecans, maple syrup, and a few other things into my quarter sheet pan with my bright red spatula two days before, I envisioned myself in this moment, relishing the afternoon pick-me-up. I'd been waiting all day for the sweetness paired with the biting warmth of the coffee.

"So..." He crossed his arms and leaned against the cherry wood cabinets. He looked nice with a white button-up shirt under a light gray suit. He had an olive and black striped tie that brought out the green of his eyes. Yes, Rick was cute, there was no point in pretending he wasn't.

"So?" I emptied the pod and moved to get a small plate from my shelf inside one of the cabinets.

"I want you to go out with me this weekend." He didn't move, didn't ask. He just tossed it out there, like he was giving me his Christmas wish list.

"Oh?" I wasn't sure what else to say. I still didn't know how I felt about going out with someone. I tried not to add the *else* as in *go out with someone else*, but that was how it felt. Someone other than Luke.

"Yes. And I think you might want to go out with me, so I think we should." This was fast becoming one of the weirder lead-ins to a date I'd ever had, but ok. He wasn't entirely wrong in that I thought he was acceptably cute and we hung out in groups together and got along, even if he was a whole lotta presumptuous.

I was having a good day, and I was riding the wave of success. I didn't want to deal with rejecting him, and after all, I was single.

I turned to him and gave him a hesitant smile.

"What did you have in mind?"

~

The hostess showed me to the table, and I took in the atmosphere of the hip little place as I slid into my seat across from Rick. Butcher block community tables stretched in rows across the surprisingly small interior of the room. Mason jars filled with silverware were grouped in threes every four or five feet. Wild flowers were spilling out of tin watering cans, and overall the place looked down home chic. I'd read their décor was simple, but their food was fastidiously made, everything hand-pickled and baked and seasoned and smoked to perfection.

"You look great," he said from his seat as his eyes swept over me in a more than obvious appraisal of my outfit.

I was wearing dark jeans and a t-shirt with a long gray short-sleeved cardigan over it. In other words—I had not dressed up. My enthusiasm for the date as it got closer was nil. I hadn't heard from Luke in four days, so I'd started to worry about him. I decided he had been injured, was in the hospital unconscious, and I wouldn't hear about it for weeks until he was ok and got home.

Clearly, I was *totally* rational when it came to Luke.

Only about twenty minutes before I was due to meet Rick, I dragged myself off the couch, swapped my sweat pants for jeans, combed my hair, and put on mascara and lip gloss. With a kiss to Lemon and one last regretful glance at my couch, I left.

And there I was, meeting Rick and his open perusal of my body for dinner. And there he was, sitting at the end of one of the long tables with a nicely fitting short-sleeved polo and jeans that suited him—he looked good. He did.

By the time Saturday morning rolled around, I was sure I shouldn't be going out with him and would have canceled if he hadn't mentioned he was going to take me to Robbie's Kitchen. I liked Rick as a friend, and yes he was cute, but I knew it wouldn't go anywhere. At the same time, I felt much worse bailing on him now. Plus, the new hipster barbeque place had been on my list of must-eats since I'd read about it a few weeks ago, and so there I was.

But as soon as I sat down, I felt instantly annoyed to be there with him, which was not fair to him. I was annoyed with his shaggy light brown hair and his green eyes. He needed a haircut and an iris transplant, stat.

Or, he needed to be someone else. But whatever, *let's move on.*

"I wanted to surprise you, so I already ordered for us. I was just picking out some wine." He gestured to the wine list in his hand, his nicely shaped arm reaching out to point to a name on the list.

I stared at him, unable to speak, dumbfounded by the sheer wrongness of everything he just said.

First, who drank wine with barbeque? I was all for wine, truly. But with barbeque? I wanted a coke, or a beer, or water, or all three. But ok, that was fine and easily remedied.

The far greater sin was his ordering for me.

It wasn't so much that I was so modern or independent that a man couldn't order for me. I could see how maybe, in some cases and with the right person, that could be nice or even charming. After all, one might say the way to Alex's heart was through her stomach.

But this dude didn't even know me. We'd become friendly at work over not quite two months of my working at B&W. I had to bite my tongue not to say just that because *You don't know me well enough to order for me* was on the tip of my tongue. His telling me he'd ordered for me was akin to telling someone you'd done a nude drawing of them and you couldn't wait to show them, but you'd never, in fact, seen them naked.

See me: not naked. See Rick: showing me a drawing of me naked, draped on a couch and wearing nothing but the The Heart of the Ocean.

No. Just no.

I breathed deep and shut my eyes for a second, willing my internal outrage to remain internal. This guy was trying to be charming. He was failing on so many levels, it wasn't even funny, but it wasn't totally his fault he jumped the gun. Maybe most girls liked that on a first date. Plus, maybe he chose well. If this place was as good as it was rumored to be, then he probably couldn't go wrong.

I swallowed my ire and said, "Oh, did you? That's interesting." It was basically as nice as I could be. My voice was about an octave higher than usual, but he didn't notice.

He looked at me with a small smile like he knew I was happy, and it was one of many moments that night that told me Rick and I had no future.

"So... you were picking wine?" I tried to address at least one of the issues at hand.

"Yeah, I love a good red, thought that'd go with our meals." He smiled at me enthusiastically and leaned over a bit with his finger pointing to a pinot noir on the short, laminated list.

"Would you mind if I just had a beer?" I asked, wondering why my voice continued to climb into the rafters.

"Oh, no, of course not. I should have asked you. Beer's great." He flipped the drink menu and handed it to me, and I took it gratefully.

The rest of the night followed suit. After we made it through the typical hoops of where we'd grown up, and how I was settling in, the conversation became stilted and surface-level. Maybe I had no patience for first dates anymore, but this one seemed particularly lacking.

True, I hadn't been on more than one or two first dates since I was engaged to Marcus, and my date with Luke didn't count since we knew each other. So maybe it was me. In a group, I hadn't noticed Rick and I didn't have much in common.

Or, again... maybe it was me.

"Do you like movies?" he asked.

See? He really asked that. He asked if I liked movies, like there was a huge subset of the population who *doesn't* like movies. And I felt terrible about it because he tried to get me talking about some TV show he watched—*Black Mirror*—and I hadn't seen it. That stalled out, and so he was justifiably searching for something else.

"Yeah. Yeah, I like movies a lot. Love a good movie." I tried not to sound sarcastic. I did try. At this point I was feeling furious with myself for ever agreeing to come, and I also felt guilty as all get out for subjecting Rick to my charmless presence at all.

"Have you seen the newest *Transformers*?" He was attempting to set up date number two to go to a *Transformers* movie.

Trans. Formers.

I loved Josh Duhamel as much as the next girl, but if we were resorting to the common ground of Michael Bay's latest filmsplosion within the first twenty minutes of a date, this might signal we had little in common.

"You know, I'm not huge into *Transformers*. What number is this? Number five? Six?" I wasn't going to lie because I knew I'd already been doing that to myself, and by extension, to him.

The lure of hipster barbeque and my own hurt pride had

been too much to resist, but I'd learned my lesson. An hour after we arrived, we hugged, and I gave Rick the friend pat as he leaned in, making clear, I hoped, that he was a great guy, and we'd be friends. I walked the twenty-minute walk home feeling guilty and stupid and lonely and supremely angry with myself.

Lesson learned.

CHAPTER TWELVE

Luke: *What'd you do this weekend?*

It was Monday morning just after I got in to work. I had mounds of work to do and was trying not to dread seeing Rick. He might not even have realized how bad the date was, but it was bad. I was still reeling from how stupid I felt for agreeing to go. He was a nice enough guy, if a little unobservant, but we had *not* clicked in the one-on-one setting. I didn't typically see him in this part of the building anyway, so there was hope I could avoid him for a few more days. I felt the awkwardness of the situation settle in around me when I arrived, but I'd pushed it away and was focusing on reviewing the new account and the work my account leads were working up for a local hospital's nonprofit foundation's yearly fundraiser scheduled a few weeks before Christmas. They'd won the bid just two weeks ago and we hit the ground running.

Whether I wanted Luke to know I went out with someone was an entirely different conversation I was having with myself. Part of me was hoping for him to ask this very question so I could say something coy about going out with a friend. I wasn't trying to make him jealous, but I did want to see what his reaction would be.

Ok, maybe a small part of me was trying to elicit a reaction, and I might have been not altogether upset if he was a tad jealous.

Me: *I went for a long run and then out to dinner Saturday. Church and some baking Sunday. You know, Earth-shattering stuff. You?*

I settled on "dinner Saturday" because that could be anything, date or not, and it was up to him to ask if he wanted to know more. If it was just casual conversation, I didn't need to explain and he clearly didn't need to know.

Luke: *What did you bake?*
Me: *I made some peach cobbler that I brought to work because if I keep it at home I'll eat it all tonight in one sitting, and some granola, and I made some triple berry muffins for my boss's daughter who just had a baby.*
Luke: *That's a lot of baking.*
Me: *Yes. It kept me occupied. Thrill a minute over here.*

He certainly didn't need to know it kept me occupied from thinking about him and his perfect lips and his glacier-blue eyes and his perpetually warm hands. The fact I had to avoid one of my silicon mixing bowls that was a bright shade of blue because that shade reminded me of him was still niggling at me and was not something he needed to know, either.

Luke: *How long was your run?*

Me: *Nothing like your long runs, I'm sure.*

I returned to my emails and focused on my current pet project, a fundraiser for a local private school's arts program. It was a small event, but I had freedom, and I loved that the outcome would be more than just champagne-fueled CEOs like so many of my corporate events in NY were. It was essentially exactly what I wanted to work on when I made the move here. The account lead was Willa, who was shared with Janie's corporate team. They were in an all hands on deck planning mode so I offered to take the event off Willa's hands, and she was grateful. So was I.

I liked my little office too. It was an improvement on the cubicle I had at my last job, though it was probably about as big. It was like a large walk in closet, but it had big windows and good light in the afternoon. My light wood desk was an L-shaped thing with shelving on top of the side that rested against the wall to my right. My computer was facing forward, which I liked because it let me look out the door into the hallway and see if people were approaching my office. I had a laptop and a desktop computer that shared information so I didn't have to rely on the desktop for weekend events. I had a desk calendar to my right and typically documents and contracts spread out over the desk to my left. Sometimes I even had the binders full of event center offerings like table cloth colors and photos of cakes, but in my more managerial position here, I had a lot less of that than I used to. When I wasn't working with them they lined up neatly in the floor to ceiling book shelves.

It was all a bit less tactile than how I did things in New York when I showed clients a swatch of the emerald green table cloths they wanted or showed them their seat cover options, but that was fine. That also meant I didn't have to be at every weekend event, and that I had a little more control over the bigger picture of events instead of just those small details. I was quickly relishing this smaller company, the community feeling that built up on the teams and in the office over all, and with Nashville itself, which felt like the perfect big little city to start over in.

The fact that I had already identified someone I wanted to date was also an interesting one. If I was honest, I'd made the move to get a life, essentially. I wanted the job change, but I wanted the life—I knew I wanted a family and knew I wasn't going to be able to have that if I kept up the pace I had in New York. That Luke had popped back up in my life like he'd never left, but was frustratingly elusive both physically and emotionally, was the only real imperfection.

I chose not to dwell on that.

My phone buzzed, and I saw it was after five, time to leave. I gathered up my things and read the text.

Luke: *Where'd you go to dinner on Saturday? Anything good?*

Ah, there it was. My opening. I felt pleased he asked, though maybe his motive really was just about the food.

Me: *It was Robbie's Kitchen, you know that hipster place that everyone has been raving about? But I didn't end up getting what I was planning to.*
Luke: *Why not?*
Me: *Someone else ordered for me.*
Luke: *Was it for work?*
Me: *No.*
Luke: *...?*
Me: *I was on a date, and the guy ordered for me. I had some*

kind of grilled chicken salad thing. It was good—surprisingly
good, but a total waste in the context of the other options.
Luke: *He ordered for you?*

The response came fast. I'm not sure what I was hoping
for, but it didn't seem like that was it. But how could he
display crazed disappointment and lifelong longing over text?
What could I reasonably expect from him?

Me: *Yeah. Awkward. I mean... chicken? At a barbeque place?*

Just as I was closing my office door, I saw Rick coming. I
thought about ducking back in but thought his coming into
my office while much of the rest of the building was empty
might be worse. I took a bracing breath and gave him my
friendliest close-lipped *hey there friend* smile.

"Alex! I was looking for you." He slowed down and
brought his hand to my arm and squeezed it lightly, then let it
drop away.

"Hey, how's it going?" I asked.

"I just wanted to tell you I had a great time this weekend,"
he said and inched closer into my space.

"Yeah... the food was great. Thanks again for taking me." I
pulled my purse up on my shoulder and used that as an
excuse to shift away from him. He wasn't inappropriately
close, but I still needed more space.

"Yeah, sure, anytime," he said, and I saw a look of uncer-
tainty cross his face.

"Hey, I'm gonna head out. This Monday just...
wiped me."

"Oh, yeah, totally. Have a good night," he said and
nodded enthusiastically.

"You too," I said and turned down the hall. Once I got to

my car I tossed my purse into the passenger seat, ripped off my blazer, and tossed it on top of my purse. I could feel my shirt sticking to my back thanks to my discomfort and now the still blazing heat of an early September evening in the South.

I drove home and ignored the next buzz from my phone, waiting until I was parked in my spot in front of my building to read it.

Luke: *Will he get another chance?*

Ok, that was *something* at least.

Me: *Definite no.*

I was hoping to hear more from him, but nothing else came. The rest of the week flew by and aside from the one uncomfortable meeting with Rick where it became clear he likely had no idea how bad the date was, I felt good. I felt more in control of my work and ready for the weekend.

"Are you coming with us tonight?" Emily asked from the doorway to my small office.

"Where are you going, and who is 'us'?" I asked, standing up from my desk to stretch. I shut down my computer for the weekend and closed my laptop. I wrote a few notes on a post it to remind me of where to start when I came in Monday.

"We're doing Mexican—Janie's craving fajitas. I know Janie, Colin, Jeff, Rick, and I are going. I'm not sure if anyone else is."

"That sounds like a good group. I hope it's not awkward

with Rick though." I told her about his ordering for me and my general awkwardness/irritation the next time I saw him.

But I also definitely wanted a margarita and some guacamole.

"Nah, don't worry about it. Just come out with us, take down a margarita, and the world will be a better place." She widened her smile into an obnoxious open-mouthed smile as she waited for me to respond.

"Ok, fine. But let's go to Rosita's, if no one else has somewhere in mind?"

"Oh, yes. So good."

Yes, it was good. It was also a few blocks from my apartment, so I wouldn't have to drive or ride with anyone else. I could get home early enough to snuggle up with Lemon and watch a few episodes of something dumb on Netflix while I mindlessly put stuff in my Amazon shopping cart I'd never end up buying before going to bed.

"Are you telling me you've never had bourbon?" Rick asked me, a little too loudly, sitting a little too close to me on our side of the booth. We were working on round two during happy hour and happily snacking on chips and salsa and Rosita's glorious guacamole.

I'd had it once before and then the next day had a day dream about waking up and finding a bowl the size of my head filled with it just waiting for me on my counter in my kitchen. It was sitting there with a little tented sign like we used for buffets and said, "please enjoy," and next to it was a never-ending bag of blue corn tortilla chips. In the dream I also knew this would be a no-consequence binge in a dream world where chips and guac were calorically inconsequential.

The disappointment of that little mental escape coming to an end was a mild form of heartbreak.

"I have not. I've had a Jack and Coke or whatever. But I've never had bourbon just to taste it." Rick had weaseled his way into sitting next to me, despite my best efforts and glares with sharply raised eyebrows and pursed lips at Emily and Janie. They were no help, and Jeff and Colin were oblivious. I decided I'd play friends, and maybe he would too.

"This, we must rectify. Waiter!" he shouted and raised his arm comically, if sloppily.

"Hear hear, time for some bourbs," Jeff said and smiled lazily at Emily. He was clearly interested in her and had polished off a margarita and a beer in rapid succession, so he sounded veeeery relaxed.

"No, no, no, I'll be just fine without it for tonight. I'm enjoying my margarita, thank you very much." My phone buzzed just as I checked it for the time. 8:00. Unlikely that I'd end up eating dinner because my mental schedule had me getting home by 8:30 to properly relax before I had to go to bed.

As a morning person, staying up super late held no allure for me. Plus, I planned to continue stuffing myself with guacamole and chips at an aggressive rate so I could call *that* dinner and move on to dessert when I got home.

Luke: *What are you up to?*

Ah, sweet, sexy, smart, sexy Luke.

Uh oh. My thoughts were alliterating, which meant I was feeling the tequila from my one and a half margaritas on a chip and guac-filled stomach.

Me: *I'm at a little place called Rosita's. It's in my neighbor-hood—super cute! BESSSST guacamole. And good margaritas.*

"Fine, fine. Don't taste the best liquor. Don't have the true southern experience, Miss New York transplant," Rick teased and nudged me with his shoulder.

"I'm not actually *from* New York," I said, feeling annoyed. Rick went from ignorant to willfully ignorant at some point, and that plus feeling the ticking clock of my own Friday evening timeline—I was done.

"I know, I know." I stood up and he grabbed my hand. "Where are you going?" I pulled it back immediately.

"I'm going to head out. I'm exhausted. Don't want to be a killjoy for the rest of your evening." I smiled at them and everyone nodded kindly and mumbled their, "no problems" and, "have a good evenings." I passed Emily some money for my part of the check and waited. Rick just sat there, blocking my way from the booth.

"You can't leave." He looked at the table, not at me, when he said it.

"Well, I *am* leaving. Up you go," I said, shooing him with my hands. "Really, Rick, move." My voice was a little harsher than I'd planned. He looked up at me like I'd offended him.

"Now I'm the fifth wheel," he said in a pleading voice, giving me a mock frowning face. If I was in the mood to be begged, it might have worked. As it was...

"Sorry buddy," I said through my teeth, trying not to have a tantrum of my own as he moved in painfully slow motion out of the booth. He stood up and stayed just outside so I had to slide past him to get all the way out. I tried to touch him as little as possible, his whining and ignorance grating and clarifying even more my lack of interest. He grabbed my hand again.

"I'll walk you home."

I kept moving, trying to extract my hand from his as I moved toward the door. "Thanks so much, but I live super close, it's no problem." I pushed out the front door and he followed me out into the night.

"No, I want to. I'll walk you." He said it like he was doing me a favor. He still wasn't listening.

"Rick, listen. I appreciate it. But I'm good. Please just go back inside and enjoy your evening." I widened my eyes for emphasis and gave him a close-lipped "do you get it?" kind of smile.

"All right, yeah. I'm going to head back in then. See you at work." He seemed a little put out, but I felt relief he might have gotten the message about both tonight and our future dating prospects. He'd been a little touchy all evening like he thought there might still be hope. I watched him go back inside before rolling eyes to myself, shaking my head, and turning to make the quick walk home.

Then I ran into a wall.

A human wall.

I was looking down at my purse, still walking, when I hit a human wall of muscle (and I guessed bone and a lot of other stuff too, sure). I grabbed the person's arm instinctively, both to steady myself, and him, and so I could apologize.

"I'm so sorr—"

"Well hi there. Not the welcome home I was expecting, but I'll take what I can get."

It was Luke. Luke was the wall. Luke was the wall in jeans and a dark gray shirt with some kind of emblem on it that I couldn't be bothered to notice in the face of his truly astounding chest and arms. I forced my eyes back to his face where I was then ensnared by those familiar glacial blues. He was holding me by the shoulders, smiling brightly back at my undoubtedly stunned face. My body perked up, my nerves lighting at the sight of him. He smelled so good.

So. Good.

"What? What are you doing here?" It came out as a kind of over-excited shriek, but he laughed as he pulled me, and I leapt, into his arms for a hug. He squeezed me as tight as I squeezed him, and then we released. I took a step back to give us space to talk (and me to breathe). Holy taco Tuesday, he looked good.

"Well just a minute ago I was watching you let some poor sucker down easy." He crossed his arms and looked at me through his lashes with a provocative half-smile.

"Ah, you saw that, huh?" I squinted up at him, then started to slowly meander in the direction of my apartment.

"Yeah, I almost felt bad for him." He turned to walk next to me, arms still crossed as we strolled.

"Almost?" I looked down the quiet sidewalk, all of the din and bubbling sound following behind us from the restaurant. I tried to calm my heart, clear my still-fuzzy margarita-influenced head.

"Well it's not like I'm rooting for the guy or anything."

"Why not?" I couldn't stop the words from spilling out. It was too direct a question, and I felt my cheeks heat at the consequence of my loose lips.

"I would think that's obvious." He said this with finality and something else, an edge, in his voice. I wasn't sure I could say anything else without embarrassing myself. I wanted to say *Is it because you want to date me?* but just the thought made my cheeks flame even more.

"I'm sure he'll be just fine. He didn't get the hint before, but I'm hoping I was clear enough this time." We turned the corner, and I saw my little porch with my pot of herbs happy and hunter green in the fading sunlight.

"That's the guy who ordered for you?"

"Yeah. But enough about that. How was your training? How are you? You look good." It all just tumbled out. I wanted to be done talking about Rick, and I wanted to talk about Luke. Or more specifically, I wanted Luke to talk to me so I could look at his gorgeous face and watch his lips-of-perfection say words.

So... still feeling those margaritas.

"Thank you." He chuckled and stopped at my place, waiting for me to climb the two steps to my door and unlock it. "Do you mind if I—"

"—Have you had dinner? I can make you something." We spoke over each other and smiled. I tried to swallow down my nerves as I opened the door and we walked into my apartment. I couldn't escape the thought of our last time here, both the very heated encounter in the kitchen and the thoroughly disappointing conversation in the living room where he told me he was leaving two days later.

But here he was, back in my apartment, seemingly soon after he got home.

"I'm ok. I had a little something before I came, just in case you ate already." He stepped in and closed the door behind him and looked around like he was expecting to see someone else. In an uncharacteristic move, Lemon hopped down from the back of the couch and greeted Luke with a small rub on his leg before disappearing to my bedroom. Luke looked at me with a genuinely pleased grin.

"Well, seems like Lemon remembers you fondly enough," I said as I poured red wine into two glasses and handed him one.

"Does that mean you don't?" His brow furrowed with the question and he looked at me.

I waved him to the couch with a nod. "Of course not. I'm

still pretty fond of you—always have been." I could feel the small quiver in my voice, but I hoped he hadn't noticed. "When did you get back?"

He sat down *right* next to me, not giving me any space on the more-than-big-enough couch. "Today. Tonight. About three hours ago." He set his wine glass down without taking a sip and looked at me, his eyes a little hazy and his focus narrowed to my lips as I sipped my own wine, then set the glass down.

"I wish you'd told me when you were going to be home. I could have met you at the base, or wherever, so you wouldn't have to drive all this way. I'm sure you're exhausted." I swallowed, feeling my hand tremble a little as I patted his leg nearest me.

I folded my hands in my lap, not sure what to do with myself while he was sitting so close and definitely not wanting to leave my hand on his impressively muscular thigh. Our bodies touched from ankles to shoulders. Then he shifted and put the arm closest to me around the back of me on the couch, not quite around my shoulders, but... come on. What was this, *Saved by the Bell*? It wasn't like he had to trick me into letting him put his arm around me.

"I didn't know what the timing would be and didn't get a chance to charge my phone until I was in the car on the way here." I could feel him studying my profile, looking for something.

"Oh," was all I could manage, both because I had no idea what else to say, and because he was sitting so close, and he smelled so good, and all I could think about was his lips.

"I missed you." He breathed it, more than said it, and I turned to look at him.

CHAPTER THIRTEEN

He was still studying my face, his eyes moving back and forth between my own. He must have seen the confusion in them, but it felt like he might kiss me. I stood up abruptly, the confused and hurt side of my brain winning out over simpler desire to crush my body against his now that it was in my vicinity.

He watched as I walked to the kitchen, took another sip of wine, and put my half-empty glass in the sink, studiously avoiding his gaze.

"Alex."

I ignored my name on his lips, even though the sound of him saying it did things to my insides. Not altogether bad things, but things I was choosing to ignore. He stood up and grabbed his glass, still full of wine, and brought it with him into the kitchen. He stopped so our chests were no more than six inches apart. He reached past me, not moving his feet, to place his glass in the sink, his arm brushing the side of my arm, sending goose bumps over my skin.

"Alex. I missed you." He tilted my chin up toward him so

my eyes eventually had to look at him. His look was concerned and gentle and frustrated. He threaded the other hand through one of mine and squeezed it as if it would elicit a response.

"Ok." I took a deep breath and let it out slowly, looking down at our entwined hands. "I guess I'm confused."

"What about?" He wandered back to the couch, pulling me along with him. He sat sideways, pulling me down so I'd sit too. I sat and then scooted away a few inches to give myself room to breathe.

Being so close to him was making it hard to think, and I hadn't decided what I wanted to say or how I wanted to handle his coming home. I assumed I would have some notice before I saw him and that it would force me to make a decision. I thought he would be gone at least another week. That was a miscalculation and it left me feeling adrift.

I didn't want to have to spell out the fact that he'd hurt me by not telling me he was leaving. I didn't want to have to ask him what he wanted from me, or how he saw us. I wanted him to have the emotional intelligence and the mindreading powers of a fantasy, somehow knowing what I wanted and what I needed before I even recognized it.

Ok, so apparently, I wanted him to be God. Not altogether fair, but there it was.

"You can't think of any reason I might be confused about you showing up after being gone for almost eight weeks and saying you missed me, and... and looking at me like *that*?" I gestured with my chin and my elbow since my hand was still in his.

"I'm sorry I caught you off guard." He looked contrite enough, but it wasn't the answer I was hoping for.

"That's no big deal," I said it quietly to myself, wishing I knew what to do next.

"So, you dated that guy? The one outside Rosita's?" He squeezed my hand and then let go. Even though holding his hand was making me nervous, I was sad when he released mine.

"We went to dinner just the one time." I wanted to make sure he knew it wasn't an ongoing thing. I certainly didn't need that misunderstanding further confusing things.

"Were you not on a date tonight?" He now had his arms crossed, questioning me, but it felt less like they were crossed in judgment, and more like he'd done it because he didn't know what else to do with his arms.

"No. Definitely not. We were with a group. He just decided he wanted to walk me home, and I refused him—which is what you saw when you were walking up."

"Ok." His arms were still crossed. Something had changed in him—his energy had moved from kind of gooey and warm to a little more reserved.

"Ok... what?" I crossed my own arms, closing myself off to him even though I was sitting facing forward on the couch and he was sitting sideways.

"Ok, I'm glad you're not dating that dude anymore." I watched him and saw his jaw clench then, and I could tell he was irritated.

"I wasn't *dating* him. It was one date." I didn't know why I felt the need to clarify, but I did. I was feeling more frustrated by the minute.

"Ok." He still hadn't relaxed again, his arms crossed and jaw ticking away like he was angry with me.

"I'm sorry, but *what* is happening right now? You're acting like you're mad at me, and I do not understand what you're trying to tell me with your crossed arms and your manly jaw and tight t-shirt and all of that." I waved at his general position, huffing a bit as I looked at him and trying not to notice the edge of his t-shirt had pulled up just enough to expose a gap of ridiculous, annoying, totally distracting abdomen. I pulled my eyes away when he spoke.

"My manly jaw?" He raised his eyebrows in challenge, his arms *still* crossed, looking covertly amused.

"Yeah, so not the point. What is up?" I demanded.

"I'm not allowed to be glad you and that guy didn't hit it off?" He was squinting at me, masking whatever it was he was thinking or feeling.

"Why would you be glad about that? That's where my confusion is coming in." I felt my heart rate increasing and could tell I was getting more and more upset. Paired with a long week, a half-empty stomach, and general emotional exhaustion, I was in danger of crying out of frustration, which was absolutely not on my list of things to do in front of him tonight.

He was silent for a moment and so still I thought maybe he was holding his breath. Finally, he let out a breath and his look grew more severe. "Because you should be dating me, not some idiot who tries to order for you." The edge in his voice was harsh, like he was really mad.

"Uhh, ok. But you realize we weren't dating when you left, right?" I was reacting to his tone. Even as I felt my heart race with his statement, I felt completely annoyed he was pissed at me for dating someone while he was gone when we weren't even dating. "We never talked about *anything* like that. Anytime we did talk about anything even remotely related to our relationship, you pretty much ran away." I was getting mad. How could *he* be mad at *me*?

"I—" He started, but I interrupted.

"Don't sit there like I did something to betray you. We weren't dating! I would absolutely not go on a date with another man if I was dating you, let's be clear about that. I barely went out with him to begin with because all I can think about is you. So don't guilt me about something that doesn't matter anyway and I already regret because it was a total waste of time and energy." I ended, and I was breathing heavily, riled up from my rant and frustration and a twinge of embarrassment at revealing my preoccupation with him.

Before I could calm down, his hand was pulling my face to look at him, and he was kissing me. It was a crushing, exhilarating, infuriating kiss. He practically inhaled me, like he'd been thinking about kissing me for those same eight weeks I'd been thinking about kissing him. But I was mad, and he clarified nothing, and I couldn't ignore that, as much as most of my body wanted to. I pulled back and glared at him.

"You can't just kiss me!" I gave him a push on the shoulder as I said it, and he grabbed my hand with both of his.

"I know, I know, I just..." He looked down at our hands, then back up at me. "I'm mostly mad with myself. I'm mad I didn't talk to you before I left. I wanted to, and I should have, but I wussed out. The night of the ball was surreal for me, and I was confused, and I didn't know how to talk to you about it. And then when I told you I was leaving you seemed so unaffected, and I thought that meant you didn't care. So... I just didn't bring it up."

"Trust me, I was affected. I guess I did a decent job of hiding it, though." I felt my heart lightening up a bit, relaxing its clinch.

"I figured if you weren't worried about me being gone that long, then you didn't care about... us, or the possibility of that, and that was sign enough for me."

"I didn't want you to see how upset I was. I felt so thrown when you said you were leaving and you hadn't even mentioned it was a possibility before that. I just... I felt like you not telling me before then meant *you* didn't want... a-anything else." I stuttered at the end, trying not to put a name to whatever it was we were hinting around at.

"I found out the day before the ball, the day before I told you. Honestly, I found out that Friday, and then I didn't want that to be the focus of our night. I wasn't originally slotted for this trip, but it fell to me because someone else had to pull out last minute, and I tend to get tasked with last minute stuff since I don't have a wife and kids. I was nervous enough taking you to something like that, and I didn't want to pressure you by then also saying I'd be going away for two months like I had big expectations of you." His thumb ran across the inside of my wrist and I was mesmerized by the feeling and by this new revelation.

"I—I can't believe this. I should have just asked you. I felt so stupid." I rubbed my free hand over my face and then through my hair and glanced at him.

"Why did you feel stupid?" His voice was gentle and so compassionate I almost sighed out loud like a crazy person.

"We'd had such a great time at the ball, and then we... kissed... and that was... good." I let out a shaky breath and glanced at him, then back down at my hands. "And I felt like maybe, you wanted something... I don't know. But when you said you were leaving it felt like a blazing sign pointing to Friendsville. I didn't want to be the one to push in another direction."

"I did. I always did. And I do. I've had plenty of time to think about it and I do. Want something else." He sat up with this, emphatically gripping my hand and pulling me so I edged closer to him.

"What?"

"Well, the point is moot unless you want something else

too," he said, hope unmissable in his tone. But then his voice hardened a little. "Unless you wanted to keep going out with whatshisface."

"Uh, no. I didn't even want to go out with him before. If you'd been an option, I definitely wouldn't have." I flashed him a smile, hopeful it would clarify my meaning.

"You have no designs on anyone else then?" He was smiling victoriously, despite his question.

"Just you." I held his gaze after saying this, a small smile on my lips. His smile faded at that, though, so I pressed. "Do you want to...?" I felt embarrassed at having to outright ask him.

"I want to date you, but I know that if we date and it goes wrong—"

"It'll be awful," I finished for him. I felt it too. I felt like my veins were studded with crystals, some of them melting, some of them exploding. I felt ecstatic and breathless layered over a profound fear.

"But it won't be. We're not going to let dating come between us. We've come back together as friends after years apart. Plus, that's assuming it won't go well, and I don't think that's something we need to worry about." Every word out of his mouth echoed one in my own mind. I wanted this. I wanted him. I was scared of it, but I was hopeful.

The glaring issue of *how* it might work and what it might mean in the long run, felt too large to confront in that moment. So we didn't.

"Ok then," I said, my voice textured with nerves and hope.

"Ok then," he confirmed with a graveled, deep voice that wrapped around me.

Something shifted then, like the neutrons in the air could tell what was coming and charged.

He leaned forward and pulled me to him. His lips met mine softly, like a question. I turned toward him, trying to get closer, and his arms, one on my shoulder and the other on my back, urged me forward. He kept kissing me, even as he pulled me into his lap with hands moving my thighs and settling again low on my back, his tongue and lips exploring my mouth with urgency.

His hands moved to my neck, into my hair, and he held my head in his hands. He deepened the kiss and made a sound as I slid my fingers in to the soft, short hair at the nape of his neck. He pulled me closer, his hands skimmed down my back and slipped under my shirt so he touched the skin of my lower back. I shivered at the feeling of his skin touching mine and pulled him closer, our bodies now crushed together, chest to chest. He groaned, or maybe growled, something primal, and I heard myself whisper his name.

"Luke."

The sound of my whisper nudged me out of my kiss-induced fog, my alternating thoughts of *yes* and *finally* awakening to the rapidly escalating moment. I pulled back from him a little, enough to see his eyes were closed. He trailed kisses from my mouth to my ear and down my neck, his hands had moved around to my sides and his thumbs swept lightly along my ribcage. I moved my hands to his chest and savored the feeling of him under me for a moment before I found my voice.

"Luke, stop." I said it just above a whisper, but it was loud enough to make him still completely. He froze, his eyes fluttered open, and he looked at me with confusion. He took several breaths, searching my face for an answer.

"What's wrong?" His voice was gruff, and he looked disoriented, blinking at me as though trying to clear his vision and mind.

"Uh…" I wasn't sure what to say, but I knew I had to get up and move before we progressed physically far past where we should without serious consequences. We'd just acknowledged we wanted to be together, but I wasn't mentally prepared to *be* together before I'd had time to understand what that really meant. I started to stand, but he pulled me back down to sit on him again, his hands never moving from my waist.

"Don't go. Just stay here and tell me what's wrong." His eyes were pleading and he looked desperately worried now. "What's wrong?"

"I'm… concerned," I said weakly, my voice raspy and unsure. My left hand pressed against his chest lightly, my right fiddled with the crew neck of his t-shirt.

He looked at me, waiting for me to continue. When I didn't, he prompted me. "What about?"

He smiled at me as I felt my face flush. Obviously, it was time to talk more directly, but suddenly I felt like I was too immature to even think about sex, much less talk about it. Somehow we weren't adult Luke and Alex, but in my mind had been transported back into the awkwardness of age twelve when Luke had come over to play with water guns the summer before seventh grade. He ran with me upstairs to my room to grab a hat and tripped on a pile of laundry my mom had set outside my door. Pristine white training bras and brightly colored underwear topped the pile, and the shoulder strap to one bra caught on his shoe while the others spread out in a mangled mess. I knew he saw what it was, and I don't think I've ever blushed as deeply or felt the singe of humiliation as I did in that moment.

Well maybe until now, when I had to talk to this gorgeous, fully grown version of that same friend about a perfectly normal thing, but something that had never been a part of our relationship.

"I feel like we need to take a breath, maybe. And... talk?" I shifted, moving to stand up, but he held me in place again. "I need to move. I can't think... like this."

Silently his hands released me, and I leaned so my right foot touched the floor, then lifted my left leg over him, and walked to the kitchen. I shook my hands and arms at my sides, shaking out the nerves and desire. He was watching me—I could feel him tracking me, even with my back to him.

"Tell me what's going on in that head." His voice was commanding but not loud. He was firm, sure, and even though he was still sitting on the couch, leaning back and surveying me, his voice was anything but relaxed.

I dumped out the wine glasses we'd barely touched, loaded the dishwasher, and poured us each water. I topped off Lemon's water bowl. I considered going out and trimming my herbs, but that was probably taking it too far, so instead I took the glasses with me when I went to sit back down on the other side of the couch. I propped my feet up on the couch, my knees almost to my chin, creating a barrier between him and me.

"I think... we should wait. A while. Before we... go any further." My voice was shaky and I kept my arms locked around my knees like I was keeping them safe with my relentless grip.

He watched, taking in my arms wrapped around my knees and what must have been a face full of worry. "Can you tell me why?"

"It would..." I took a deep breath. "I think it could ruin our friendship."

"Why would it ruin our friendship?" He looked at me, studied my face, and didn't move.

"Don't play dumb. You know that moving beyond being friends is already a risk. If we date, that's one thing. But if we sleep together, and then break up? There's just no recovering from that." My voice was quiet, but confident. I was feeling the wear of the week, of the surprise of seeing him, and of the rollercoaster of emotions and hormones. Now I just felt tired and a little unsure and ready to sleep.

"I'm not playing dumb." His look was steady and he didn't break eye contact.

"Ok, well, what do you think?" I heard the edge to my voice. I felt just shy of hysterical from both wanting him and fear. I was afraid to talk about this and more afraid of what he'd say.

He sighed and ran his hands over his face and through his hair, then they found their grip at the back of his neck. "I understand what you're saying. I'm not happy about that because... I mean, damn Alex. It's you. I can't pretend this isn't something I've thought about for... a while. But, I get it. I don't want to hurt you or put pressure on us before we even get a chance to enjoy dating." He sounded resigned, but sure, and he stood up.

"Ok, but... now you're leaving?" I felt relieved by his response, but extremely disappointed he was unmistakably ready to leave.

"Yes, I'm leaving. Because I haven't seen you in eight weeks, and I have been wanting you for essentially my whole life, and now in some small way you're admitting you want me too. I'm exhausted, and my willpower is minimal, and I do have to get back home because I promised Harrison I'd workout with him early tomorrow. But I want us to make plans soon." He walked to me and grabbed my hands and pulled me off the couch. When he hugged me, he pressed me with both hands against him, his whole body wrapping around mine, warm and reassuring. Then he gave me an all too chaste kiss and was at the door.

"Ok, let me know when you're home." I smiled at him as he swung the door shut, feeling a swirl of disappointment, relief, exhaustion, and elation.

CHAPTER FOURTEEN

My phone was in my hand before I even thought to grab it. I dialed and waited until I heard Ellie's sleepy voice on the other end of the line.

"Why, in the name of all that is sacred and beautiful, are you calling me at midnight?" Her voice sounded tired and disoriented but mostly extremely annoyed. I liked my sleep, but Ellie was a bear if she didn't sleep. She was an ideal college roommate for me because, like me, she never partied, required silence to read, and needed at least eight hours of sleep to function.

"Luke just left. I think we're dating now." I heard the words and felt a trill of nerves run through me.

"What? He's back? You're dating? Tell me everything!" She perked up, her determination to get caught up winning out over her frustration over losing sleep.

"I was leaving Rosita's and literally ran into him. He looks so good. We hardly even talked about his training, but it must have been the eat-protein-and-spinach-and-workout-so-you-look-like-a-marble-statue training because wow. He saw me brushing off Rick—"

"Ughhh, this guy needs to get a clue," she interjected.

"I know. I think he finally got it. So Luke saw me reject him and then basically told me I should be dating him, not Rick, and—"

"Oh my Goooooo—"

"I know! I know. So, I basically said, 'Yeah, I agree' and then he kissed me, and then we had to talk about the whole him leaving without telling me. Turns out he didn't find out until the day before the ball and didn't want to tell me before the ball, and then when he *did* tell me I acted all too cool for him because—"

"Because you were devastated he wouldn't tell you and ask you to be his girlfriend or fiancée or mother to his future children..." She couldn't help but interrupt me, and I couldn't help but smile at her runaway train of romance. Ellie was perpetually ready to find the love story in my situation, and she'd been rooting for me and Luke since I met her freshman year.

"Ok, crank it back a notch there, killer. Anyway, we cleared the air, it was both of us just being stupid, and it sounds like essentially wanting the same thing, but being scared to risk our friendship. So... I think we're dating now." I could tell my face was beaming from the smile I wore.

"You *think* you're dating now? What does that mean?"

"We haven't been on a date since he left and obviously not since we mutually agreed to *officially* date each other. And he didn't formally submit an application to be my boyfriend or anything. But I feel like we left it at that—he clearly didn't like me dating Rick, and I assume that extends to other people. And then I kind of made it awkward at the end..." I trailed off, thinking about the last few minutes of our time together.

"How did you make it awkward?" she asked, and I could hear her skepticism. Ellie had endless faith in me, despite my persistent ability to prove her wrong when it came to my inter-actions with and feelings for Luke.

"Well, I told him I thought we probably shouldn't sleep together." My mouth felt dry as I thought about his response, and I prayed silently he really did understand and agree.

"Wow, ok. I can see that being a little awkward, but you know what? You needed to say something if that's how you felt," she confirmed.

"I know. It might have been better to say something not like, in the heat of the moment, and not like three minutes after we decided to go for it with the whole dating thing, but... I've never had great timing with him. And I felt myself get so caught up in him, like... I couldn't think of anything else, until I *did*, and I felt terrified of losing him if something happened. I don't think I could be his friend if we, I mean, if we were..." My voice had gotten softer as I felt the fear of losing him all over again.

"I get it. I do. And I know that you felt like that dynamic was confusing in your relationship with Marcus, even after you were engaged, especially when you felt like you didn't want to be engaged anymore. I understand why you said it, and if Luke is as awesome as you say he is, then he'll under-stand." Her voice was firm and affirming, and I loved her so much in that moment.

"I miss you El. I want you to come visit me. I need to look at your face when I talk to you." I sounded whiney, I knew I did. I'd known she'd be the biggest thing missing in my life when I moved. We saw each other often when I lived in the city.

"I miss you too. I need a break from the city—I am feeling so burnt out and over basically everything. So maybe I can start looking at tickets. Maybe over fall break? That's the second weekend in October, I think." She sounded thoughtful and I realized she meant it.

"Really? Oh, my goodness, yes. When you can come, I will be here. I haven't taken vacation days, and I'm not planning on taking many at Christmas anyway, so I could totally take a day or two! *Please* come. I'll buy all your food and won't charge you rent for the couch. It's an unbeatable deal."

"I'll look. It could be very good timing for me."

We hung up soon after that, and I felt sure she'd come. She was my best friend and seeing her after months apart would be soul-restoring. I felt hopeful and excited and relieved that I finally had something good to tell her in terms of Luke. I told her how I missed him, and how much I disliked the date with Rick, and how I wanted Luke. She didn't need me to tell her that—she probably knew that better than I did at this point because she wasn't blinded by my irrational fear of the change of status in our relationship, but still. She knew it all, and I knew she was rooting for us.

I heard my phone buzz as I was getting in bed.

Luke: *Home safe and sound.*

I liked hearing from him right before bed. It felt cozy and like he was mine to end the day with.

Me: *Good. Glad you didn't fall asleep at the wheel.*
Luke: *I'll call you tomorrow so we can make plans.*
Me: *Ok. Night Luke.*
Luke: *Night Al.*

I couldn't stop beaming around my room. He hadn't called me Al since we were about eleven. He started calling me Al because I got my hair cut short, and even though I thought it was an adorable pixie cut, he said I looked like a boy and called me Al. At first, I didn't like it, but as we got older, he kept calling me Al, even when my hair had grown out and I'd gone through puberty and was unmissably female.

I went to bed feeling hopeful and excited with an undercurrent of nervous anticipation. I pushed away the bigger questions. I didn't think about where we could go, and whether I could actually love him, and what I'd do when he inevitably moved to his next duty station. I locked those away and let myself have at least one night of just simmering in the happy.

The next morning as I scrolled the headlines over breakfast of a blueberry muffin and some scrambled eggs, Luke called.

"So, are you free next weekend?" Hearing his gruff voice, unused so far today if I had to bet, felt like the perfect way to begin a Saturday. Then I remembered I was working the event for St. Marks school all next weekend.

"Unfortunately, no. I'm working the whole weekend. I have an event Saturday and I'm helping Janie with her event Sunday. It's going to be a long couple of weeks."

"Well crap. I want to take you out, but I can't come during the week this week or next, and it sounds like you'll be swamped anyway." He sounded genuinely disappointed and I won't lie—I relished it.

"What about the next weekend?" It would be a long time to wait to see him, but I knew the next ten days would be madness at work.

"I have this tournament thing..." He sounded a little... something. Shy? Chagrined? I couldn't tell over the phone.

"Tournament? Are you jousting someone?" I teased.

"Yes. Whoever wins gets to marry the princess and inherit the kingdom."

"Wow. You Army folk really are all about tradition."

"If you want, you could come. It's not formal like the ball, but it'll still be work. I got tasked to do it because I'm one of the only guys who is level two certified from the battalion staff," he said like I knew exactly what he was talking about. I did not, but the *why* didn't seem all that important.

"Certified in what? What is the tournament for?"

"Sorry, I fall into Army speak easily and forget you don't know everything." I felt a little bump of disappointment in that and realized I wanted to be able to understand this other language so he didn't have to worry about explaining everything all the time. "It's a combatives tournament. Kind of like wrestling but a little more interesting in the later rounds, more like MMA. But I won't get that far. It has been a long time since I've done anything in the way of training. My buddy Harrison—you met him at the ball—he's amazing and it's awesome to watch him just destroy people." He sounded enthusiastic at this point.

"Well, I do love a good destruction of my fellow man."

"It's not too violent. There's not usually blood and no one gets hurt, just a little dinged up, at least until those final rounds. But it's fun, and it's exciting, I promise. No pressure, you'd have to drive up here and everything, so—"

"Luke, I want to come, and I can absolutely drive up there. I haven't seen much of your life, and you've been to my house several times now. I'd love to see where you live and maybe you can show me where you work too." As I was talking I realized just how little of Luke's life I had actually seen. I'd gotten a small taste of the Army tradition at the ball but still had no sense what an Army base or an office building (were they office buildings? Did they just run around in the woods all the time?) or anything else looked like. And I was more than a little curious to see what Luke's living situation was like.

"Yes, I'd love to show you around. It's not glamorous, but Fort Campbell is cool. It's a pretty typical big Army post. I'll send you directions next week, and in the meantime, I guess we'll just... text?" He sounded unsure and my heart responded by jumping in my chest. Even on the phone, he was adorable.

"Yes, of course we'll text. And we can talk on the phone sometimes, too, if you want." I felt the same trepidation. It was strange to decide that we were dating, but not actually get to date yet. But maybe the distance and time apart would help us adjust to this very new phase. Maybe it would give us confidence.

Or maybe it would just make me even more awkward and nervous when I did show up to see him wrestle people on his turf surrounded by other soldiers and Army wives.

Because that wasn't at all intimidating.

Work was insane. It was insane the week rolling up to the event, and the event itself was typical but enjoyable insanity, and the week after was, *shockingly*, a bit insane. I felt... say it with me now, *insane*.

Part of the insanity was that I felt growing satisfaction with the tasks and processes of work but an antsy feeling I couldn't pin down nagged at me. I had been warned it took some time to settle in and that I needed to give it a good six months before I made any judgments. I'd been there a little over three, and I didn't think it was that I wasn't settled.

I liked Nashville well enough—much more than I'd expected to so soon, actually. I liked the people. I liked my boss quite a lot and the accounts I was assigned were exactly what I was looking for when I'd made the move. They were the kind of smaller, interesting events I wanted and could never get a hand in at FixEvents in New York because I was tasked with corporate, typically one person on a team of at least ten, and that was all the company did. I liked my little team with Willa and Scott plugging away at the nonprofits with me.

I loved the little private school fundraising gala we put on. It was exactly what I was looking for when I made the move to Burney and Wilks in Nashville, and even one of the upcoming projects they teased me with during the interview. I'd basically made a lateral move in pay, but I was guaranteed the position of non-profits and education team leader, which I was so excited about. It didn't hurt that cost of living was significantly lower in Nashville, so it felt like a raise in some ways.

I had a smaller focus, and that focus had purpose, or at least more than what I felt I'd had after over three years at FixEvents where I was stuck calling vendors for the cheapest champagnes and best deals on menus for 350 for a bunch of Fortune 500 dudes to congratulate themselves on being wealthy.

Ok, so it was possible I was a little cynical.

When I left FixEvents, my boss, Brenda, swore to me she was going to get me back. I laughed it off and took it as the compliment it was, not thinking she'd meant it since I was a realist and recognized that while I was good at what I did, I was not irreplaceable. Already I knew I couldn't even entertain going back, but I'd started getting messages and quick emails from friends there saying my replacement wasn't hacking it, and Brenda had openly said she was working on an offer to lure me back.

She'd need to double my salary and give me weekends off. This, I knew, wasn't happening. So... no real temptation there (never mind the fact that a return to New York would undoubtedly be the end of me and Luke before we'd begun).

To say I was done with New York was putting it lightly. I missed Ellie, but I didn't miss the old job.

But I was beginning to find that the new job wasn't all I'd hoped it'd be. Or, maybe it was exactly what I'd hoped it would be, but what that did for me, and how that helped me or changed me or filled me up wasn't what I'd thought it would be. My mind knew that work wasn't all there was, and it couldn't be the thing to give me meaning and purpose, but my heart felt I'd come to Nashville to work *and*. Work *and* a life. Work *and* a partner. I wasn't there yet—not yet. And the usual exhilaration I felt during these busy times was missing because of my impatience.

Maybe part of that was the lack of certainty when it came to Luke. As much as I tried not to let it, my concerns about the future, about where our relationship could go, were ever-present in my mind. It was impossible to ignore, and in the sweetest moments of my job—when the party was in full swing and things were going best, or just after we won a bid for an event, or seeing someone on my team blow their part of a presentation out of the water—after these moments, I always thought of Luke.

I'd think of how I wanted to talk to him about that. I'd think of his work and wonder whether he loved it like I loved mine. I'd wonder what his favorite parts of his job were.

And then, inevitably, I'd wonder how much longer he'd have that job, be in that place, be close enough for me to see, even if it was only every few weeks. And that? That was where I got sad and shut down the thoughts and then couldn't shake the sense of impending doom about us before we'd ever even gotten going.

I moved to Nashville to free myself up for a relationship, and here I was, entering one that likely didn't end in marriage, but instead ended with a big fat *Dead End* sign when he moved away in a number of months or years. Would I move with him? Would I follow him around and lose myself? I cringed away from that every time, but it kept coming back.

My phone buzzed on the bathroom counter as I rinsed my face of makeup, and I grabbed it, my heart already beating a bit faster as I dried off and then accepted the call.

"Alex Moore's phone, how I can I help you?" I answered in my most nasal, secretarial voice.

"I'm looking to speak with Alex. Or, really, I should call her Lexy because I know she loves that." I could hear the smug smile in his voice. He knew I'd been called Lexy by Calvin Cranford in the fifth grade, and it drove me up the wall.

"Sir, I think you have the wrong number." I plunked down on the couch in my living room and ran my hands over Lemon who was snoozing on the cushion next to me.

"No, no, Lexy Moore. Sexy Lexy as she was always called around town. Or maybe you know her as Alexandra. Sometimes she likes to be more formal."

I laughed lightly. People always assumed I was Alexandra. "No, sir, there's no one here by that name." I felt myself relax a bit. I'd been wound tight for ten days straight and was so ready to see him. Two more days.

"Ah, then, maybe Alessandra? Alessandra Vittoria Moore, is she in?" He said it just right. Just the way it was meant to be said. He said it with the accent just right, pronouncing every

letter individually instead of anglicizing the names. Juuuu-
uust right.

I almost died. I almost melted into a little puddle and
slipped away, soaked up by my medium-pile carpet.

I cleared my throat in order to find my voice. "Yes. Yes,
I'm here." I couldn't say anything else since I'd so recently
liquefied.

"Good. I was beginning to worry." He sounded pleased
with himself, but I hoped he had no idea how much his saying
my name had affected me.

"Your accent's still good," I said, still a little breathless,
and kind of hoping he might say it again.

"*Grazie, cara. Non ho mai smesso di parlare Italiano.*" His
voice was unbearably smooth and seductive, and his speaking
Italian, my language, the language of my family, my bones, felt
like an assault on my reason. He said *I never stopped speaking
Italian.* We'd spoken a little as we grew up, my mom always
trying to teach him some when he came over, but I didn't
realize he could speak it.

"I don't think I knew you could speak Italian that well."
Panting? Who, me? That wasn't a thing real people did, so no.
I wasn't having a full body response to his voice layering me
with words in my mother's language.

I ran a hand over my face and fluttered my eyes to focus
and return to Earth.

Just another day—nothing to see here.

"Well, it's rusty. I wouldn't trust myself for much more
than to order a good meal, but I always loved the language. It
reminds me of you and your mom and being at your house
when we were kids. I brushed up on it now and then over the
years, I guess because it made me feel connected to you." He
sounded so painfully sincere I almost felt embarrassed by it,

except I then felt totally and completely like mush and had no time for anything else.

"You kept up your Italian for over a decade, during which you barely communicated with me in any way, because it made you feel connected to me? Are you kidding?"

CHAPTER FIFTEEN

I couldn't stop myself, because as soon as I recovered from the mush, I felt frustration. If he'd missed me that much—even just missed our childhood, why not tell me? Why not email me? Why not call my house and find out if I was there? Get my phone number? Join the modern age and stalk me online like everyone else in the world did?

"I guess it's weird. I always just liked the language, too. I didn't mean to freak you out." Now he was legitimately embarrassed, but I had to clarify what I was getting at. I didn't want him to stop being honest, or God forbid, for him to stop speaking Italian to me.

Per favore, Dio non voglia.

"No, you're not freaking me out. I'm just so confused about why you would do that but then barely respond to my emails or come see me when you knew I was in town if you were there too?" I felt the real hurt rise again as I remembered him saying we had been home at the same time once or twice, but it was only this last time he'd tracked me down. I'd never known we were in the same place at the same time other than the one time we'd run into each other years before.

"I'm sorry. I wish I had. I guess it felt safer to just keep doing what I was doing and keep our emails simple. When we saw each other, I knew you were dating someone, and I was too. It just... but it's not like I didn't still miss you." He sounded a little hollow and sad, maybe actually regretful, and I decided to move on before we ended up frustrated with no way to fix it. The phone was not ideal for conversations of any real depth.

"Ok, let's just move on."

"Ok. Tell me about how your week's been." He was clearly relieved by the topic change.

"It's gone ok." I felt the rush of disappointment and frustration flood over me again. "I don't want to talk about it."

"Do you miss New York?"

"I miss things about New York. I miss Ellie. I miss the deli down my old street that made the most perfect sandwich with green apple, real turkey breast, not lunch meat turkey, and melted brie—I would kill for one of those right now. Sometimes I feel like if my old boss makes good on her threat to woo me back I might welcome it for that sandwich alone. And sometimes I miss the *stuff* you know? Restaurants on every corner, weird artsy stuff everywhere, not needing a car. But Nashville has its own vibe I like a lot, and that's not the issue, if that's what you're thinking. I should, by all rights, feel totally proud of and satisfied by the work I did this past weekend. The school raised almost $40,000 for their arts program and they were happy with the event, but I just feel..." I couldn't name it. Not to him. It felt too much like something a kid would say, too whiny and ungrateful to be at a new, awesome job in a place I'd chosen to be and not be happy.

"It's ok that it's not perfect. You don't have to pretend it is." His voice was steady but quiet.

His response was perfect. He didn't try to prescribe a way

to improve the situation or pepper me for more information so he could try to solve the problem. He just listened and gave me permission to be honest with him and with myself.

"Thank you."

"No need to thank me for saying something true."

"Well, what about you? How has work been for you? I still don't have any idea what you do, or what your job is, even. But maybe you can show me this weekend?"

"I will show you my very luxurious, dilapidated office, sure." I heard him let out a breath and I pictured one hand gripping the back of his neck, his feet kicked up on a coffee table I couldn't yet see in my mind. "My week's been ok. Major Flint is still being a jerk, and I swear it has nothing to do with me or the work I'm producing. It's like something crawled up his—no. You know what? No. I'm not going to spend my time complaining about him. I should be leaving that office anyway, but they're trying to get me to stay and take a second command—whatever. The point is, I hope that whatever is going on with Flint resolves soon, because I do not want to deal with Bad Mood Joe anymore."

"Ugh, that sucks."

"Yeah, it does. But... there's always something, you know? Always someone you don't agree with or get along with. That's part of real life and being a professional." He sounded very matter-of-fact, and I smiled at his attitude. It was so *him*. He saw things in a black and white way—if you could fix a problem, do. If you couldn't, then deal with it, or get out of the situation. Done.

I'd always envied him that ability to see things so clearly, and I wondered if that wasn't why he sometimes seemed to short circuit when we were together—we were loosely draped in all kinds of gray.

"I guess I agree to some degree, but at the same time, it's

not a given that you hate your boss or they're a jerk, is it? Am I naïve about that? I didn't love my boss in New York, but she wasn't awful. She was one small part of a whole situation that wasn't right for me anymore."

"I see your point. I feel like I always disagree with someone in my chain of command. If it's not my direct commander, it might be an overarching methodology. Or, lately, it's more likely to be the president, who is ultimately my commander in chief."

"How do you do it? Why stay in a job that you're constantly conflicted with? Especially one that demands so much of you." It was mystifying to me.

"I know it sounds crazy, but I think that's what happens in an organization as big as the Army. One of my commanders once said that we take our oath of office and we swear allegiance to an *idea*, not a person. I'm not fighting for the president. I'm not fighting for a political party's agenda. I'm serving in the Army and working for the ideas in the constitution, the idea of upholding the republic. And then there are more personal things, like my family, my freedoms, my sense of duty, and those more immediate motivations. But when I frame it that way in my mind, it's a little less painful when I staunchly disagree with the power players in Washington or even on the battalion staff, at the very least."

"That makes sense. It does. That's... reassuring. Thinking of the Army as fighting for that higher ideal is reassuring." His words made sense to me, and I could hear the conviction in his voice. And hearing him say it did make me feel more confident in him, in the fact that what he was doing had value beyond this moment. "You're kind of amazing. Have I told you that?"

He made a dismissive noise. "You haven't. You don't need to. Plus, if you were constantly telling me I was amazing I'd start wondering what you're up to." I could hear him smiling, and I felt a tug of longing to be with him and see his face.

"I've missed you. I can't wait to see you Saturday."

Me: *What does one wear to a combatives tournament?*

Luke had texted me the address and directions to his house the night before. I felt the flood of nervous energy hit me as I'd showered that Saturday morning and then realized I had no idea what to wear.

Luke: *Your ball gown.*

He was quick to respond and I shook my head at him. I guessed he really did like the dress.

Me: *Or... option B?*
Luke: *Or jeans? It's casual. Whatever you'll be comfortable in. Unfortunately, it'll probably be hot.*

I stood in front of my closet. It was mid-September but frustratingly hot. Summer in Tennessee really did last until a third of the way through fall, and I'd heard more than one of my coworkers claim this was the worst extended summer in years.

I didn't want to be sitting there sweating all day. I was already nervous enough.

I settled on a navy-blue sundress. The straps were thin over my shoulders, but it was still modest. It cinched in at the waist with elastic, it had pockets (because any comfortable dress does), and it hit a few inches above the knee. It was comfortable and relaxed, and it would keep me cool. I wore my hair down, some flat sandals I could walk in, and grabbed a gray cardigan to throw on if we went anywhere with air conditioning.

"Well Lemmy, wish me luck." I nuzzled his forehead with mine and heard his purr accelerate in a low rumble. "Love you too, buddy."

~

The drive wasn't too bad, but it did take me a full hour to get from my house to Luke's. When I pulled up to the apartment building, I saw his truck and my heartbeat kicked into high gear. I hadn't even seen him yet, and I was already starting to sweat and feel weird.

"Hey," he called to me as he walked out of a first-floor door close to where he'd instructed me to park. I fumbled with my seat belt and threw the door open. He was at the door and opening it too before I was out of the car. He grabbed my arm and pulled me the rest of the way out and right into a hug like he couldn't wait another second.

"Hi," I said into his shoulder as he crushed me to him, lifted me up, and twirled around a little as he hugged me. He smelled so good. He was wearing his uniform—the one I'd mistakenly referred to as camouflage and he'd explained they were "ACUs," but really, they were just camouflage in my world that didn't yet grasp the nuance of the difference—and he looked like an action figure in it. "It's so good to see you."

"It's good to see you too. It feels like it's been weeks." He squeezed me once more and then set me down. He beamed back at me, but his smile fell a bit as he took in my dress.

"What's wrong? I do have jeans in the car just in case you

meant that literally. I just thought I might overheat in them if it gets hot like it did yesterday." I started toward the car to grab my jeans and show him, but he stopped me.

"No! No, you don't have to wear jeans. There's no uniform for you." His eyes were bouncing between my dress, my legs, and my lips. When he finally met my eyes, I felt that familiar feeling of stepping off a stair and missing one so I ended up lower down.

"Ok," I said, not sure what he was thinking, but feeling increasingly more self-conscious. I licked my lips and was searching for something else to say when he grabbed me gently by the back of the neck and pulled me in for a kiss. He pulled away although his hand fisted in my hair in what felt like frustration, and then he grabbed my hand.

He stood there a moment, his brilliant blue eyes piercing, and he let out a little puff of air and cleared his throat. "I just have to grab a bag and my water, and then we can go. We'll go in my car and that'll make signing you in easier."

We walked into what must have been an airplane hangar, and they had bleachers set up around a bunch of mats, each grouping of mats creating a different ring where rounds could be held simultaneously. Soldiers milled around restlessly, awaiting the competition's start. Luke led me to the bleachers where I saw Megan, Ally, and a few more women I was introduced to at the ball. Megan's eyes lit and practically glowed when she saw us, and she gave me a knowing smile when I sat down by her.

"So." She leveled me with her bright blue eyes and Cheshire cat smile.

"So," I said, not willing to let her win right away, although I couldn't help meeting her smile with my own.

"So now you're his girlfriend," she said. Her dainty hand patted down the hair along the side of her head and smoothed down her long, blonde ponytail. Even in capri pants and a tank top she looked polished. How?

"Yes."

"Good." She beamed at me and then introduced me to a few people milling around I hadn't met.

"Did you meet Captain Jackson at the ball?" Megan asked me as she nodded to the woman sitting a few rows down with a few other soldiers.

"Oh, yes, hi. It's nice to see you again, Captain Jackson," I said to the striking blonde woman sitting in front of me.

"Please, call me Rae," she said and extended her hand. I shook it.

"Ok, Rae. Good to see you again."

"Likewise. I'm sure Waterford's happy to have you here," she said and smiled at me. Good grief, this woman was pretty. She had sparkly blue eyes and bright white teeth. She looked like G. I. Jane Barbie.

"Glad to be here," I said and smiled back. I had to stop myself from asking if she was a model for the Army.

I mean really, get this girl on a poster.

"Rae was in the battalion with our boys. She and Captain Richards there," Megan pointed a perfectly painted nail to the left down the bleachers to another woman in uniform who I thought was the other female captain I'd met at the ball, "were the only female officers in the battalion. Richards left last week. Rae, I heard you're about to leave us too, is that right?" Megan turned back to Rae.

"Yeah, I'm already over at the BSB. Probably do some staff

time there," Rae explained.

"Oh that's where you go since you're not infantry, right?" Megan asked.

"Yeah it's the brigade support battalion so that's where logisticians usually go after a company command. I transitioned over a few weeks ago."

"Well we'll miss you, honey, but I know we'll see you around. You holler if you need anything, all right? I know you're a self-sufficient, badass woman, but still." Megan gave her such a motherly look I had to laugh just a little. Megan narrowed her eyes at me, but Rae laughed too.

"Yes ma'am, I'll be sure to let you know." She turned to me and said, "Nice to see you again, Alex. Enjoy the day." Then she pushed up off the bleachers and walked toward one of the mats. I watched as several heads turned to follow her movement, just as I did.

"She's astoundingly pretty. I hate for that to be my first thought, but..." I trailed off.

"You're not wrong. She is. She's also damn good at her job, which is the good news." Megan's eyes were still on Rae when we heard a loud buzzer signaling the start of the event.

As the competition got started, I saw how fun it was. The grappling or... combating, was very entertaining. Luke sat with me for a few rounds, and then he moved off to stretch and warm up a little before his turn. I was getting nervous on his behalf as I saw him bouncing around at the corner of the mat where his match would take place in a few minutes.

"Are you nervous?" Megan asked as I watched Luke stretch his long legs and tried not to let my mouth hang open in appreciation of how devastatingly sexy he was in his regular, every day uniform.

"Yes, I'm so nervous. Why am *I* nervous? Should I be

nervous?" I rambled and gripped the metal bleacher on either side of my legs to brace myself.

"No, you have nothing to worry about. He won't get too banged up, and it's all for fun until the later rounds anyway. This kind of thing? No nerves required." She seemed so seasoned at that moment, and I wanted to hear more.

"What kind of things do you get nervous for?"

"Mmm, not much anymore. I used to get nervous for jumps or air assaults—where they jump out of the helicopter and fast-rope to the ground—and sometimes even helicopter rides because there are accidents during training. But that's so much work. You learn to block that out. And even during deployment, it's different. It's like you get inured to the feeling of danger. You pray every damn day, but by the end it's like you're always humming with that *please God, keep him safe—please God, let him come home.* You can't possibly always be putting it into words or even letting it become conscious thought because you'd never do anything else. So you just keep it there, tucked at a low roar in the back of your mind and keep on keepin' on until he's back and you're touching his face."

I took a moment to process her words. I thought about the moment of a soldier's return, of finally touching him again. I felt a pang in my chest at the thought of the goodbye and at the joy of being reunited. I didn't let myself imagine the soldier was Luke and I was the one touching his face, kissing his lips, being reunited with him.

"It makes sense that you can't constantly be scared of the things that most people would be. It's their job description to do some of these things the teacher or banker or corporate guy would never dream of doing," I said.

I had thought a little about that dynamic—that what Luke did was entirely different from anyone I'd dated or even considered dating. Different from my father, who'd been an engineer at a local plant for decades, always in the same place.

"Yeah, military life isn't for the faint of heart, I can tell you that." She looked at me pointedly, and I shifted my eyes to see Luke, still stretching and talking to a few soldiers.

"No, I guess it's not," I said quietly.

"Girl, you are intense today. What's on your mind? I know you don't know me from Eve, but I like you. I'm not tryin' to scare you away from that gorgeous man, so don't let what I just said freak you out," she said with a chin-nod to Luke.

I raised my eyebrows at her. "You're not trying to scare me away? You sure?"

"I'd never do such a thing. I already told you I think Luke's about as gone on you as a hog on slop. Based on the way you walked in here and that sweet smile that keeps creeping up on your face every time you catch sight of him, I'm guessing you feel the same way." She watched me and all I could do was nod at her assertion that Luke was "gone on me" and her very correct assessment of my own feelings for him.

She nodded to herself then. "I thought so."

"But what if I am 'the faint of heart'?"

"Are you asking me if you're strong enough?" Megan's voice echoed a thought I'd had to repress a lot lately. I turned to her and found her eyes serious and concerned.

"I don't know. How could I know that?" It was a question I asked myself every time I wondered about the future I had with Luke. I swallowed down a surge of panic and gripped the bleachers until my knuckles were bleached of their pigment.

"Well, you don't. There's no way to know, but you can start by figuring out what you're willing to give up. Because to have this," she gestured around us to the chatting soldiers, the giant flag waiving outside the hangar doors, the other women talking and waiting for their soldiers' turns, "and to have Luke, you'll have to give up a lot." She let that sink in for a minute.

I felt the weight of her words, and I knew what she was saying was true. I knew it from the beginning, and like it or not, it was a big reason I felt like I was constantly pumping the mental breaks on thinking about a future with Luke. I didn't like that we were having this conversation there, in the midst of the tournament and at a time I couldn't think or process anything.

"It's not that it's not worth it. I wouldn't trade my life, this military life, for anything. I wouldn't trade it for the career of my dreams, I wouldn't trade it for a house near my folks and my grandparents and free babysitting and great school systems. I wouldn't trade it for a safe job for James and a predictable future for our family. I love the adventure and challenge of moving. I love the pride I feel in my husband's job, and honestly, the pride I feel in myself and my kids for all the crap we deal with and how we figure things out and make the most of every situation. I love the hell out of my Army wife friends and in so many ways, they're closer than family. But that doesn't mean that sometimes what I've given up doesn't feel like a loss, like something I need to mourn now and then, even when I know what a beautiful life this is." Her voice was thick, and I looked over at her and saw the sincerity written on her face. She seemed desperate for me to understand her, but she wasn't warning me away from Luke.

We sat quietly for two rounds. Then she turned to me and said, "I guess I would say to you that the question isn't whether you're strong enough for Army life. No one knows that because you don't get strong enough for it until you're in it. It's kind of like having a baby—you're never actually prepared no matter how many times you babysat or helped with a sibling or how many books you read. You just do it. Then you figure it out, and you keep doing it because it's real life and there's no other choice. The real question is what *aren't* you willing to give up for Luke?"

Her question was rhetorical, and I knew I'd be mulling it over for a while. I couldn't think about it here, so close to her, surrounded by people and heat and noise.

CHAPTER SIXTEEN

We heard, "Waterford! Harrison!" and I snapped out of my self-focus. I looked up to see Luke and his friend Jake walking onto the floor.

"Wait, he's going against Jake Harrison? I thought Harrison was some kind of expert-level guy?" I felt my nerves rocket back full force as I watched them each pull on and strap down head gear and mouth guards. They attached the pads that by now I'd gathered were required, and they moved to the mats.

"Yeah, he typically wins the tournaments. I think he's even competed at national levels and stuff. Luke has no prayer," she said and winked at me. That damn wink!

The bell sounded, and the two separate men became one muscled mass of energy as they met each other in the center of the mat. I could barely tell what was happening because Jake Harrison moved so quickly, I couldn't see him. I saw his open hand strike Luke's ribs, and then grab Luke by the back of his head, sweep his legs, and pin him. Then he pulled the collar of Luke's uniform tight around his neck, and Luke almost immediately tapped Jake on the side.

"Waterford did well! Most people don't even last that long with Harrison," I heard a voice from the small group of soldiers sitting near us say. I recognized the voice as that of the other female captain I'd met, Captain Richards.

I felt stricken and hoped Luke was ok. Jake reached out a hand and pulled him up and patted him on his back. Before I knew it, it had happened again—two more times. Then, they both pulled out slimy mouth guards and I could tell they were talking. Luke clapped Jake on the back, and then looked my way. He held up a finger and I nodded at him.

"You made it through," Ally said as she sat back down with a hot dog and soda. I hadn't actually talked to her yet, but she'd waved to me from across the hangar when I walked in earlier.

"I can't believe it's over that fast," I said, still trying to process what just happened.

"All I can say is Luke did hold his own. It's so hard to tell what's happening, but the fact that he made it almost a full minute each time is impressive. Jake Harrison is a beast, and I think Luke was probably the sacrificial lamb to go first. He'll be one of many to go down fast at Harrison's hands," Megan confirmed.

I felt a little better after seeing Luke smiling and laughing with Harrison, but when he came and sat down, I turned my full attention to him. His face was still a little red, his uniform disheveled, his mouth curved into a wry smile.

"Are you ok?" I asked and put a hand on his shoulder.

"Yes, I'm fine. I knew it was coming, but I'm always surprised at just how fast it happens." He shook his head and wrapped a hand around his ribs and winced a little.

"Are you hurt?" I touched the hand that rested on his ribs lightly like it would tell me the truth if he didn't.

"Not bad. I'll just be sore tomorrow. He pummeled me in

the ribs before I let go of his arm so he could sweep me and pin me. You know, my glorious ten second hold out before the fall." He laughed lightly and just that little smile and laugh lit me on fire.

His total humility in that moment was incredibly attractive. His willingness to laugh at his defeat instead of pout or complain or even try to justify his loss by the fact that he'd apparently faced an expert, was so appealing. It showed me he was secure and confident and not afraid to embarrass himself. He didn't take himself too seriously, at least not in this area of his life.

"I'm impressed. Not everyone can lose so gracefully." I grinned at him and kissed his cheek. He made a frustrated sound as I pulled away and pulled me back to him to kiss his lips.

"I'm not a sore loser generally, but I'm definitely not when I know I'm going to lose, and lose badly, ahead of time."

His statement made more and more sense as the day wore on. Harrison defeated everyone he came up against in minutes, if not seconds. He didn't seem to have any trouble. The last few rounds of the fighting were far more intense than the earlier ones. The fighters wore only their green undershirts on top instead of their ACU tops, and this meant there was less to hold on to and pull without the bagginess and pockets of the uniform. They could also throw full punches and kicks instead of the open-hand versions allowed in earlier rounds.

Harrison was like a weapon. I loved watching the fights, especially because there was no real animosity. We cheered for our guy, Luke's friend, but everyone enjoyed the spectacle and the demonstration of skill.

When all was said and done, Harrison took first in his weight class, and he would go off to a regional tournament in a few months—good for him. He came to shake hands with Luke before we left.

"Good work man. At least I can say I lost to the champ."

"You put up a good fight." Jake Harrison's voice was deep and surprising. He spoke like it cost him to spend his words.

"Great job." I smiled at him, feeling like I wanted to say *it was so fun to watch you beat all those guys* but thought that might sound a little too weirdly eager for violence.

"Thank you, ma'am," he said.

"Sergeant First Class Harrison, this is Alex Moore." Luke put his hand on my back and smiled at me.

"Pleased to meet you, ma'am." Then he nodded to both of us and disappeared into the crowd.

"He just ma'amed me twice in less than a minute," I said, surprised that someone who was clearly my peer would call me ma'am.

"Yeah, he's perpetually courteous. It's drilled into all of us, but he's so stubborn, I wouldn't be surprised if he ends up calling his wife ma'am someday." I laughed out loud at that.

"No, thank you. I do not want to be ma'amed by my future husband," I said as we stepped out of the hangar. The wind gusted around us, and I felt my dress swirl around my legs. I pulled the hair that had blown into my face out of my mouth and held my dress close to my body. Luke wrapped an arm around my shoulders.

"Whoa! It's picking up. Let's get to the truck." We sprinted to the parking lot and both hopped in and slammed the door just after the downpour started. My hair was wet, my shoulders shining with rain drops.

"Sweet steak frites, it's crazy out there!" I yelped as I pushed my now totally wild hair out of my face and looked over at him. He had rain drops running down his face and dripping onto his shirt, which was also turning dark green at his shoulders and chest where he was wet.

"Did you just say 'steak frites' as an exclamation?" He looked at me like I was crazy, and sure, yeah, I maybe was.

"What of it? It's a habit I may or may not have developed over the last decade. Deal with it." I met his look with a bold one of my own and crossed my arms against the air conditioning blasting away as we drove.

"I can deal with it. Is it always steak frites?" He kept his eyes on the road and both hands on the wheel. The rain was coming in rough sheets that blasted the truck every few seconds. We could see the wind bending trees to the side. I was thankful he didn't live far from the post.

"No, not always. That's maybe the first time I've said that one."

"That makes it even better," he said, genuinely delighted by my oddity. My chest warmed at his response.

One of the things I loved about our friendship when we were kids was we were both weird kids, even though all kids were weird. We managed to love the weirdness in each other when we were small. I used to wonder if maybe my weirdness had scared him off when we hit high school, and that was something that had truly gutted me. The thought that he knew me better than anyone, and that he maybe didn't want me because of what he knew, was terribly upsetting. But I was an expert at pushing negative thoughts away at that age, so I dove into the distractions of high school and assumed we just drifted apart.

He pulled into his apartment complex and looked at me. "I'm so sorry, but I don't have an umbrella." He looked genuinely regretful as we both looked outside at the utter deluge.

"I'm not sure it would make any difference. I think we've

just got to run for it. But I'm going to run to my car and grab my other clothes because by the time we get inside we'll be soaked, and I won't want to come back out." I mentally mapped my path from his car to mine just three spaces away, and then to his door.

"Ok. One, two, three... *Go!*"

He slammed the door behind me and we stood there, absolutely sopping wet, dripping on the linoleum entry way to his apartment. I must have looked like a drowned rat with my hair stringy down my back, my dress stuck to me, and probably some mascara running down my face. I wiped under my eyes, and then I giggled.

Luke ran a hand through his wet hair and I heard him let out a laugh.

Then, it just sort of bubbled out of me, and kept coming— I started laughing so hard I could hardly breathe. I could see him watching me and laughing too, his eyes bright and his face alight with the humor of the moment.

I felt my knees give way, so I leaned against the wall on the other side of the door, dropped my little bag full of clothes to the ground, and slid down the wall. He was standing directly in front of me, watching me laugh hysterically while he did the same. I couldn't breathe, couldn't see, couldn't think. I just laughed. When I came out of my laugh coma, I saw him standing with his arms crossed, laughing with me, though he was evidently not incapacitated with the hilarity like I was.

"Oh man, I'm sorry. I just... it's been a stressful few weeks, and so heavy and tiresome. Today has been so fun, and... I don't know. I guess I needed the relief of a good laugh." I stood up and grabbed my bag.

"Don't apologize for laughing, crazy. And that's not me saying you're not crazy, because you totally are, but I'm glad you can collapse in a hysterical fit of laughter with me. I can't imagine that's something that happens with just anyone," he said, still watching me.

"It's true. Only the privileged few get to witness such a miracle," I said. His smile faded by degrees as we stood there, and I felt that familiar charge light up the air around us. It was like we'd stepped into the spotlight in the room. The sky outside was dark from the storm, and he hadn't turned on any lights. His face was shadowed, but I could tell he was focused on me.

"I'm honored," he said, his voice low and smooth and dangerous. His shirt was plastered to his chest, and it was too alluring to ignore. I bit my bottom lip before I realized he was clearly watching me and looked up at him. If ever there was a heated stare, a charged moment, this was it.

And I wussed out.

"Ah, bathroom? Do you mind if I change?" I asked, clearing my throat of the desire that had flooded me.

"Of course. Yeah, let me get you a towel. If you want to shower or anything, go for it. You do your thing in here and..." He walked me to the door and grabbed a clean towel and set it on the counter. Then he looked at me and said, "and I'll be... I'll be out here." He left and closed the door behind him.

I took a deep breath letting out a bit of frustration, a bit of relief. He was overwhelmingly attractive sometimes, and I felt like a fumbling goon when faced with his intimidating looks, not to mention the *looks*. The way he looked at me lit a match in me, one that had never been struck by anyone but him. Maybe one I never knew was there, lying at the bottom of kindling that was flammable only for Luke. I had certainly never felt this out of my mind for Marcus, or anyone else.

After I showered quickly and changed into my jeans and tank top (not ideal, but I figured if I was wearing jeans I'd want something cool on top for the tournament. I didn't plan on the downpour), I wandered out, toweling my wet hair and surveying his apartment. He must have heard me come out because he came to the hallway with a bundle of dry clothes and I heard him say, "I'll be out in a sec," as he took his turn in the shower and I wandered his small place.

It was nice. It was neat, but not too neat, but definitely a mature bachelor's place rather than the dreaded *bachelor pad*. He had some actual furniture, but some IKEA (but I wasn't judging because what red blooded American didn't love Swedish particle board?). He had a few things hanging on his walls—an old-timey looking map of the US with pins in different cities, and another map of the world with similar pins. He had some kind of flag on one wall with a plaque underneath that I definitely wanted to read.

But first, I studied his maps. His US map had pins in a lot of cities. It looked like he'd been to almost every state in the West, Midwest, and South. He had work to do in the North-east for sure. Then I moved to his map of the world, and I sucked in a sharp breath.

Ireland.

Iceland.

Germany.

Kyrgyzstan.

Kuwait.

Egypt.

Afghanistan.

Iraq.

These each had green pins in them. Everywhere else—

England, Scotland, Germany, France, Denmark, Mexico, Canada, the Caribbean—these had yellow pins.

He emerged from the bathroom and I was still standing there, thinking about those green pins, not seeing anything.

"Do I have you beat?" he asked, suddenly right behind me, his warm breath on my ear.

"I think so. I've only been to about eight countries, I think." I leaned back just a little so my back was pressed to the front of him, and he wrapped his hand around and held me to him, his arm crossing my collar bone and his hand resting on my opposite shoulder. He took a deep breath.

"Well, not all of those are places you'd want to go. And some of them don't count because I didn't get to see the actual country."

"The green pins?" I asked, holding his arm in place with my hands.

"Yeah, they're all the places I've either deployed or stopped in on the way to or from a deployment. So Kuwait, Ireland, Iceland, and Germany are countries where I barely stepped foot outside the plane, basically for refueling. But of course, then I did visit Germany when I did that other trip, so I count that as an actual visit too."

We stood there a moment longer and looked at the map together. I felt an overwhelming sense of grief when I looked at the little green pins. I felt my eyes prick with tears and tried to force them away before I turned toward him. He wrapped his other arm around me and held me to him.

"I'm so sorry." My voice was a rough whisper. I was choked with the emotion and I wasn't sure how to verbalize it better than that.

"Why are you sorry? I'm not sorry for the places I've been. There are some places I don't want to go back to, and there are people I wish had come back with me who didn't, but I'm not sorry," he said gently.

"No. No, I don't mean that you deployed. I assume that as a soldier who has chosen to make this your career, that's just part of the reality. I'm not saying I assume that means it's easy, but I guess I think it'd be difficult to be in the Army if you were going to regret every experience that forced you out of the Western world. What I mean is, I'm sorry I wasn't there for you. I'm sorry I didn't write you or send you mail or support you through those times. I feel like I'm looking at a little list of all the ways I've failed you as a friend." My voice shook. I felt a dreadful sense that I was making this about me, and I didn't want him to think that. My heart was aching because I'd missed loving him, even as a friend, during what must have been hell at times.

"You can't apologize for that. I missed your life too. I didn't do a damn thing to support you through your moves or education or anything." He ran his hands soothingly up and down my back.

"That is so completely different. I was here, doing everyday things. I wasn't risking my life. I wasn't surrounded by a different culture and fighting a war."

"It doesn't matter. It was your life, and I wish I'd been a part of it. I wish you'd been a part of mine too. But I can tell you with full conviction that dwelling on things you can't change is completely unproductive. It won't get us anywhere, and it certainly won't make our relationship *now* any stronger." He paused then and ran a thumb over my cheek bone, then traced the shell of my ear. "Thank you for being the kind of person who would feel the need to apologize, but please believe me when I tell you I understand what you mean, and there's no reason to apologize." He practically glared at me, trying to impress me with his words, trying to make sure I understood and believed him.

I did.

He lifted his hand to the side of my face and ran his thumb across my bottom lip. His eyes were that crevice blue, the depths inescapable and gravitational and irresistible. Fireflies lit up in my belly and I leaned into his hand. He leaned forward slowly, slowly, slowly until his lips were nearly touching mine. My body was pressed to his, and I tried to breathe like someone who was good at it—who knew how to take and expel breaths without conscious thought.

My mind was buzzing with anticipation, overwhelmed with his nearness after what felt like an agonizingly long day without much contact. I was just about to close my eyes when he said, "Are you hungry?"

I may have groaned.

In frustration.

Because... seriously?

"Uhhh..." I just stood there, looking at him, my chest rising and falling like I was in mortal peril, and all I could say was, "Uh." My mind did feel a kind of peril, the kind that comes from having Luke Waterford stand *that* close to me and not kiss me. Especially after either watching him or sitting next to him the entire day, but not really touching him since he was in uniform and technically working.

My nerves threw themselves off a cliff.

His smirk grew into a grin that grew into a sunrise-level self-satisfied smile.

"Is that a yes?" He loosened his grip on me and stepped back just a little.

"That was mean. You know that was mean," I said, shaking my head at him as he bounced away from me, clearly proud of himself for getting me riled up.

"It wasn't mean. I just wanted to make sure you're still interested." His voice was obnoxiously confident.

"Well, I *was*..." I stood in the same spot and crossed my arms.

"Come come, now Al, be a good sport. I promise I'll kiss you tonight." He raised his eyebrows a few times for emphasis.

"Oh boy, you are full of yourself. You'd never know you'd been knocked on your butt and nearly asphyxiated in less than a minute just hours ago." I sat in an overstuffed chair and watched him shuffling around the kitchen.

"Now that's low. I thought you said I was a good loser?" he said in a mock-hurt tone.

"I did, that."

"Well I'm just proving to you that losing hasn't hurt my manly confidence. I've still got some left." He sifted through a drawer and pulled out a menu.

"Yes, I see you have just a little left," I said with a roll of my eyes.

CHAPTER SEVENTEEN

We continued to tease each other as he ordered pizza and handed me a beer. We sat in his living room talking about the tournament, his coworkers, and he told me more about what he did day to day. The plan for him to take me on a tour of the post after the tournament was postponed since the rain made doing anything other than escaping to his apartment a non-option.

I finished a beer and switched to water. I'd had a hotdog about seven hours before for lunch, and I was absolutely ravenous. He didn't have much to eat because he'd been working nonstop after getting back from his trip, and I ended up basically guzzling my beer in search of caloric fulfillment. It went to my head and I'll just say, I got a little bold/awkward.

He was sitting in the chair and I was on the couch, but after I went to the bathroom, as I came back, I stopped right in front of where his legs rested. He was reclined comfortably in the deep over-stuffed chair after the long day, his long legs outstretched in front of him on the ground. He eyed me from where he sat and one eyebrow quirked up.

"Can I help you?" he asked and took a sip of his beer.

"Yes," I said, my voice remarkably sultry, which served my purposes perfectly. I took a step forward between his legs to the edge of the chair. As he watched me, he straightened and sat up and set his beer down on the table next to him. His eyes never left mine.

I moved to straddle his legs, resting my knees on the outside of his hips in the chair and ran my hands over his chest. I tried to ignore the tantalizing dips and swells under his t-shirt as I gave him my most predatory look and bit my bottom lip just a little as I leaned forward. His hands came to my hips, and I could feel his heart beating increasingly fast under my hand. I leaned down and brought my face to just an inch from his.

I had to swallow down a gust of nervousness as I looked in his eyes, now hooded with desire, because his face was intense. I had meant to tease him. I had planned to whisper in his ear and then do something obnoxious, but his eyes stilled me. I felt the heat between our bodies, now ironed together, and thought about moving, about pushing off his chest and stepping back, but I couldn't convince myself to do it.

Being that close to Luke was like being caught in a rip current—it was all fun and games until you were caught, and then the only thing to do was swim sideways with all your might. But here I was, realizing I had forgotten how to swim and felt myself being pulled out into the depths.

He was determined not to move. He sat there, watching me intently, unnervingly. His hands hadn't moved from my hips, but as we stared, so close together, our breathing increasing even though nothing else in the world around us was moving, his hands slid up my sides, over my shoulders, and settled at the base of my neck. He pulled me the last inch to meet his lips, and then we were kissing like it was the end of the world—his hands in my hair, on my back, on the backs of my thighs, pulling me closer even though that was impossible.

Somewhere in my mind I heard a sound, an annoying one, and wished I had a flyswatter, or some way to make it stop. Then it registered—doorbell!—ringing to tell us the pizza was here, and we'd have to stop or starve. I pulled back from Luke, and he loosened his hold on me, but his eyes were searching mine for an answer.

"Doorbell," I said, blinking away the fog of desire and excitement and stepping away from him.

He stood up and grabbed his wallet, and he must have paid and thanked the pizza delivery guy, although I don't remember him doing that. I was staring out at my car, the rain still pounding, trying to slow my jackhammer heart.

"You ready to eat?" he asked, and my distracted staring ended as my stomach growled in response.

"Yes please." I piled pizza onto my plate and refilled my water. No more beer if I was driving home in this, or at all.

"Do you want to watch a movie while we eat?" he offered and took a place on the couch. I walked over to the living room, and before I could opt for the chair and gain a little space from him, he took my plate and set it down next to his on the coffee table in front of the couch. Ok, so we were going to sit together. Fine. Good.

"Sure." It wasn't like I was not excited to sit next to him, because I was. But being next to him apparently made me a little crazy.

As he fiddled with remotes, I saw him give me a glance or two.

"What?" I asked.

"Uh, well, I wanted to ask you something, actually," he

said, and I could tell he was nervous when he brushed his hands over his jeans.

"Ok. Ask me," I said.

"I have this thing..."

"Another ball?"

"No. It's a dinner, actually. It's not a formal event—no gown required. But it's for the battalion, and it's kind of turning into a big deal, I guess. It's called a Hail and Farewell, which is where they say goodbye to the soldiers leaving the unit and welcome to those who are arriving. It's a catered event at Lieutenant Colonel Wilson's house. Major Flint has told me like five times to bring a date so I didn't look like a 'sketchy single captain,' as though he isn't a sketchy single major." He raked his hands through his hair and then gripped his neck, and I noticed he was sitting up, his spine straight, even though his words seemed purposefully casual.

"Ok. Well for one, you're not a sketchy single captain— you're just a sketchy captain," I said and gave him a smile. He gave me just a ghost of a smile in return, and I knew whatever this was, it was important to him. "Of course I'll go."

As he pulled up the movie and chatted, I could tell my agreeing to be at this dinner with him was significant. I couldn't tell why, and he didn't say any more about it, but I was glad he asked and glad I had a chance to say yes.

"Alex," I heard a far-off voice say in my ear.

"Al."

There it was again. I took a deep breath and tried to roll over but I was trapped, and I couldn't move. My eyes sprang open and I sat up. The room was dark, but I could feel warmth—Luke all around me. There was a leg next to me, his chest must have been behind me, and his hands on my arms, pulling me back toward him where I was nestled before I jerked into consciousness.

"What time is it?" My voice was rough from sleep.

"It's two. We fell asleep watching the movie, I guess," he explained as he ran his hands up and down my arms and then gently through my hair. I swung my legs to the side of the couch and stood up.

"I'm sorry. I should definitely get going." I grabbed my long-forgotten plate with the discarded crusts and glass and walked to the kitchen. I moved as quickly as I could in the darkness lit only by the small clock display on the oven and muted light outside the shut living room blinds.

He scrambled up and after me and took the dishes, setting them on the counter. "No, you definitely shouldn't." He held on to my arms to keep me in place.

"No, I should go."

"No, you're not driving an hour back to Nashville at 2am. Not happening. Plus, it's still raining. That's insane." I heard his words, and they made sense, but I felt a mounting sense of panic.

"Well... I mean, I can't stay here," I announced, like that was the most obvious thing in the world. And it was, wasn't it? That would be... significant.

"Of course you can."

"Of course I can't."

"Why can't you stay here?" I heard the edge in his voice and saw his impatience in the bunch of his shoulders.

"It's just... I just... you're just..." I stuttered and struggled to find some sense, some explanation that could verbalize why the thought of staying at his apartment made me feel like the bottom had dropped out of the room under my feet.

"You are a grown woman. We are in a mature relationship. We live in the modern age. You can stay at my house overnight, and you can leave in the morning unscathed." He crossed his arms and was smirking at me like my nervousness about staying the night was some small thing. I felt a little annoyed with him. Ok, no, I felt a little embarrassed, and a lot a bit pissed.

"Don't patronize me. I know I'm a grown woman. I'm not worried about my reputation or some such nonsense. I'm a big girl and make my own decisions. What I am a little worried about is..." And suddenly, I felt foolish. In my newly awakened mind, I'd forgotten who Luke was. Perpetually looking after me, even to the point of making me insane at times.

"Don't stop talking. Finish your thought." He seemed genuinely concerned with what would come next.

"I just don't know what your expectations might be. I feel so dumb saying that, by the way, but there it is." I tried not to crumple up into a little ball and throw myself in the trash like a bad first draft. He still held my arms so I couldn't move anywhere.

He smiled at me, a painfully sweet, adoring smile, like I was a delightful little creature he'd found in a glen. I huffed an exasperated breath. "It's not like I'm going to jump you and steal your virtue in the night," he said, and I could hear the twinge of a laugh in his words.

"That's not what I—never mind. Fine. I won't drive back tonight." And then I felt it. My insides hit an ethereal boiling point and turned to a roiling mess of nervousness.

Luke must have sensed my anxiety, and he steadied me with his hand on my arm while he flipped on a light. "Al, chill. We're going to *sleep.*" He stopped there and leveled me with his most reassuring look, his flaming blue eyes pouring into mine. "We're going to go to bed, and we're going to sleep, and then in the morning we're going to go to breakfast and fill you up with pancakes and coffee before you drive back to Nashville."

~

Luke's bedroom. Not a place I'd ever been after the age of ten, but honestly, it was a place I may or may not have imagined myself being in a few (hundred) times over the years. It was strange walking in and seeing it. He had a dark wood queen-sized bed with a navy comforter and crisp white sheets. He had a night stand on one side—presumably his side—with a reading lamp set on it. The room was a decent size and had a large closet that took up one wall. He had a window covered in blinds, and a few large black and white nature photographs framed around the walls—ones I recognized as scenes from back home.

"This is a good-sized bedroom. Mine is a little smaller," I said and ran my hand along the comforter. It was soft.

As if it needed to be soft for me to want to be in there.

Right.

"I'm guessing everything is a little smaller in the city," he said conversationally, and he stepped in to the bedroom. He'd given me a toothbrush and a t-shirt and some shorts, so I was dressed in his clothes that smelled like his fabric softener, standing on the side of his bed in his room. And there he was, stepping out of his bathroom in basketball shorts and a loose t-shirt, his hair sticking up in all directions, his eyes tired but warm as they looked at me.

He let out a breath, then turned on the lamp, and threw back the covers on his side. "Don't be shy. We used to have sleepovers all the time." He smirked at me again, and I willed my heartbeat to slow. I was exhausted, but at that point it was hard to imagine actually sleeping.

"True, but we were four," I qualified as I pulled back the covers and slid between them. My leg brushed against his, and he turned and shut off the light. I lay there, eyes wide open, staring up at the ceiling, unseeing in the new darkness.

"That's true. It's a little different now." His voice was soft, but tired, and the sound of it made me relax.

"Goodnight Luke," I said quietly as I rolled on my side and enjoyed how incredibly comfortable his mattress was. *Way* better than mine. I'd have to ask him what kind he had and jot that down for future reference.

"Goodnight, Al." He was silent then, and the room was silent until I heard the rasp of his skin against the sheets and felt his hand grab mine. He laced our fingers together, and I felt myself relax even further, sinking into the sheets and mattress with full abandon.

I woke up before Luke and let myself lie in the bed that was warm with our shared body heat, let myself savor the sounds of his relaxed breathing, memorized the way he curled into himself on his side and how his dark eyelashes looked even longer than they usually did when his eyes were open. I left as quietly as I could and showered, then changed back into my own clothes. My chest felt tight, and I tried to ignore the feeling as I jerked on my pants and brushed my teeth.

He woke up looking handsome and sleepy and basically perfect, and I felt another jolt of frustrating pressure in my chest but swallowed it down and willed myself not to think about all the things grabbing for my attention. I had an hour-long car ride and the rest of the day to mull over things.

He took me to breakfast at a local diner and asked me to let him order something for me with a little twinkle in his eye.

He ordered sweet potato and pecan pancakes with maple butter and real maple syrup for me and eggs benedict for him, and then we split them evenly. How could he have known I liked something savory to balance out sweet things in the morning? Likely because he was discerning about food too. Everything tasted like heaven, and he was charming and adorable and just the right amount of affectionate, and I had to give myself a talking to in the bathroom so I wouldn't cry.

I was totally and completely undone by the last twenty-four hours, and each bite of those damned sweet potato pancakes drilled home what I knew I knew but didn't want to acknowledge. Couldn't yet. Not 'til I was alone.

When I came out of the bathroom feeling more than ready to leave, he gave me a serious look.

"What's wrong?" he asked, and I knew he could see I was flustered, or crazed, or whatever it was I was.

"Nothing. The food here is mind-blowing. I don't know how you're not here every weekend," I said, covering the intense inner turmoil I was experiencing with a too-wide smile.

He studied my face and squinted just slightly.

"I meant to ask you last night—what did you and Megan talk about yesterday?" He said it like he'd accidentally forgotten, but I could tell he'd been waiting based on how not-casual he sounded.

"She told me about the combatives stuff a little, about how good Harrison is, and introduced me to Captain Jackson. Man, she's beautiful," I said, swirling the cold coffee in my mug.

"She's a coworker."

"I didn't assume she was anything but. Just making the observation."

"You seemed pretty serious at one point with Megan."

"She was talking to me a little bit about... you know, about what it's like to be an Army wife, or whatever," I said and felt the linoleum floor shift under me. I studied my coffee.

"Oh really?" The tone of his voice made me look up at him, and I smothered a smile when I saw him working hard to seem nonchalant. His bouncing knee under the table and his death grip on his coffee mug gave him away.

"Yeah," I said, completely unwilling to play into his hand. I didn't know how I felt about the whole conversation, and this morning, stuffed full of perfect pancakes and the smell of his soap still on my skin, I couldn't say anything else.

"What about it?" His voice was higher-pitched than normal. I wasn't trying to be evasive, but it felt insane to talk about this with him before I'd sorted it out for myself.

"She said she loves being an Army wife. She said it's a sacrifice and that it asks a lot of anyone who is one, but that it's worth it." I took a sip of water and then waited for him to respond.

When I raised my eyes back to him, I saw what I could only describe as a pained look on his face. He nodded a few times and said, "It does ask a lot."

Before I could say anything or he could say anything more, the waitress brought his change, and we both stood with a mutual nod.

He kissed me sweetly, still tasting a little like maple and coffee, before sending me off back to Nashville with a hug and an admonition to watch for flooding on I-24.

I called Ellie the second I pulled out of his apartment complex and put her on speaker so I could drive.

"Ellie," I said it like a plea when she answered.

"I knew it."

CHAPTER EIGHTEEN

"I know. It's bad." I could hear the whine in my voice, but my heart was aching.

"Why is it bad? You love Luke. You've always loved Luke. This is great news!" Ellie couldn't hold back her excitement, and I could hear she was thrilled.

"I have always loved him, but I like... *love* love him. Completely. Totally. Kill me now and bury the body because I am not going to be able to keep this secret from him. He's going to know. I almost said it today at breakfast." I could hear the misery in my voice. I hadn't had time to think, but I needed someone to talk me down.

Also, no wonder I'd never fallen in love before. It was *the worst*. It felt heavy and so corporeal it hurt. It wasn't a light, ebullient thing. It hung on me like one of those lead aprons they make women wear before dental X-rays.

"How do you know he doesn't feel the same? I can almost guarantee he does, Alex." She sounded so sure, and I felt my whole body reach out and try to snatch the words from her and make them be true.

"I mean... maybe he does," I eked out. "Oh, pancake freaking pizza, what if he does? What then?"

"You sound like this is the end of the world, but it is fantastic. This is the fairytale everyone wants. This is a love story that ends with happiness and bunnies and rainbows and *babies*!" She yelled the last word and I felt myself wince. She was a hopeless romantic for me, but never herself. If I tried questioning her about her own love life, she'd shut it right down and accuse me of changing the subject.

Did I want a fairytale? Did I want bunnies and rainbows and babies? Well... yes, and yes, and sure, yes, I'd always planned to be a mom. But with Luke?

It echoed in me—*yes*.

But if I had that with Luke, what would I be, then? If I gave up everything like Megan said I'd need to, who would I be?

"I know that's the idea, but he's in the Army, Ellie." It was the giant, patriotic, moving, deploying elephant in the room.

"So?"

"So, he's going to move around and probably have to deploy, and... I don't know." I didn't let myself think about what a life with Luke, married to Luke, might be like. I hadn't had any time alone to process my conversation with Megan from the day before, but I knew her questions were ones I did need to seriously think about.

"Yes, that's all true."

"I was talking to Megan yesterday—she's one of the wives I met at the ball. She asked me what I wouldn't give up for Luke." I could hear her voice in my head, her earnest eyes as she explained the sacrifice, but also the reward, of being a military spouse.

"Well? What wouldn't you give up?" Ellie's saying those words made them sound different. Hers was a voice I heard, who'd known me for a decade, and I felt the question settle into my bones, down deep to the marrow. I expected to feel *un*settled, like I had when I realized that yes, I did love Luke. I wasn't broken and unable—or unwilling—to love. I just hadn't loved Marcus. We didn't fit.

"I don't know. Honestly if I had to tell you right now, I'd say... nothing." I swallowed down the madness I felt bubbling up inside me. I let out a wild sounding laugh.

"You don't have anything to say? Or, you wouldn't give up anything for him?" Ellie sounded perplexed and a little deflated.

"No. There's nothing I *wouldn't* give up for him. Ellie, he's amazing. He's honest and so kind and thoughtful and irritatingly humble and good *Lord* am I attracted to him. I mean, the babies part? Yeah, that'll come naturally. And he *knows* me. It's not just that we grew up together—though that obviously gives him a perspective on me someone who hasn't known me my whole life wouldn't have—it's that he takes time to ask me questions, and then he listens. He knows me, and I think I know him."

"Well there's your answer." Ellie's voice was firm, almost demanding. It was a declaration.

"But that's insane. We've only been dating for like two weeks, and during those two weeks, we haven't even *seen* each other except the last few days!" I shook my head and tried to stay focused on the road ahead.

"That's crap, and you know it. You've basically been dating since he first took you out when you were home in Utah months ago. And I know you haven't seen each other for years and years, but picking up a relationship that has as strong and historic a foundation as yours does—that understandably accelerates things."

"I get that, and part of me agrees with that. But do you

hear me? 'I'd give up everything for him?' Who is that? I wouldn't stay in Boston for Marcus. I wouldn't give up my job for someone I was *engaged* to. And now I'm talking about giving up any plans I have for my own career or future for Luke and life as an Army wife?" Even as I said it, I knew it wasn't as ridiculous as I was trying to make it sound. I had been increasingly discontent with my career being my whole life for the last few years. But could I just abandon it, essentially run away from everything I'd worked for since high school?

"You know you and Marcus weren't right. We're done talking about him, so stop referencing that like it has any bearing on this situation. Luke is different, you are different with him, and you clearly feel things for him you didn't ever feel for Marcus." Ellie's voice was still firm, but I heard her compassion and love for me too, and my heart warmed. My pulse slowed, and I remembered what an ally I had in her.

"I know. I think I've made peace with the Marcus thing. Realizing that *everything* with Luke is better and more intense and exciting and terrifying has made me realize what a shell of a relationship that was with Marcus."

"Good. And as for you giving up your career—you kind of already did that, didn't you?" Her voice was soft now, but I felt a stab of guilt for some reason.

"Because I left New York? It's not like I don't have a career. I might have moved laterally in terms of paycheck, but I moved up in responsibility, title—it's exactly what I wanted." The words sounded weak in my ears, but they were true. I'd wanted a change. I'd wanted to step away from the madness, the pace, the competition, the financial focus of my old job.

"I don't think it was just a job change you were looking for, and I think you know that. I know you love the job, but is that enough? If Luke walks out of your life tomorrow, is your job going to be enough?" Her gentleness broke my determination not to cry, but I kept it together so my eyes didn't blur.

"It's not an easy answer. I can't just say I'm willing to give up my career for a man who, yes, I've known my whole life, but as a *man*, I've only known a few months. And I think the stupid, crazy, infuriating thing is that I probably found what I've been looking for. I've always measured people against him, even though he was never really mine. And now I want him, and even in some strange way to share his life, so much I can hardly breathe." I took a deep breath because even explaining my feelings to my best friend was utterly terrifying. "But it's scary, Ellie, and I don't know how he feels. As much as I know he likes me, he is seriously committed to the Army. He may not think I'm right for him or for the life he knows about much better than I do."

"The only way you're going to figure that out is to talk to him."

Ellie was right, of course. I had to talk to Luke which probably meant I was going to totally and completely humiliate myself by saying I loved him, and he'd pat me on the head and tell me he had always loved me too, as a friend, or as a girlfriend-for-now, but that he had to go do tough Army stuff.

Ok fine, that didn't sound like Luke, but thinking about laying bare my feelings for him, both old and newly realized, felt completely paralyzing. Especially after the night we spent together that held a deep intimacy even if it wasn't a physical one in the usual sense.

But the other issue was the inescapable fear I was getting caught up in a fairytale and losing sight of my goals. By that evening, even though I still felt a steady drip of the love potion swirling in my theoretical IV, it was tempered with reality.

I was an independent woman. I always had been. Deciding that because I loved Luke, I was ready to dive head first into a new life just wasn't me. I needed to calm down, and take some space, and get into the work week and remember who I was.

Late that night, he texted me.

Luke: *How has your Sunday been?*
Me: *Good. Ready for the week.*
Luke: *Good. Me too. I'm glad you stayed last night.*

Hmm. How to respond? How could I tell him I loved sleeping in his bed and feeling that ownership, that proximity, and yet not betray both my love for him and my fear about what was rapidly feeling like a doomed relationship? I couldn't.

Me: *Those pancakes today were amazing. Thanks again for breakfast.*

Yep, focus on the food. Keep it light.

Luke: *I guess I probably won't see you until the thing on Friday. Can you get here by 5?*
Me: *Yep. I'll meet you at your place?*
Luke: *Sounds good. Night.*

And then he didn't say anything else, and neither did I. Not that I slept hardly at all, but eventually the night surrendered and the day won out, and I was finally sitting at my desk.

I grounded myself, gripping the metal supports that held up the arm rests of my desk chair. My morning was full of back to back meetings which was the perfect way to launch me into the week. It put my feet back on the ground.

Sitting behind my desk, I thought about how much I was looking forward to some of the upcoming projects. I thought about how busy November and December were going to be. I checked my email again and saw a note from Brenda Schwartz, my old boss.

My eyes skimmed through the message. Words like *irreplaceable* and *incentivize* and *promotion* jumped out, but ultimately, I couldn't slow my mind enough to read it closely. She was offering my job back, but with a pay raise and a team— essentially giving me the job I'd worked for and had to move to Nashville to get. What she wasn't offering was a life outside my job. When I was gunning for the promotion, working endless hours, I saw that the team leaders worked just as much, and if wanting to explore my life in Nashville more thoroughly and avoid another cross-country move wasn't enough to keep me from wanting that job, I knew I didn't want that work schedule. I made a note on one of my stickie pads to write her back when I wasn't so distracted so I could be appropriately gracious.

I made a short list on a post it of other emails I needed to write, knowing I would likely lose track of the list, but it helped me download some of the swirling thoughts in my mind. I stared at my desk, my mind taking a short vacation from the moment, and then I saw it.

There on my desktop calendar, a note I hadn't transcribed into my digital calendar, I saw my handwriting: *Janie's Campo Gala.*

Craaaap.

Weeks ago, I'd promised Janie I'd help her out with one of her bigger events of the year. It was a gala for a local outdoors company. This company was awesome, and they did a huge third quarter event to bolster the spirits of their local employees since they all worked such long hours through the end of the year holidays. She'd caught me on a conference call and begged me because she was completely stressed about it, and I of course said yes. I was even looking forward to it.

But I had broken my rule. I didn't put it on my digital calendar, which essentially meant it wasn't in my brain. Or at least, it wasn't in my brain *on the right day*.

I had the event tagged as an all-day event on Saturday. We'd be at the convention center for most of the day and then the gala started at five for cocktails.

The problem was, it was actually on Friday. And so was Luke's dinner.

Now this conflict... I mean, it was small. First, I'd confirm with Janie that it really was on Friday—maybe that little note was wrong, though I had the sinking sensation it wasn't. I just kind of *knew* it wasn't going to be that easy.

And if it was Friday? Couldn't I help her during the day, and then head to Luke's dinner?

Of course, I could. But the problem was, the most intense hours of the set up would be those hours right before the event thanks to some of Campo's planning. That meant that if I left at three, the latest I could leave and still get to Luke's on time, I'd essentially miss the biggest part of the afternoon *plus* the actual event.

Not ideal.

But... could I even consider missing Luke's dinner? He was unusually nervous to ask me about it. It seemed like he was feeling pressured to bring a date—maybe he wouldn't normally if that Major Flint hadn't ribbed him about it?

So... maybe it wasn't a big deal?

I started to feel a little wave of guilt splash at the shores of my conscience when I shook my head. No. No! This was exactly what I was worried about. Yes, I'd made a mistake when I told Luke I could go in the first place, but in the end, I had to prioritize my job, didn't I? Helping Janie on this project was not only a show of good faith as a team member of the company but also an important opportunity for me to meet some of the vendors I hadn't met or used yet.

I knew in my gut I couldn't miss it. If I did, it'd be a clear sign I wasn't a team player. In events, that just wasn't possible —you had to have a team, and you had to be willing to help. It was the only way things succeeded, and that was all the more true at a smaller company. That was, yet again, one of the perks of being at a smaller company—a closer-knit staff that worked well together. Was I willing to jeopardize that and come off looking self-serving or even like I didn't value my own career?

Was Luke's job more important than mine?

Hell no.

And it wasn't like he was asking me to say it was—he had no idea there was even a conflict. But now that there was, it was building in my chest. I felt the weight, the heaviness. I knew if I told him I couldn't go, he'd be disappointed. But maybe he'd understand. After all, if I had told him no from the start it wouldn't even be a question—I just wouldn't be going.

That night when Luke called to check in, I missed the call.

On purpose.

I texted back some excuse about the day being long, hoping he was doing ok, blah blah blah. Basically meaningless stuff, the kind of nonsense that, if he wasn't as perceptive as he was, might have flown. But I knew he knew something was wrong. He was just kind enough, or maybe patient enough, not to call me out on it.

~

By Wednesday, I hadn't figured out a plan. I was a confusing mix of sad to miss Luke's dinner and angry at him for ever asking me—I knew it didn't make sense. *Non ho senso, io so.*

I woke up that morning feeling like I needed to tell Luke, sooner than later, that I couldn't go with him. The dinner was two days away, and it seemed cruel to wait any longer. It was already bad enough that I'd waited two days at this point.

But wait I did. I waited until I got home, into my sweatpants, post-dinner, Lemon on my lap. Then I called him.

"Hey, I'm glad you called," he said, his voice light.

My heart squeezed in my chest, tightening at the sound of his words.

"Hey, yeah, sorry it's been such a crazy week."

"Everything going ok?" The weight of guilt settled heavier on my shoulders when I heard the concern in his voice.

Oh, God, but I loved this man. Why was I about to tell him I couldn't be at his event?

"Yeah, it's fine. I'm so sorry about this, but I got some dates mixed up, and I realized I'm supposed to be helping Janie with an event on Friday." I hoped he could hear the regret in my voice.

"Oh," he said. And then nothing more.

The silence hung there, and my mind rifled through things to say.

"Yeah, I know the timing sucks, but I'm the newest

employee there. I can't have them thinking I'm not prioritizing my job after they just hired me, you know?"

"It's Janie's event though, not yours? Could you cut out a little early and still come?"

"I wish I felt like I could..." I did wish that. I did. And I didn't know what else to say to him.

"No, I don't want you to feel bad. You've got to... you know, do your thing." He sounded deflated but was trying to be supportive, and I felt sick.

"I'm sorry. I am. And if I *can* get away, I absolutely will. I want to be there for you," I said.

"Well don't do anything you're not comfortable with, ok? The dinners are paid for, and I've RSVP'd for both of us to be there, so if you can come, there'll be food. If not, it's just the way it goes sometimes."

He was so calm and reasonable, and I felt another injection of guilt that I was even thinking of not being there for him.

"I'm so, so sorry," I said again.

"Listen, don't worry about it. This is... this is probably better anyway. I have to actually jump off, but I'll talk to you soon, ok? Can you just let me know for sure Friday?" His voice was different now, his words clipped, and I felt a flare of alarm go up.

"Oh. Ok, yeah. Yes, I'll let you know. Talk to you soon," I said, trying not to let my voice betray my hurt or surprise.

I stared at the phone for a minute, then set it down. I couldn't tell what I was feeling other than surprised. Was he mad at me? Did he really have to go? He said he knew I had to "do my thing," right? He seemed understanding, but also upset. *Ugh.*

By Friday morning, I couldn't breathe. Sure, my lungs

were exchanging CO_2 for O_2, but other than that, it wasn't happening.

Before you tell me that doesn't make sense, just go with it. You know the feeling. It's like there's a shuddering, hacking feeling with each breath, like there's a labored pressure in your lungs. In my lungs.

I hadn't heard from Luke since the call. That was the longest we'd ever gone without at least texting, even on a busy week, since we'd been together. Well, I texted, but he didn't respond. I'd sent him a "hey how was your day" the night before and got no response. It was a major sign something was wrong.

Worse yet, I was starting to feel pretty clearly like I'd made the wrong choice even telling him I might not be there. All day I'd felt the ticking of the clock pushing against my ribs, drilling into my mind that I was one second, then one minute, then one hour closer to when I *should* be leaving to go meet Luke.

I'd been glad-handing Campo execs and team leaders all morning and making contacts with the vendors Janie had set up, when I just couldn't take my own spiraling thoughts anymore. I needed a voice of reason.

I needed Ellie.

"Ok, I know I'm calling you during your office hours, but you know I wouldn't call if it wasn't—"

"What's going on? *Dimmi!*" Her voice was urgent.

I told her about the dinner for Luke. I told her about the event that day. I told her I'd said I couldn't go, and then that I'd try to make it but wasn't sure, and that I was feeling horribly guilty about it.

"You know why you're feeling guilty? This is easy. You love Luke. You want to be there for him. You don't feel good about not being there for him. Done." She was in professor mode, and there was no stopping her.

"Ok, obviously, yes. But I can't just neglect my job." I felt angry. Angry with Luke. Angry with Ellie. Angry with myself. Angry that some idiot had put a bunch of fake indoor potted plants around the podium at the front of the ballroom.

"Nonsense. You're not *neglecting your job* if you choose to go to his dinner."

"Yes, that's exactly what it is. That's saying 'ok, I have this commitment I made long before Luke asked me to this thing, whatever it is, but since I'm in love with him, I'll just toss the baby out with the bathwater and do whatever he asks me.'"

"Mmmkay, first, I don't think you're using that saying appropriately. Second, that's just crazy talk. It's ok to make changes in your life and accommodate someone else's plans into your own. That's a thing people do when they love someone." Her voice was a little exasperated with me, but she was being patient. I could tell she was working on staying calm in the face of what she thought was my irrationality.

"I know that. Don't think I don't—I do know that. But this feels like one of those small examples of what it would be like if we were... you know, married, or whatever. Like, if I start ditching my own career *now*, what hope do I have of ever maintaining my own identity? How do I move forward feeling good about the fact that I've crapped on every goal I've ever had because Luke Waterford decided to hold my hand?" I was pacing back and forth on the sidewalk outside the convention center, gesticulating wildly, my adrenaline racing through me so hard I shook. I absolutely looked like a crazy person.

"Ok. Ok... I have to just—ok. I'm going to say something to you, and I need you to *really* listen to me. Can you do that?" Uh oh. I knew this voice. This was hammer-dropping, take no prisoners Dr. Kent. This was truth time.

I swallowed hard.

"Yes. I can."

"I'm calling bullshit on all of this black and white... bullshit, ok? None of this is easy or clear, but there are no black and white, fully right or fully wrong versions of this story. You choosing to show up for Luke is not you ditching your career. I don't know if you choosing to marry Luke, should the occasion arise, would mean that you were sacrificing your career, but you know what? No one's life goes exactly how they planned when they were eighteen years old."

"I know that—"

"I'm not done. You keep talking about being with Luke like it means not having a career. I'm guessing that if you were to marry him, it would be a very different thing. I don't know—I hadn't thought about the ramifications of what military moves might mean for you in the long term in regard to this *one part* of your life. But I do know that man is someone you love and have *always* loved. And if he is as special as you say he is, then you need to get your head out of your sweet Italian ass and talk to him about it. You need to figure out what life might look like, and *then* start making decisions. Don't decide that your relationship is doomed just because you have this *idea* of what your life might look like, especially when I suspect it won't be as awful as you think it might be."

I could feel her let out a deep breath, and then she started again. "And just one more thing, and then I'm done. You have to stop talking about your job like it's who you are. I definitely understand the very real tendency to equate what we do with who we are. I do it too. You've watched me do it, especially the last year or so. But you are much more than your job as an event manager. Your value extends beyond the bids you win and the events you produce. I think if you let yourself off the hook on that one, it might help you feel more free to make changes in that area."

The little timer on my iPhone call timer ticked away. I couldn't respond, my emotions paralyzing my vocal chords. More than anything, she'd made me feel hopeful.

"Alex?"

"I'm here, I just... you're right. You are. It's not black and white, and I'm getting way too far ahead of myself. I feel horrible for not going, and I feel like... like I've messed up everything, and ugh, Janie is going to be so pissed, but I feel like I need to be there for him."

"That's not a surprise to me. Last weekend you told me you thought you'd give up just about anything to be with Luke. I don't know what happened between then and now, but I think in *both* cases, you have... you know, just *maybe*..."

"I know, I know—"

"You *might* have jumped the gun."

"I know! Ok? I need to talk to him. He doesn't know how I feel, and now that I do, I'm getting too in my head about it. I'm overanalyzing and getting freaky, and I know it. Thank you for talking sense into me," I said.

"That's why I'm here. But hey, crap, I gotta go—student's coming in to talk about why his paper is alarmingly similar to his friend's paper who is in another section of my class." I could hear the edge of irritation in her voice.

"Ugh, cheaters. Good luck, my friend."

I hung up and took a big breath. I knew what I had to do.

CHAPTER NINETEEN

"Will you think I'm crazy if I ask you if I can still come tonight?" I was pacing the sidewalk outside the convention center, still amped up on adrenaline in the wake of my call to Ellie and my subsequent realization I needed to show up for Luke.

"Uh, no. But I thought you had Janie's event?"

"I did. I do, really. But I feel terrible, and I—"

"Don't worry about it, Alex."

His voice was friendly enough, casual even, but it stopped me in my tracks.

You know how people rarely say each other's names? Like, they just don't. We just talk to each other, and when I'm directing my voice at a person, they know I'm talking to them. When I talk on the phone, I rarely say the person's name. And it seems like the more affectionate or close you are with a person, the less you say their name?

Luke's saying *Alex* to me felt like a punch to the gut. A straight up upper cut just below my rib cage.

"Really? I feel terrible for getting my schedule messed up..." I trailed off.

"Really. Please don't worry about it. Just take care of your event, and I'll talk to you later this weekend, ok?"

"Luke, I want to be there for you. I can make it there, no problem."

He was quiet on the other end, and I registered the fact that I had not anticipated his hesitation. I'd expected him to be overjoyed at my sudden availability.

Arrogant, much?

"If you can be here, then I want you here." His voice was low and somehow resigned, but I felt it pour over me like simple syrup.

"Ok. Good. I want to be there. I'll see you this afternoon at your place around five."

After I hung up with Luke, it was time to deal with Janie, who I knew was going to be frustrated, but I'd made my choice. I stalked back into the convention center, a woman on a mission, and tracked her down.

"I'm going to have to head out before things get going tonight." I watched Janie typing away frantically at her phone, but when she heard me, her head jerked up. Her black, curly hair was in a tight bun at the nape of her neck, but little curls escaped in all directions giving her a harried halo effect.

"Hilarious," she said in a dead-pan voice and then dove back into typing like her life depended on it.

"I'm going to have to leave by three. I'm so sorry, but I got my schedule mixed up, and I have to be at an event about an hour away this evening." I smoothed down my black dress and met her eyes again.

"For B&W?"

"No, something personal." I clasped my hands in front of me to steady them. I didn't want her to see that I was upset or frazzled.

She stood there for a beat, no expression on her face.

"Well, ok then. I guess you'll leave when you need to." Then she turned back to her phone again, and I practically ran to the other side of the ballroom to start knocking out my to do list before I had to leave. I could make it work—I could do it all—but it'd be close.

I was driving home. It was 4:30 when I left the convention center. Janie was actually a little more pissed than I'd expected based on her subtle shaking head as I told her goodbye and her refusal to respond in any way but that, and while that made my gut roil in discomfort and frustration, I knew leaving was the right choice, even if it was late in the game. I sprinted out the door. I was going to be late, but I would make it.

Once I was home, I messaged Luke.

Me: *Running late but I will be there. ETA 6ish. Still meet you at your place?*
Luke: *Meet me at Gate 3 at Fort Campbell where I signed you in for the tournament. I'll have to sign you in. Dinner is on post and I'll need to be there at 5:30.*
Me: *Will text you from the gate.*

Had there not been traffic, I would have arrived at 6:15. I'd made it home by five, changed into heels, refreshed my deodorant and makeup, checked that my hair was still in a smooth ponytail, and jumped back in the car. I'd decided I didn't have time to fool with changing clothes, so I stayed in my fitted black work dress—it was nothing special, but it looked professional and paired with flats wasn't a bad option for walking miles around a convention center. With heels, it looked a little nicer, if still more on the business end. But I was coming from work, after all, and since I had no idea what I should be wearing anyway, I went with it. It cut out the time I would have spent deciding and changing, and I needed every minute I could get.

The problem was, there was traffic. There was an accident at an exit ramp on I-24 north that stopped traffic completely for a full twenty-five minutes. Literally, it stopped. People got out of their cars, popped sodas, sat on their hoods or dangled feet from their truck beds. Then, when things got moving again, it took another ten minutes to get up to freeway speed.

I messaged Luke from the visitor's center outside of Gate 3 at 7:02. I was so late. I was embarrassed and nervous and so frustrated I couldn't even think straight. Ten minutes later, he walked through the door looking hassled and serious and effortlessly appealing in dark gray chinos and a white button-up shirt.

"I'm so sorry. The traffic was crazy, and I—"

"It's fine. Let's get you signed in." He ushered me to the window after a thin man behind the Plexiglas waved us forward. Luke signed me in, led me to his truck, and opened the door for me. I climbed in and exhaled slowly, focusing my mind on calming down and not freaking out.

I knew it was totally reasonable for him to be frustrated. I was frustrated too. I completely understood. But that didn't stop the disappointment from flooding in. He hadn't kissed me on the cheek or even smiled when he saw me. He hadn't said but one thing directly to me, and now we were going to go socialize with his coworkers and act like we were hunky dory. *Perfect.*

"I'm so sorry I'm late. I hate that I hit traffic, and I feel like I messed everything up." I glanced at him to check his face and was relieved to see it, at least, wasn't angry.

"I know you couldn't control traffic. It happens." He stretched his neck to one side and adjusted his hands on the steering wheel.

I ignored the flare of alarm that shot up in my mind. He was saying the right things, and I think he wanted to believe them. But I wasn't convinced. I didn't want to pick a fight about that, so I kept talking to cover my wariness.

"So, did I miss everything?"

"They've done most of the formal portion, yeah." He was still speaking to the road in front of him, not to me.

"I'm sorry."

"They've already served dinner, but I saved your plate. We'll hang out for another half hour and then we can leave." He pulled onto a street lined with cars, and I didn't say anything again. He parked and hopped out of the truck and walked around to my door. I unbuckled and when he opened my door I turned to face him, grabbed his hand, and pulled him toward me so he was standing right next to the seat. I put my hands on his cheeks and one of his eyebrows popped up in question.

"I'm sorry I was late. I'm sorry if I embarrassed you by being late." My eyes shifted back and forth between his, and in them I could see a flash of something—confusion? Frustration?—before the look cleared and he gave me a nod. I kissed him lightly on the lips, still holding his smooth cheeks, and then pulled back. He took my hand and led me inside.

"Good to see you made it!" I heard a familiar voice say. I

turned to see Megan smiling at me and felt a wave of relief I actually knew someone else there besides Luke.

"Barely, but yes." I smiled back at her as she approached me with her arms open for a hug. She leaned in and squeezed me, her floral perfume light and pleasing.

"I thought your man might discombobulate just sitting there. I think he checked his watch every three minutes," she said with a hand to the side of her mouth like it was a secret. I felt a pang of guilt for making him anxious, especially so anxious someone noticed.

"I feel like such a jerk."

"Honey, don't feel like a jerk because of traffic. Nonsense. Get over it. Move on. Be here now." She waved her hand in my face and then all around, typically matter-of-fact.

"Ok. Yes, ma'am," I said and mustered a smile. She winked at me and gestured to a round table with six chairs. There was a lone plate wrapped in tinfoil at one seat—likely my dinner. Luke found me before I had a chance to wander awkwardly and sit down without him.

"Waterford, this your date?" a gruff voice behind me barked.

"Yes, sir. This is Alex Moore," Luke responded, pivoting me to the right where the infamous Major Flint stood. I extended my hand to him.

"Pleased to meet you," I said and watched as his face responded with a blank, bored stare.

Ok, then.

We stood there a moment longer, Luke's energy near me clearly on edge, his fingers pressed against my shoulder blade, his face once again serious. Flint just stood there, eyes flitting back and forth between us with alarming apathy.

"Yep," Flint said and then turned on his heel and walked in the other direction.

Luke and I stood there a moment, and I found I had absolutely no idea what just happened.

"Is he always like that?" I asked.

"Part awkward, part rude? Yeah, pretty much. Unless he's just being a dick, but that only happens if you're a soldier," he said, his voice quiet but clearly annoyed.

I heard a muffled laugh and looked up to see Captain Rae Jackson watching us. She smiled at Luke and raised her eyebrows.

"What?" he asked her as he shuttled me closer to Rae.

"Nothing. Just a little ballsy to be handing out accolades so openly," she said and nodded toward the living room where Colonel and Mrs. Wilson were now standing with Flint.

"I'm sure his ego will survive, should he hear me," Luke grumbled.

"Good to see you again, Rae," I said, smiling back at her. I tried not to let myself feel the raging, choking jealousy I felt smoking in my gut when I looked at her in her black pants and button-up white top. She was nice and she was pretty and she was clearly friendly with Luke. She wasn't wearing provocative clothing or flirting or anything, but it was hard to imagine how Luke could work with her and not think of her as something else. How any of them could. For that matter, maybe they *had* dated, and I had no idea.

"Likewise. Luke said you were helping out a colleague tonight. I'm so glad you could make it after all. Lieutenant Colonel Wilson said some nice things about him that I'm sure Luke won't share with you." Her voice was kind, and she was smiling at me, but I felt her words settle in my belly like gravel. I'd missed his boss talking about him?

"Thanks. Me too."

She turned her attention back to Luke. "Congrats on the nomination. You deserve it."

"Thanks. You too." He smiled warmly at her, and my stomach sunk.

"Nomination?" I asked, trying to make sense of both their conversation and the sinking sensation I couldn't escape.

"We were both nominated for the MacArthur award. They announced that tonight. We won't find out if we actually get it for a while because a board convenes to review the submissions and it's quite a process." Luke said this looking everywhere but at me.

"What he's not saying is it's a pretty big deal. Most people are never nominated, and, at the risk of sounding incredibly arrogant, only really excellent officers get nominated," Rae explained.

"Wow. Yeah. Congratulations to you both."

Rae left us to mingle and we made the rounds after that, spoke to the Wilsons and a few other familiar faces including Ally and Jose. I ate the salad that came with my meal, but that was it. I had no appetite. I couldn't touch the now-cold entrée, which made me feel worse.

By the time we were in the car on the way back to Gate 3, I was more miserable than I'd been that morning before I'd decided to come. I felt my own indecision wrap around me like a rope, tying my hands and keeping me from enjoying any given moment, so wrapped up in my lateness as I was.

"Captain Jackson's nice, I like her." I immediately regretted letting the words slip out. I'd promised myself I would not bring her up.

"Yep. She's a good officer."

"Are you guys... friends?" Oh, kill me now, why was I digging at this?

"Sure. As much as anyone in the battalion I guess. We were in command at the same time in Afghanistan last year. She's moved to a different battalion now but was here for the farewell, and the news of the nomination." He seemed unaffected by my questioning, but I saw his eyes slide toward me and narrow a bit, trying to read my intention.

And what was my intention? What was I after? To hear him say she was pretty? To hear him say they'd dated when I was fairly certain they hadn't? Who was this version of me, picking at him and being jealous and suspicious? *Ugh*.

I closed my eyes and took a deep breath.

I could do this.

I could clear my mind of all that nonsense and get this back on track.

I was trying to shake off my mood, trying to feel like I could rally and enjoy the rest of the evening. I needed to properly congratulate him about his award and hear more about it. I'd missed a big moment for him, and that had to be part of his frustration. Maybe we'd go back to Luke's and watch a movie, or maybe we could talk it out and get over this hump of awkwardness.

"I'm probably going to call it an early night. I'm sure you're exhausted too..." he said from his seat and a thousand miles away.

"Sure, yeah, of course. I am. I should head back sooner than later." It was 8:15 on a Friday night. I hadn't seen him in five days, had barely talked to him, and this was going to be it for the night. My hopes plummeted.

"Thanks for coming tonight," he said, and even though it might not have been, what I heard felt forced.

"Of course." I didn't want to apologize again for being late. In the end, my lateness was frustrating, but for me, it wasn't what had me feeling so terrible. Maybe it was the same for him.

He came around and gave me a quick hug, a quick peck on the lips, and opened my car's door for me. He waited to back out of his parking spot until I'd backed out of mine and drove off in the opposite direction of his house, toward Nashville.

∾

When I got home, I sent up the "home safe text" to let Luke know I was back. He responded "good," and then said nothing else. And neither did I.

I wasn't sure what I expected, but it was radio silence after that from both of us.

Instead of waiting by the phone, hoping he'd suddenly call and say he was over being frustrated, or disappointed, or whatever he was, and that he wanted me to forget the mess of the day and the week and that he'd be right over to kiss and make up, I took a long shower during which I cried my guts out to the point of dry-heaving. I felt like a total idiot, like I'd screwed up every good thing in my life. Sure, I thought Janie would recover, but I'd flaked out on her. I couldn't go back and change things, so I had to just deal with it. Really, she was the least of my worries.

And Luke? I knew he was upset. He was interacting like he was fine on the surface, and I didn't even think he was trying to make me feel bad, but oh ratatouille on a stick, did I. I'd gone from the high of realizing I *wanted* to show up for him, and that I felt it was worth it to give a little in terms of my own schedule and life, to the low of the reality where I was late, it was awkward, and I ultimately wished I hadn't gone anyway.

Add to that my weird interaction with his boss, my uncharacteristic and raging jealousy of a woman who was always nice and seemed to have no link to Luke beyond being in the same unit, and I hardly knew myself.

A good cleansing cry was inevitable.

By Saturday afternoon, I felt physically ill. There I was in love with the guy, and I'd failed him. I knew it. I was too wrapped up in my own junk to see that at first, but I had. And if I hadn't been so confused by my love for him and the ensuing irrational fear of losing myself in that love, or whatever it was I was thinking, I might have been able to help him understand me better. I might have been able to just *talk to him* and that might have fixed everything before it was broken. I would have figured out that I wanted to go, or he would have been able to reassure me that it was just fine and I wouldn't have felt so mixed up about staying.

Saturday evening, I sent him a text. I was restless, and I could feel that my level of upset was growing and would soon balloon so far out of control that nothing would be able to stop it. I raised a little white flag to see if he'd come out and play.

Me: *How has your day been?*

I checked my phone over and over and didn't hear back for another eighteen hours.

Eighteen. Hours.

Torture.

Luke: *Sorry, went camping at Land Between the Lakes.*
Me: *Oh, nice. Did you go with friends? How was it?*
Luke: *By myself. Helped me clear my head.*
Me: *Ok. Do you want to talk?*
Luke: *Probably not tonight, ok?*

That text felt like the kiss of death.

Me: *Ok. Looking forward to the movie next weekend, if that still works for you.*

He didn't respond. I cried for most of the rest of the night.

On Monday morning, I sat ram-rod straight in my office chair, my left knee bouncing, my nerves a pit of snakes in my belly. I had a meeting with my boss in an hour, and it was scheduled that morning—this didn't bode well. All I could think was that Janie really was *that* pissed.

I knew she was upset but... I had the sense this meeting wasn't one where I was going to be winning an award.

So there I was, feeling like my heart was ripped open by my own stupidity and feeling woefully underprepared for a meeting with my boss for some unknown reason.

Ok. Not entirely unknown.

When the time came, I padded down the hall in my black flats and straightened my suit jacket. I said a silent prayer of thanks that I actually looked decently professional despite my end-of-the-world crying jag late last night that left me feeling raw and exhausted.

"Alex, have a seat." Mr. Burney gestured to the comfortable chair across from his desk. I sat down and waited with a pleasant smile on my face.

"I'll get to it. I need to know you're here—you're in this," he said as he squinted at me and nodded his head like he was willing me to confirm that I was. He pinched one side of his glasses—a gesture I'd seen him make when he was irritated or stressed.

"I am, Mr. Burney. I absolutely am," I said, feeling the knot in my gut double in size. I folded my fingers in my lap, preventing me from emphasizing my words with my shaking hands.

"Your performance so far is as expected, if not better.

You've delivered on everything we've asked." I felt a fleeting sense of relief before I realized his serious face hadn't changed. He reached to finger his glasses again, and my stomach sank.

"Can I ask where your concern is coming from?" I kept my voice steady, low, calm.

"I know you left the Campo event on Friday..."

"That was—I had a conflict, and it's not something I anticipate being an issue again," I explained.

"It's not something we can afford, Alex. We've brought you here, and we want you to be a part of the team."

If possible, I sank deeper into my seat. I might have sunk into the floor if the chair I was sitting in wasn't reinforced steel or some other immoveable force beneath me.

"I understand. I want that too," I said, willing my voice to remain clear and not cloud with the flood of humiliation and shame I was feeling.

This was what it must have felt like to be sent to the principal's office, a thing that had never happened to me except when she wanted to ask me to convince the student body to do something or notify me of an award I was receiving.

"I'm glad." Mr. Burney's voice cut through my self-condemnation. "And I want you to have a life. I know you left New York because you felt like you had none. I'm not saying that—I'm not saying *don't have a life*. I'm saying, if you say you're going to be there, then be there."

"Absolutely," I said, and I felt my cheeks brighten with my embarrassment. "It wasn't my intention to leave. I didn't handle the situation well, and for that I'm sorry." I felt my nails digging into my palm.

"I know it won't happen again. When I heard you left, I remembered we never had our first quarter performance review, and I wanted to give you some feedback. You're doing well, and everything you're bringing to the table is good. I'm checking in to see how *you're* doing. I know leaving New York was a big change." He raised his eyebrows and waited.

"It was that, yes. But, I'm happy here. Really, I am, and I appreciate you speaking with me. This shouldn't be an issue again." I gave him a wide-eyed look that probably looked more like exhausted raccoon than convincingly earnest employee, but it happened.

"I'm sure it won't be," he said and stood. He extended a hand and I shook it, and then I all but ran back to my office and planned to hide out until it was reasonable for me to leave.

I shut my door and leaned against it. I breathed through my nose and gritted my teeth against the tears I could feel pricking in my eyes.

I was humiliated. I was embarrassed by my flaking on Janie, by my inability to figure out what mattered most to me until the last minute, and by my boss's need to talk to me, even if it was couched in mostly positive feedback. I'd never had anything close to a reprimand before. I was a goodie-two-shoes and I was happy with that. This was a prime example of why I spent my life overachieving. I'd much rather get accolades than reprimands.

Duh, who wouldn't? But still.

I didn't regret leaving in terms of my attempt to go support Luke. What was clear now was that I'd bungled everything beyond repair. If I had simply talked to Janie beforehand, maybe found a replacement... Who knew when Janie would ask me for anything again, and I was sure I could check her off the list of supporting staff for future events for me.

The fact that it took so long for me to figure out I should be with Luke, that sacrificing a little something, something I *could* give on, was the right choice... that was embarrassing. And it was disappointing. That showed me my failing in terms of being a generous part of the relationship, which I desperately wanted.

How could I have messed everything up so deftly in the matter of a week?

That night I sat on the couch and stared unseeing at the TV while Lemon purred over my shoulders. He seemed to sense I needed his heavy, fury warmth to comfort me.

By Friday that week, I was running on fumes. I might have stalled out because I couldn't get anything done at work. I'd cried more tears in those seven days than I'd probably cried cumulatively in my entire life.

That might sound dramatic, but it was true. I hated feeling so clueless, so unmoored, so unsure. I hated feeling so completely in love with Luke and yet knowing I'd hurt him and messed everything up between us. I felt humiliated by my questioning him about Rae Jackson and the jealousy I felt despite my total faith in Luke (and for that matter, my overarching positive view of Rae, which only made things worse). I felt angry with myself for missing the announcement of his nomination for the award, which I'd since looked up and discovered was, in fact, a very big deal. I felt angry with him for not understanding my showing up late even though I knew I'd done something wrong. I felt furious that he wouldn't just *talk* to me. I felt embarrassed by my fumbling of the Campo event, and my ego was a long way from recovering from the meeting with Mr. Burney.

I felt stripped bare and I didn't know what to do. I was longing to be with Luke—I knew if I could talk with him, I could explain myself, and he would understand where I was coming from. Maybe we could talk about what life would be like, and he could help me understand what my life would be like if we stayed together. If he wanted to stay together.

He had always been a good listener, and he had always been reasonable. Maybe it was that ability to see black and white so clearly. His freezing me out, his minimal, one-word responses to texts were killing me and infuriating me. And with each volley I sent out, I felt a piece of my hope turn to dust when he responded with a forced, singular word.

I felt angry, and sad, and scared. Because this *wasn't* like Luke, and at this point, it was past the point of concern or alarm. It was a full-on panic attack-inducing situation, and I was barely keeping it together.

Luke and I had planned to go to the newest *Avengers* movie that night after work weeks ago. We'd missed opening weekend of the movie by a mile and never saw it in theaters, but we'd made plans to go when we stumbled upon a random showing we thought we could make. In one reluctant word (who knew if it was, but at this point every text was read as reluctant or begrudging since I couldn't hear his voice or see his face and give it context), he'd confirmed he was still planning to go, and I felt almost giddy at the thought of him.

Or, I would have felt giddy if I hadn't felt so much anxiety and dread.

Why dread? Precisely because I didn't have any idea what he was feeling. Because I was a bumbling mess of overwrought emotion and bubbling with love even as I was feeling embarrassed, sad, and angry with him. I still wanted him desperately, but his choice to essentially cut me off made it feel like this was the *last* of something and not the beginning of something.

More than all of the other emotions I was feeling, I was missing him with an ache I couldn't ignore. I felt like I was missing a limb. I know, I know—that sounded so cliché, but it was like sending him off to basic training all over again, except I didn't know when he'd get back. And worse, my love wasn't some childish, unspecific, friendly and familiar crush. My love for him wasn't ignorant.

It was swallowing me whole.

By the end of the day I was toast. I was put on a new account and trying to suss out what the people—a music charity for underprivileged Nashville residents—really wanted out of their event. They came in expecting Carrie Underwood, Brad Paisley, and Wynn Reynolds, an up and comer in the city, to donate time and all kinds of things that were just *not* going to happen on their timeline, so I had my work cut out for me. It was a great organization, but it was going to be an uphill battle to make them see they couldn't order up country music stars for their cause just because their organization had to do with music and was located in Nashville.

This was exactly the kind of problem that typically exhilarated me. I loved figuring out these puzzles, and sometimes I was even able to enjoy the clients who had these absurd demands because it forced me to figure out alternatives and think creatively. It appealed to my Miss Fix It personality. This week, it felt nothing but draining and frustrating.

I also got an email from my friend back at FixEvents in New York. She pressed me to respond to Brenda's offer, and I remembered it was on a long list of emails to deal with—I'd been so unproductive in my fog of emotion that week that I'd be working from home that weekend, no doubt.

I gathered up the large pile of to do list post-its accumulated over the last week or so and shoved them and my laptop in my bag. I shut my office door at five o'clock exactly and made for my car, trying to remember that being face to face with Luke would give us the chance to figure things out, get our heads together, and... fix things.

It'd be good.

Right?

~

I heard my doorbell ring right on time, and my entire body reacted. My mouth felt dry, my eyes felt wet, my skin felt tight, my heart raced, I had to pee, my palms were sweaty, and honestly, I wanted to puke—I was a mess.

What if he took one look at me and could tell I was hopelessly and completely in love with him, that I was pathetic enough to be ready to give up my life for him—or at least, to talk about what it might be like.

What if he was repelled by my desperation?

Or, what if I'd burned the bridge? I didn't want to believe my mistake could do that, but he felt so far away. It'd been two weeks since I spent the night at his house, but it truly felt like it had been at least a month.

What if, as the sinking sensation in the pit of my stomach had been telling me for the past six days, he was done with me?

I tried to loosen up by shoulders and steady my breathing as I opened the door.

And of course.

Of course he was standing there, stunning in jeans and a dark green button-up shirt, holding a small bouquet of mums. He'd styled his hair just a bit since it was slightly longer on top lately, and his face was freshly shaved and smooth. He stood tall and straight and muscular, and even with a serious look on his face, the corners of his mouth turned up into the suggestion of a smile.

Basically, he was asking for it.

But instead of jumping him right then and there and declaring my apology, undying love, devotion, and attraction to him, I smiled, and waved him in, and tried not to be further claimed by his subtle cologne and the way his eyes swept over me, then jumped away.

"I missed you," I said quietly and leaned up on my tiptoes to give his cheek a kiss.

"Are you ready to go?" he asked, not quite looking at me.

Not a great start.

"Let me just run grab my purse, and then we can make the seven o'clock at Green Hills." I grabbed my work bag that had slumped down in one of the dining chairs, the only evidence left of my formerly-messy house.

"Ok. Do you have a vase?" His voice felt remote as I walked down the hall, and I swallowed down the anxious impulse to hide in the bathroom and give myself a pep talk.

"Yes, under the sink, and thank you for those, that's... sweet." And maybe the kind of gesture Luke would make, some effort at appeasement, if he were going to tell me we were done dating?

Oh, God, help me.

I grabbed my purse and heard the cabinet clinking shut. I brushed my long hair back out of my face and smoothed my duvet cover on my bed. I'd cleaned the apartment obsessively after getting home from work in an attempt to funnel some of my nervous energy. One sparkling apartment later, I was no less anxious, but a little more addled thanks to the nostril-scorching fumes of Clorox. Fortunately, I knew I'd probably shovel a full bag of popcorn during the movie, and that should bring back my ability to taste.

I wandered back into the kitchen and saw him staring at a

sleeping Lemon on the back of the couch, the green and yellow mums sitting in a small vase.

"You ready?" I asked, and he turned toward me slowly. I couldn't tell what, but he seemed different. Even more guarded somehow, and I had no idea what had changed.

"Yep." His face was impassive.

That was it. That was all he said. So, when I thought he was guarded? Yeah... I was right.

"Ok. Is everything ok?" I mean, why wait to deal with this? If he was going to let me down easy, if he could tell what a mess I was, we should just get this over with. I felt like I'd been waiting for this, and I just wanted to be done with it.

"Just fine. Let's go."

And it went like that. For the rest of the evening. I tried to talk with him in the car, in the line for the tickets, as we sat before the previews, but everything he gave me was terse at best. We sat silently during the movie, not speaking, not touching, and I don't think he ate a single bite of popcorn.

I vacillated between hurt, embarrassed, and angry. By the end of the movie and with a belly full of popcorn, I had leveled out to a low burn of frustrated anger. I decided I was going to force him to talk to me when we got back to my apartment. His continued silence in the car only confirmed my determination, even if it meant I unloaded my full confession on him.

He walked with me to my door but stopped there.

"I think I should probably go."

CHAPTER TWENTY

He was standing there, feet planted, looking at the ground instead of at me as I turned back to him from inside my house. I felt the frustration and fear and confusion boil over.

"I don't know what's happening Luke. I know we have a lot to talk about. And I can't tell what changed between when you got to my house and when we left for the movie, but please just come inside and tell me what's going on." I grabbed his hand then, hoping that the physical contact might shake him out of this mood or whatever it was.

He stood solidly there, not moving, for what felt like a good ten minutes. His hand was rough and warm in mine, and my heart raced at the contact despite myself.

It was probably only about twenty seconds. I'm not sure exactly what conversation he was having with himself, but it must have been a lively one based on his frowning face and tense energy. Fear unfurled itself like smoke in my belly, and I knew something was *really* wrong, and he had to come in and talk to me. I knew I'd messed up by being late to his dinner, and by the way I handled things going forward, but I didn't expect it to be this bad. I had braced for the worst but didn't think I'd be facing it. And Luke was typically levelheaded and reasonable...

He couldn't leave. I pulled him toward me, over the threshold, and he let me. I closed the door and locked it behind me, as though my doing that would keep him there. He pulled his hand from mine.

"What is going on?" I tried not to let my voice shake, but it did. My heart was pounding, and I felt shaky and weak and almost out of my mind with the need for him to talk to me. I walked to him but stopped before I reached him when he flinched.

"I think we're done here." His voice was low and it had a sharp edge to it. His words made no sense.

"What do you mean?" I searched his eyes for some hint. What the hell had happened? I knew, but I needed to understand how it could be this quick, this sterile.

"This shouldn't be a mystery. First, the thing last weekend. Your entire life has been about your job, and I knew that wouldn't change but thought maybe we'd figure it out. But the last few weeks have made it clear that's unlikely, and even if we did, I refuse to be what holds you back. And now, I see you're going to New York. There's no reason to draw this out and make it worse for both of us when you actually leave." He nodded to the floor where a little pile of purple stickie notes sat. They must have fallen out of my work bag.

"What?" I waited for him to explain.

"You're going back to New York," he said like it was fact. He said it like he knew it was true and inevitable. My eyes focused on the stickie note on top of the small pile: *respond to Brenda re: New York offer.*

"No. I'm not going anywhere." I moved to him and put my hands on his shoulders to hold him in front of me and force him to look in my eyes. "I'm not going to New York. I didn't even consider it. That was a note to respond to the offer my old job sent me. My response is *no,* and I just didn't take the time to send the email—I've been distracted at work and am working tomorrow to make up for that, so I brought all of my reminders with me. I realized yesterday it's been a few weeks since my old boss emailed me and didn't want to put that off any more." I tried to cover all the bases, leave nothing out, so he would see the truth. I could at least get that one very easily-solved issue out of the way before we dealt with what I thought was the *actual* issue.

"But you told me you miss New York. You loved it. Why wouldn't you consider it?"

"I miss Ellie. I miss things about New York. But I feel like that chapter of my life is closed. I made a conscious choice to move here, even before we got involved." I explained it as best I could, not quite ready to spill my guts all over the floor when he was still frosty.

"Are you sure?" His voice sounded smaller, but with a twinge of hope in it.

"Yes, I'm sure. Why on Earth would you think I would accept an offer to move back to New York and not mention a word about it to you?" I felt the frustration with him hit now that I'd clarified things. Was he that ready to end our relationship, and all because of a stickie note? Before he could respond, I said, "I'm hungry, and I'm making pasta." I moved into the kitchen and pulled out a pot for pasta water and a pan for sauce, waiting to hear him say *something* to make this better.

"Your career has always been the priority for you."

His words felt like a slap across the face. I turned from the stove, and I must have looked as shaken as I felt because he continued.

"That's not wrong—not a bad thing. I do the same. And I

respect you for always going after what you want. I always have. It's one reason I've—we've—it's one reason I've kept my distance. I just... I don't think I can keep doing this. I think we're better off stepping back before either of us is... too upset to be friends again." He was standing on the other side of the counter, looking over it at the floor between us, not at me, his hands shoved deep in his pockets.

"It's one reason you've kept your distance? What is? What reason?"

He just looked at me and shook his head, then swallowed. Maybe he wouldn't answer my questions, but he could listen to my apology, at least.

"I can't tell you how sorry I am that I messed up last weekend. There's no way I can fully explain to you how frustrated I feel about not understanding that going to your event instead of mine was the right choice, and I should have changed my plan from the beginning. I didn't realize it until I was in the midst of things and just *felt* how wrong it was. Once I did, then my timeline was messed up, and then I was late and missed them announcing your nomination for the award..." I turned the nob of the burner and searched his face, willing him to look at me so he would see how sincerely sorry I was. When I heard the click-click-click of the igniter and the whoosh of the gas flame lighting, I set the pot of water on to boil. I moved to the fridge to gather ingredients and kept talking.

"But I will tell you, I can't change what happened. At this point, I can't undo that. I can only tell you that I feel like I've learned the lesson. I understand that it's ok for me to compromise some things for you, and I hope you'll be willing to do the same for me. I know that's not always possible with your job and life in the Army, but I think that's the only way a relationship works. I'm going to mess up again, and my guess is you will too at some point... we have to compromise. And you would have known this if you'd let me call you and talk to you some time in the last six days." He was looking at me now, finally. He'd moved into the kitchen and was leaning back against the counter, watching me smash cloves of garlic with the side of my chef's knife into a bamboo cutting board.

"I agree. I shouldn't have shut you out. I just couldn't have this conversation over the phone and didn't feel like we could do much before having this conversation. I also agree that compromise is important and we're human, so we're going to mess up." He ran a hand through his hair.

"And I'm not even a little bit interested in the New York job. Truly. Don't you think I would have mentioned I was thinking about it?" I ran my knife through the garlic to mince it and grabbed a bunch of basil from a mason jar in front of me. Some grew in my pot outside, but I kept a bunch in water near the sink since I used it so often.

"I guess that's kind of what I was wondering, but then I thought maybe I didn't have the right to feel like you should be consulting me on job options." He was still watching my hands bunching and chopping ingredients.

"Why wouldn't you have the right to feel that way?" I felt a little ill asking the question, afraid of what he might say. I focused my efforts on chopping sundried tomatoes.

"I don't know. I'm just your boyfriend. I have no real claim on you." He cleared his throat, and I saw he was nervous. He took a few steps closer to me, brought his hands to my sides and gripped me, and I felt a little relief at his touch. So far, he'd just stood there with his hands in his pockets while I moved around the kitchen to burn my nervous energy. His response made me bold.

"But you could have," I said, setting down my knife and wiping my hands on a towel.

"What does that mean?" he asked, his eyes skating back and forth between mine, searching for clarity.

"You could have a claim on me, if you wanted to. You kind of already do." My heart beat faster and my throat felt tight, but I got the words out, and I saw his eyes ignite. I felt his grip at my sides tighten like he was keeping himself from pulling me toward him, but then he frowned at me.

"Don't say that Alex." His voice was rough and a little too loud with frustration.

"Why not?" Luke of today was a totally incomprehensible being to me. Maybe I was blinded by my own feelings and couldn't read his because of them.

"Because I can't have you, and you know that." He shook me a little and then turned away from me to examine the pot of now-boiling water behind us on the stove.

"I don't know that. I don't know what you mean." I tried to keep my voice calm. I walked to the stove him but thought better of touching him again. I reached around him to the bowl of kosher salt I kept at the ready. I grabbed a large pinch and tossed it into the water.

Luke was quiet for a few minutes, and I couldn't tell if he was retreating into himself again, or if maybe he was just trying to figure out what to tell me. He held on to the back of his neck, his elbows jutting out on either side of his head. As he paced around the small space of the kitchen, I could see his hands clasped together and turning white from the tension.

While he fought whatever internal war he was fighting, I sautéed the garlic with some Parma ham, crushed tomatoes, chili flakes, and sundried tomatoes. I splashed in some red wine and set the pan to simmer.

Finally, he let his hands drop and the look he gave me made me stop. Stop moving, stop breathing, stop picking at my nail polish as I stood there waiting for him to say something, stop thinking.

"I told you I was in love with you when we were growing up. I never stopped loving you. I have always loved you, and like an idiot, I'm in love with you now." He looked pained and miserable as he said this.

"I—"

"No, listen. I've always loved you, but I've always known you had your own goals that didn't necessarily mean being someone's wife. You were always heading for somewhere different—bigger than our hometown. You had ambitions and dreams. You were so talented and smart and you were absolutely made for more than some stifling high school relationship with me. I saw what happened with Jen and Louis—they both sacrificed their plans for the baby and to get married. When I heard him crying in his room night after night when he thought no one knew how upset he was, I vowed I wouldn't be like him, and I wouldn't ever put you in a place where you had to stay home with a kid instead of pursue your dreams."

"I'm sorry about what happened with your brother, but they got Tessa out of it, didn't they? And she's awesome, even if they ended up divorced. I know Louis has had a hard time accepting the way his life has turned out, but I don't see why that changes our situation now. I'm sorry we didn't date in high school. I kind of wish we had. I know I certainly wanted to, but you weren't around—and I guess now I know why. But that's beside the point. Why does that have any bearing on our relationship now?" I didn't let my voice get shrill and screechy. I wanted to have a little tantrum right there and knock some sense into him. Why were we belaboring our lack of relationship in high school *now*?

"You said yourself that being together was a big deal. I think I've deluded myself into thinking I could be with you, and not be in love with you, or at least just keep things casual enough to survive when it's over. I thought I could have it both ways—have you, but not cause you to compromise your goals. I realized the other night that's impossible. I'll always want you with me, and you'll always have a conflict. I don't want you feeling bad because you can't do both—constantly conflicted like you were last week." He said this like it would make sense to me, too.

He said it like I heard anything more than that he was in love with me.

My heart was pounding out of my ears and I could. Not. Understand. Him.

"Why does it have to be over? Why do you keep talking about this like we've broken up already?"

"Because it's over! You're not going back to New York, but eventually I'll get orders, and I'll leave here, and you'll still be here. You'll be doing the job you've worked for practically all your life. I'm not going to ask you to give up what you've worked for since high school and then be miserable. It's just a matter of time, and I don't think I can keep being with you and then give you up."

"So, don't give me up."

"What the hell? You know what my life is. You know that being with me isn't an option for you." His voice shook with frustration and anger, and I knew my wide eyes betrayed the shock I felt at his comment. I felt a flood of sadness and frustration all over again.

"Why can't I be with you? What makes that so impossible?" My voice was steady and calm. I felt buoyed by the fact I wasn't begging. I needed to know, yes, but it wasn't me who was the illogical one. I could be calm, if he'd just help me understand.

"Because you're... you. And I'll be damned if I'm the one

to stand in your way of whatever it is you want. I won't have you look at me like Jen looked at Louis—like he'd stolen something from her—like he'd ruined her life. I saw it eat both of them, and she still can't be in the same room as him without shredding him with her anger. She wasn't like that before. She was nice—and she loved him." He sounded resigned, leaned a hip against the countertop, and I felt my inner fighter rise up.

"Ok, I'm sorry, but this is bullshit. You're telling me I can't be with you because I don't want to be, right? You're saying, in essence, that being with you means giving up what I want and becoming some old embittered shrew because you've stolen all my hopes and dreams. Is that it?" I stalked toward him from where I was at the other side of the kitchen—yeah, stalked, because I had a hellofalot of adrenaline coursing through me, and it propelled me in his direction. We stood a foot apart, and I felt myself shaking with adrenaline and energy.

"Uh, no, I mean—"

"That's what you're saying. You're taking the choice away from me. You're assuming what I want is my job, or some other kind of person for a partner. You're also assuming, as you usually do, that it's black and white. That it's either, or. You've made up your mind that it's black—that we can't be together, period, or I'll eventually resent you like Jen resents Louis, and vice versa. But have you noticed how I've been unsettled, and conflicted, even? I know I haven't unloaded it all on you, and we've barely seen each other the last month, but I haven't been happy at B and W. I've actually been miserable because I've realized this dream position in this cool city at a great company with awesome coworkers and appealing accounts *isn't* all that I want in life. I mean, it totally is in terms of a job, but in terms of a *life*? No—it's not enough anymore. And it's damn frustrating to have worked so hard and had this dream only to get here and realize it's not what I thought it would be–it's not enough. It's disheartening, and annoying, and disappointing." I waited for him to understand. I waited for a signal of some kind that he knew what I was saying, but it didn't come. I grabbed hold of the counter next to me to anchor me. He just kept watching me, studying me. So, I kept going.

"You don't get to decide for me, Luke. You decide for you, and I decide for me. And I've decided. It's terrifying and honestly I have no idea what it means, but I want you. I already knew that, but when I screwed everything up last week, I got the message, loud and clear. I should have put you first, and if I'd tried, I could have, from the beginning. I wouldn't have had to flake on my job, and I wouldn't have had to do it last minute. It's been messy with all kinds of black and white and gray in my mind, but I'm figuring out that's ok." I ran a hand over my mouth and then looked at him. He was standing there, frozen in place by my rant. *Time to go for it.*

"You're what I want. I love you and I'm in love with you, and I want you to have a claim on me because I want a claim on you. I don't want a life where I have a great job but you're not in it." Before I could even take a full breath after my tirade, he pulled me into his arms and crushed me against him, his mouth covering mine in a possessive, passionate kiss. Then he set me back away from him.

"That was—You were... I don't know what to say." He ran a hand through his hair again, and a smile grew on his face as his chest rose and fell.

"I think you've had me on some kind of weird pedestal. I don't want to be there. I want you to talk to me and not assume you know what I want, or what's best for me. I get to have a say in that. And we're not Louis and Jen. They had a baby just out of high school and that changed all the dreams they had growing up. We've both gotten our degrees, laid down the foundation of our careers. It's different. And yes, I'm going to have to compromise and change some things to have a life with you, and that's a huge unknown, but I trust that we can figure it out... together." I crossed my arms and glared at him, wanting to make sure he understood the problem with him deciding everything on my behalf without talking to me.

"I don't think you want me. I mean, it's easy now, while I'm here. But let's say we stay together, and we get married. You have to come with me. I'm not going to be one of those soldiers whose wife lives in a different place. I'd want you with me wherever I go."

"Good. I'd want to be there with you. I'd go where you go."

"It could be anywhere. It could be Korea. Or Alaska. Or backwoods Louisiana." He was all worked up, his hair sticking up, no longer styled, and it made him look frantic. His face was flushed and he was practically a blur as he paced a small line around the kitchen island.

"I love Korean barbeque. I've always wanted to see the northern lights. And you know I love Cajun food." I stepped where he had stopped his pacing, suppressing a maniacal giggle I felt rising in my throat. He was trying to scare me away.

"Or Germany or Italy," he said, like *that* would scare me away.

"Schnitzel. And duh," I said, taking another step.

"It could be years and years stationed at different posts in Texas. *Texas*, Al," he said, his eyes wide.

"Austin is a gastronomic hub. Mexican food is one of my favorites, as you well know. And if you're there, then... I'm there. *Capisci?*"

"What about when I go TDY or I deploy? What about when I'm gone for a year at a time, and we can barely communicate, and you hate where you're living, or you can't find a job and you're miserable?" He ran his hands through his hair again, and then stopped with his hands on his hips.

"The job thing is a real issue. That does scare me, in some ways. But I also never would have imagined that I'd be so comfortable here in Nashville so quickly when I was starting my job in New York, you know? I *never* would have imagined voluntarily making that move. What's the difference if the Army tells me where to go? I know it won't be the way I planned, but honestly, I'm not convinced I should be in charge anymore. I've had tunnel vision, and I've missed out on having a full life." I held out my hands as a kind of sign of surrender.

"You're a good planner. You don't want to give up planning. The Army will take that away from you—you can't plan anything." He was shaking his head, his gorgeous face twisted with worry and determination.

"You're worth it to me," I said in a quiet voice I hoped would convey my faith in him, in the possibility of us.

"But what about when I'm gone? That's a very real and inevitable aspect of being with me. Other men with normal jobs—that's not something you deal with if you're with a lawyer or a banker or a high school science teacher." His face had softened, but I could see the muscles in his shoulders bunching up, betraying his concern.

"I admit I don't want to think about what it'll be like when you have to be gone. I feel like we've spent way too much time apart already. But I believe we can get through that together. And the women I met at the ball were all amazing. I admire them, and I can see why people talk about how unique the military culture and bond is. I see that they have it, that they support each other, and I believe I could easily fold into that. I feel like they were ready to fold me in already because they know you and care about what you care about. And... I want it for myself."

"You do?" He sounded amazed, one hand gripping the back of his neck again.

"I do. I obviously don't know much about what your life is like, or what it's like to be an Army girlfriend, let alone an Army wife, but I think if I was *your* wife, and better yet, if you were *my* husband, I could do just about anything. I'm already so proud of you... so proud to know you and be your friend." I moved to him then, and I could see his shoulders relaxing a little, and a small smile start at one corner of his mouth.

But I had to ask one question that had been on my mind since we'd started this conversation. "But do you? Do you think I could do it? Because like you said, I don't know what it's like, and you do, and if you don't think I—"

He cut me off with a kiss. He held me with one hand at my back, one hand behind my head. He pressed his lips to mine, pulled back, and kissed me again. They were strong, reassuring, loving kisses.

"I have absolutely no doubt you can do anything you want —anything you decide to do. I have always known that and never wanted to be the one to hold you back." His eyes bore into me, reassuring me, and I felt my heart expand as I looked back at him. "I have wanted you all my life. I knew, even in ninth grade, that I couldn't be close to you without wanting all of you. After Louis and Jen, I knew I couldn't be your best friend and not push you for more. So I removed myself because watching my brother and his dreams implode in front of me scared me. I was scared for myself, and I was scared of you ever looking at me like Jen looked at him."

I lay my head on his chest and hugged him, then tipped

my head back again to look at his face. "I always wondered if it was something with them. You disappeared so soon after, I knew it was, even though I wished you would have just talked to me."

His hand squeezed my shoulders for emphasis. "I couldn't. I couldn't talk to you without admitting how much I loved you, and the prospect of that was terrifying. As time went on, it felt like I'd made the right choice—you were happy and then you went off to New York like you'd always dreamed. It was confirmation that staying away was right." He dipped his head.

"I missed you every day. I thought about you every day," I said, feeling the familiar pang of longing I'd felt so often over the years, and so acutely those first few years after he distanced himself.

"I'm not sure I was wrong. I wish we could have been close, or that I could have explained what I was thinking, but now we've both had time." His eyes searched mine again, and I breathed in his explanation, letting it settle in my mind.

"That's true. We've had plenty of time," I admitted with a small smile. I watched as his eyes darkened and searched my face as he pulled me closer.

"If you want me, I'm yours. Always have been." His voice was low and smooth and quiet and hearing those words coming from his mouth in combination with his voice turned me into a puddle of elation and desire.

"Sold."

～

After that, we talked. Ok, we kissed for like, a while, all right? And things may have escalated, but we managed to calm down and keep talking. We had ground to cover. We decided we'd keep dating, but instead of feeling some kind of inevitable end date lingering out in the wings, we'd stay hopeful, we'd act like we were going to stay together and build a future together. I had a few moments where I felt the sheer madness of making plans to essentially marry and have babies with my childhood friend all while we'd only dated for a few weeks, and yet it didn't feel unnatural. As we spoke, so much of it came with a tunneling inevitability that I laughed.

I laughed out of relief, and out of joy, and because there were moments when he looked at me and I finally recognized what it was I saw in his eyes—desire, love, devotion, hope. It was addicting, and thrilling, and still scary. I'd never felt this way and never been with someone who did either. I didn't know what life would look like, or how I would carry on with my old routine much longer when I knew so clearly what I wanted—I wanted Luke. I wanted a life together with him. We just hadn't had time to develop the details of a future yet. We did need time. It felt like all we'd had was time, and yet, we did need time. We'd take it together.

EPILOGUE

"Al, I have a question for you," Luke said from my computer screen. We were Facetiming yet again. It'd been another six weeks since our big confession, and we'd managed to see each other at least once a week since then. We talked every night and texted through the day, and I had to use every ounce of my professionalism and adulthood to not just sit around and think about him and how adorable he was.

"What's your question?"

"How'd you like to go on a little trip with me after Christmas?" he asked from his couch. I could tell he was lying sideways, his head propped on his hand, and the phone must have been balanced on his coffee table.

"Sure. We're flying to Utah together, right? I literally just made my plane reservation because you gave me your flight information."

"Yes, yes, still doing that." His smile was blinding, and I had a flashback to Luke at eighteen. Good grief, this man had always been painfully handsome.

"Where would we go?" I wondered what he had up his

sleeve and tried to suppress any little runaway trains that might spring to life in my very active imagination.

"I was thinking we'd fly to Italy and you could show me around," he said with a growing smile.

"Wait, really?" I sat up straighter and I must have pushed at the limits of Lemon's tolerance for human movement because he jumped down and shot me a condescending look before he sauntered off with his tail twitching.

"Yes. I think it'll be a good start to the next year of our lives. New Year's in Rome?"

Something about the way he said it—*the next year of our lives*—had my heart pounding. I hoped it would be the first of many to come.

"*Certo, Amore.*"

ACKNOWLEDGMENTS

Thank you to the writer of the best love story of all time—the One who shows us real sacrifice and loves us before we ever know what hit us.

Thank you to my husband, whose encouragement and cheerleading have been at the root of my writing, and whose love has inspired me to write. Matthew, our love story will always be my favorite.

Thanks to my family, who've been supportive, even if they have no idea what I mean when I say I'm writing a romance. It's ok guys—you don't have to read it if you don't want to.

To my Beta readers Melissa, Meagan, Stephanie, Whitney, and Staci—thank you for your diligence, your insight, your honesty, and your time.

Thank you to Julie, whose friendship and love are fuel on so many levels. Thank you to Monica, Denise, and Karen for being my own personal cheering squad—for laughing, crying, praying, cheering for me, and being sweet enough to be impressed that I ever even started.

To Jamie, who kept me going and commiserated in so many ways along the line I can't even fully describe it—thank you for your incredible mind, your amazing patience, and your genuine excitement. I cannot freaking WAIT to get YOUR book in my hands.

To the Writerly Writers Write group, thank you for being persistent in our swaps, despite long distances, disparate time zones, and a whole lotta life in our faces. I'm honored to read your work regularly.

Huge thanks to Judy Roth for working with me, turning drafts around at lightning speed, and being so thorough and thoughtful. Thanks to Jeff Senter at Indie Formatting for formatting the book. Unending thanks to Rainbeau Decker for patience, creativity, and beautiful work with the cover—I'm so thrilled to be partnering with you!

To the readers who've made it this far, thanks for reading. If you have time, please leave a review. Now, back to work!

ABOUT THE AUTHOR

Claire Cain lives to eat and drink her way around the globe with her traveling soldier and two kids, but is perhaps even happier hunkered down at home in a pair of sweatpants and slippers using any free moment she has to read and cook. Or talk—she really likes to talk. She has become an expert at packing too many dishes in too few cabinets and making houses into homes from Utah to Germany and many places in between. She's a proud Army wife and is frankly just really happy to be here.

CONNECT WITH CLAIRE:

Facebook: facebook.com/clairecainwriter
Twitter: @writeclairecain
Instagram: @clairecainwriter
E-mail: clairecainwriter@gmail.com
Newsletter sign-up: http://eepurl.com/dGuIBv

Want more?
Here's a teaser for the Rambler Battalion Series,
book 2 starring Alex's best friend Ellie,
due out Winter 2019!

"Ladies and Gentleman, please remain calm. As you can tell, we're experiencing some turbulence."

The speakers crackled like something out of a 1980s disaster film and I made a point of staring straight ahead at the tray table latch, pushing a breath slowly out my nose. The plane rumbled and rattled around me and I willed myself to calm down.

I'd been on the flight for an hour now. I left DC after my first harrowing flight from Philadelphia, but it was a quick hop, more up and down than anything. That sounds easy, except that the upping and downing is a prime feature of my overall dread of flying. And now here I was, halfway through what was quickly turning out to be the worst flight of my life. The plane took a huge dip, so much so that my body strained against the seatbelt as gravity forced what was up to go down and just about everyone in the plane let out gasps and a few shrieks. Perfect. I was going to die at the ripe age of 27 having done almost nothing but read and write papers and have two crappy boyfriends.

The plane shuddered and bumped along, and I pulled on

my seatbelt one more time like it could have loosened in the thirty seconds since I'd last done it. I tried to return to my book. I gripped the small brick of bound pages and tried to turn my attention to the green cover and the soldier piled high with the weights of the world and his vocation. I read the title: *Grunt: The Curious Science of Humans at War* by Mary Roach. This woman. What a brain. So far I was approximately twenty-eight pages in. I'd purchased about twenty books on a variety of military-themed subject matter to get started on my research and also so I didn't look like a total idiot when I started my new job. And now I was unable to even crack the book back to the page I'd dog-eared during boarding (some would say blasphemy, but I say, what else is the point of a paperback book? Should I baby and preserve it, or should I devour it? I say the latter.).

I smoothed my hand over the cover and then gripped the book, wishing the familiarity of a book in hand, a daily ritual, an elemental thing, would sooth me. No dice. The plane dipped again and my body pressed back against the seat as I shut my eyes against the horrible gush of terror that swam in my belly. I breathed in through my nose and kept my eyes closed, repeating to myself what I was doing, and why I was on this plane.

I'm moving to a new job that matters. I'm moving so I can have time to write. I'm moving so I can help people. I'm more than halfway through this flight. I'm more likely to die in a car crash on the way to my new apartment than on this plane. Air travel is perfectly safe. Turbulence is perfectly norm—

The plane dipped. No, it didn't dip, it flat out dropped, and my belly, that one swimming with terror? It dropped too, like we were on a roller coaster on the biggest thriller dip, except we weren't on a track. We were thousands and thousands of feet in the air surrounded by some sham of a metal like aluminum and all that kept us there was, I suspected, the sheer will of God and the pilots, who were probably drunk or busy sexting their girlfriends.

Ok, that was going a little far. But I hated flying, and my ability to assume that every flight would end with my fiery death was a real skill. I'd coddled it and developed it into a full grown boy of paranoia.

But back to my imminent death.

The plane finally caught the bottom of the air pocket, or whatever the hell it was that made turbulence happen, and leveled out. I kept my eyes closed tight, not daring to open them, my body still tense and fully expecting the horror show to continue any second. *Eleven minutes of this crap* I thought to myself as I eyed my watch. Eleven minutes of straight up gut-wrenching awfulness in the skies. *29 minutes until touchdown, if my watch hasn't betrayed me and the drunk pilots can still tell time.*

"Ma'am?"

My body had overheated in my panic, and my glasses were smudged. My jeans felt too tight around my belly and my V-neck shirt was damp under my arms and at my back. My hair felt too tight there piled on top of my head in a bun.

"Ma'am."

I took a deep breath and talked myself down. *It's fine. Turbulence is normal. Plane travel is perfectly normal and safe. You're more likely to die—*

"Ma'am?" The voice came from right next to me and cut through my thoughts, and I realized this person was talking to me. I opened my eyes hopefully, like maybe this stranger had the ability to control whether we'd hit another air pocket or a flock of birds and go plummeting to our deaths.

"Uh, yes?" My voice was rough and I wasn't sure whether

I'd made any noises. I wasn't a screamer, so probably not, but my vocal chords felt surprised by my effort to speak.

"You...ok?" The voice spoke again, tentatively. It was deep, and a little gravelly, like it hadn't been used lately. I took another breath and breathed it out and summoned a polite smile as I turned to look at him.

"Yes, I'm ok." I smiled and took in the stranger, my seat companion in 11B to my A.

Oh.

Bright brown eyes in their own shade of milk chocolate looked back at me, hovering over a dark brown beard tinged with deep red. A mouth pulled into a closed-mouth, slight smile. I felt the familiar discomfort with my peer whizz through my already agitated belly as I registered this partner-in-row-11 was likely just a few years older than me. Max ten. Yep, a peer.

"Good. Good." He nodded his head a little, but his brow furrowed.

"Are you?" I asked, taking in his large build, his big arms, and his... oh. His hand. That I was holding. In a death grip. I released his hand as I said, "Oh my goodness, I'm so sorry. I don't even remember grabbing your hand. I'm so sorry!" I brought my hands to my face to press them over my mouth and shook my head at myself. If I hadn't already been red-faced from bracing against my impending doom, I might have blushed in awkwardness.

The man laughed quietly. "Don't worry about it. This is pretty bad turbulence."

I pulled my hand away and adjusted my glasses that had slid down my nose. "It is, isn't it? I definitely hate flying, but this seems particularly—" And again. The plane dropped and then rumbled and I rammed my back against the seat taking short, shallow breaths. I felt a hand cover my right hand, the one currently death-gripping the arm rest between the seats.

"What's your name ma'am?" I heard that rough voice say. Sometime later I knew I'd spend time thinking about why this man was calling me ma'am when he was definitely close to my age. I mean, he could not be younger than me, could he? Had the turbulence of flight 707 prematurely aged me that significantly? But in the moment, I just answered.

"Elizabeth."

"Good. Nice to meet you, Elizabeth." His voice was steady despite the plane's cruel jolting.

I couldn't respond. I had to stay braced against the seat with my eyes closed or I'd end up... I didn't know. The plane would crash, or at the very least, my body would disintegrate from terror. So I focused on bracing myself, every muscle in my body tense, barely hearing his voice.

"I'm Jake. We're going to be fine." His voice was still calm but it had an edge of command in it, like his decision that we'd be fine mattered in the context of Delta flight 707. Strangely, I believed him. I let my eyes slowly open, one at a time, and tried to relax my shoulders.

"I'm so sorry you're next to me. I hate flying." My voice was shaky.

"Where are you going?"

"Nashville. I'm moving there. I've actually never been there before, but I'm moving, so I'm flying, or at least I'm hoping we'll keep flying and not end up crashing before I ever do actually end up there." I babbled this nonsense and he stayed focused on me, his serious but patient face watching me, still covering my right hand with his left on the arm rest.

"That sounds exciting," he offered, and if I'd been in my right mind, I might have laughed at how serious and unexcited his voice was. He was focused.

"Yep." I said it in a gulp as I breathed through another series of rumbles. I kept focused on the tray table, kept focused on breathing normal breaths instead of shallow ones, and slowly let myself release the tension as the plane stayed steady.

"Should be the end of the turbulence folks, sorry about that. Pretty rough air there, but we should have a smooth flight now—'bout 25 minutes to Nashville." The captain's voice spoke life back into my brain, and I looked over at my apparently fearless seat companion.

"Again, so sorry," I said as I lifted my hand, and he quickly pulled his away. He was watching me, maybe waiting for me to freak out again, or maybe just curious about what kind of crazy person I really was. I pushed my glasses back up the bridge of my nose and pulled at my seatbelt tight, tighter.

"You going to make it?" He asked, just the smallest corner of his mouth turning up. His brown eyes studied me and my addled brain took that moment to think *he has great eyebrows* like that was pertinent to the situation. Like eyebrows had bearing on me surviving this flight. *Ugh.*

"Yes," I said, and then turned away because I realized we were locked in some pretty intense eye contact considering I had no clue who this person was other than he was willing to hold my hand so I didn't evaporate into the abyss of fear a few minutes ago. "Where are you coming from?"

"DC area. Heading home now," he said. He leaned back in his seat but kept looking at me. I half expected him to shove in his ear buds and tune me out.

"DC is a great city. I like it," I said, trying not to roll my eyes at how incapable I was at small talk. "What were you doing there?" Before the words were out of my mouth, I thought it was maybe too personal of a question. But that was something people asked a fellow passenger, right?

He shifted in his seat a little, and that serious, bearded face frowned a little. "Funeral." Just the one word, but it was enough.

"I'm so sorry," I said, and watched a pained look crossed his face.

"It was my father's. We weren't close." He said the words slowly, his voice still graveled and I felt a pang of guilt for making him speak.

"I'm sorry. Losing a parent seems like a very difficult thing." I felt the impulse to pat his hand, or something, to show him my regret for his loss. We'd already crossed the physical boundary of handholding thanks to my complete inability to maintain sanity in the face of a turbulent flight, but I didn't want to seem overly aggressive, so I looked him in the eye hoping to convey my sorrow for his loss, even if a distant one, with my eyes and face. He nodded.

"Your wife? Kids? Were they with you?" I asked, for some reason compelled not to leave our conversation there.

He shook his head. "No wife or kids. Not in the cards for me." His eyes flickered to mine, then back to looking ahead of him, past the curtain into first class, and past the nose of the plane. Based on his intensity, he could likely see beyond the horizon.

"Oh, ok." I had no idea what else to say. I just assumed he would have a family the way I assume most people in their thirties did. That wasn't really the case, but I'd realized that outside of New York, people usually did get married and start their families younger. The fact that he said it "wasn't in the cards" was so peculiar and I desperately wanted to ask him why he said that. But the situation didn't allow for that. It wouldn't help his grief to have me prying into why he thought he'd be a perpetual bachelor.

I turned my book over in my hands, then over again. I

fanned the pages and pictured my heart, which was still beating pretty quickly, and tried to slow it down. Sometimes I felt like if I thought hard enough about something, I could will it into submission. I could *make* myself calm down, if I thought about it hard enough.

"And you? Is your husband moving with you?" His question startled me.

"My husband? Oh, no. No husband. No boyfriend. Just me. Not even a cat, though I should probably get one to satisfy the stereotype. Hopefully someday I'll have a... well. Yeah. So. Nope. Just me." I caught myself before I launched into telling this unsuspecting stranger about my very real desire to have a husband and children. That desire felt all the more real in the wake of my near death experience there on flight 707.

Then, we sat there. We just sat, and didn't speak anymore, which I felt like might be his natural state of being. I couldn't read him without turning to look at him and that would have been too obvious since we were smashed together in our seats, so I just took out my book and read the same few paragraphs over and over again until we landed, layering a prayer for survival in my mind over the words of the book.

Catch more of Ellie and Jake in early 2019! Sign up for the newsletter for release info and exclusive content at http://eepurl.com/dGuIBv

CPSIA information can be obtained
at www.ICGtesting.com
Printed in the USA
LVHW11s1146111018
593105LV00001B/118/P

9 781732 771802